D1192947

SCOUNDREL

SCOUNDREL

PETER ELSTOB

JONATHAN CAPE
THIRTY-TWO BEDFORD SQUARE LONDON

First published 1986
Copyright © 1986 by Peter Elstob
Jonathan Cape Ltd
32 Bedford Square, London WC1B 3EL

British Library Cataloguing in Publication Data

Elstob, Peter
Scoundrel.
I. Title
823'.912[F]   PR6055.L7/

ISBN 0-224-02810-3

Printed in Great Britain by
Hazell, Watson & Viney Ltd
Member of the BPCC Group
Aylesbury, Bucks

For my daughters
Ann, Penny and Sukey

Every man may be a scoundrel,
and perhaps every man is a scoundrel.

                                    Dostoevsky

1

TRYING TO KEEP upright while balanced on top of a load of mixed vegetables is not the most comfortable way of travelling and by the time the old open truck reached Milan I was aching all over and covered with a dusting of good Italian soil. It was a great relief when the driver slammed on his brakes bouncing me off the back of his cab. He leaned out of his window.

'Stazione Centrale, amico!'

I jumped down and walked around to shake his hand. 'Mille grazie, Ulrico, for the lift. Now I have another favour to ask . . .'

'Ask it then.'

'Please do not tell la signora that you brought me here, capisce?'

'You bet I unnerstan'.' He smiled knowingly, a man of the world. 'Don' worry – I tell her niente – you have a good time.'

'Okay. Addio, amico.'

'Ciao, il mio Colonel.' He saluted in mock military manner and gunned the decrepit truck away as though it were a racing car.

I stood outside the entrance to Milan Central Station, shabby, unshaven and penniless. It was just before eight in the morning of what was obviously going to be a hot and humid summer's day. One or two in the crowd hurrying to catch trains gave me curious looks so I knew that I had better make some emergency repairs if I were to stay in the game.

Sometimes I compare my life to a game of Snakes and Ladders, a game in which time after time I make my way steadily up the ladders towards the winning square at the top left-hand corner, only, inevitably it seems, to land on the head of a snake. That was what had happened two days earlier. The dice had landed me on a square which must have read YOU ARE ARRESTED – RETURN TO BOTTOM LINE, and from a comfortable apartment I had been suddenly whisked to a small, scruffy cell in a small, scruffy police station.

I

God knows why but I always keep on playing; somehow, even when everything seems to be going for me, I know I'll soon slide down a long snake and have to begin all over again. It had happened before but not for some time had I slid from so high to so low.

If I were to get back in the damned game, priority was to restore at least an appearance of respectability. To be unshaven, obviously in need of a wash, dressed in soiled clothes and with empty pockets would make it quite impossible for me to follow my profession. Something had to be done.

Joining the people scuttling into the station I stopped to get my bearings. The on-duty policeman scrutinizing the crowd and I spotted each other simultaneously. His eyes stopped ranging over faces and took me in from uncombed hair to dusty shoes. Genuine travellers, even the poorest, are fairly clean at that hour of the morning and are almost never completely empty-handed. If I didn't want to be questioned by the police – and I didn't – I would have to get out of his sight quickly.

I spotted the men's lavatories and walked briskly towards them, almost feeling the policeman's eyes on the back of my dirty neck. Inside an attendant was polishing the mirrors over a line of wash-basins. He turned as I entered his kingdom and took me in with an experienced glance.

He was, I guessed, in his sixties and had more the bearing of a proprietor of an inn than of a public washroom attendant.

'Buongiorno,' I said.

'Buongiorno . . .' A slight pause and then he added, 'Signor.' I felt I'd moved one square.

We faced one another, each quietly making his assessment. He saw a foreigner in a crumpled, stained but expensive suit with a linen shirt, tie of one of the better London clubs, good shoes though scuffed and needing polish. I saw a lined, hard but not unkind face, very dark brown eyes which looked directly but incuriously into mine. He had an air of confidence or perhaps it was just lack of anxiety, the captain of a ship which was now safely in port.

'I have suffered a misfortune . . .' I began in Italian which, though I can read, I don't speak well.

'I speak English,' he said. 'Ten year in America.'

'Oh good – that makes it a lot easier.' I hadn't really thought out a story but that's never stopped me. 'Well the thing is I've been a bit of a damned fool. I'm with a party you see, on a conducted tour and our

2

guide took us to a night-club last night and, well, I'm afraid I went off with this girl, see?'

He smiled, but only just.

'Well she took me to a small hotel near here, a bit of a dump really but I was pretty drunk and when I woke up this morning she was gone, and so had my money.' He said nothing. 'Fortunately they'd made me pay for the room on arrival and, thank God, they still had my passport . . .'

'Have you been to the cops?'

'No – I felt such a fool. Anyway they'd never find her.'

He nodded and turned to wipe the white film off the glass. There were, I saw, baths at the far end of the wash-basins.

'If I could just get cleaned up, I'll go back to our hotel and see if they've left me my air ticket – the party are flying to Rome this morning. I don't want to go looking like this though – if I could just have a bath?' He finished polishing the mirror and turned to look at me again. 'I'll send you some money as soon as I catch up with my party.'

By his smile and the way he shrugged his shoulders I knew he hadn't believed a word of my story. But he had the creased look of a much-circulated banknote and had undoubtedly been down himself more than once; he'd probably never been very far up. Without a word he put away his polish and cloth, opened a glass-panelled door which led into his room and returned in a few moments with a folded white bath towel and a cake of soap.

'This way, signor.' He led me to cubicle four in which there was an antique porcelain bath with huge, newly polished taps and, with a near-theatrical bow, closed the door on me.

I turned the hot tap full on and the water gushed out, filling the room with steam. I got undressed, added the minimum of cold water and was just about to ease into the depths when there was a knock at the door: the attendant handed me a plastic safety razor.

'Give me your coat, trousers, shirt and shoes and take your time with your bath. I'll clean them up for you.'

Before I could thank him he shut the door. I let myself slowly into the scalding hot water, submerged completely, luxuriating in the ralaxing of tired, tense muscles. After a full five minutes I soaped and rinsed two or three times, finishing off with a cold shower from a leaking attachment. Then I rubbed myself hard with the rough towel and put back on my not very clean shorts, vest and socks. The razor

3

scraped rather than cut the stubble off my face. I sat on the edge of the bath and took stock of my assets.

They were a comb, a handkerchief, a worn leather wallet with my papers but no money at all, and a passport. It was my 'Lt-Col. Rokesby-Gore' one and although it had cost me two hundred pounds it was worth every penny because a hundred had gone to someone in the passport office and it would check out on a simple query.

I had other bits of paper to back up my Colonel Rokesby-Gore identity. None had been too difficult to get: a driving licence, a post office savings book, an Aldershot library ticket, an expired R.A.C. membership card and half a dozen calling cards – engraved, of course. If ever my identity were doubted someone would have to spend considerable time and money in proving its falseness. From outside Britain that wouldn't be easy to do, and I never used my Rokesby-Gore persona in England – there I was William Mackenzie, a Canadian.

Life is difficult if you have no permanent base of your own, no castle, no respectable occupation. Without a believable identity it's practically impossible to survive as an independent man in our society. That's why I'd put my foot down about the passport, and it was only because I had insisted that I'd still got it. The police captain had been going to keep it along with all my other possessions, but gambling on his basic cowardice and his greed I'd stuck out – no passport, no deal.

It had been a straightforward deal that the police chief, Captain Nicolo, had put to me just after six that morning. I had a simple choice: I could stay and stand trial for attempting to obtain money by deception, which would mean about a year if I were convicted, or I could just walk out of the police station but leaving everything I owned behind me.

'Everything?' I had asked.

'Si, tutto.'

That meant my two, nearly new suitcases, my smart black leather despatch case with R. R.-G. in small gold letters, three suits, seven shirts, underwear, socks and silk pyjamas, three pairs of English shoes and a dozen ties including an M.C.C., a Gunners and one of the less exclusive London clubs to which I had actually belonged during a rare period of respectable prosperity. Also there was an electric razor and electric toothbrush, various cuff-links and tie-pins, a gold Parker pen, and a silver cigarette case with matching lighter.

I'd tried to get my diary and, still more annoying, my keys, which

4

couldn't possibly be of any use to him, but he wouldn't yield. As a friend of Maria-Luisa's he had a personal reason to give me a hard time. I asked if I could change my shoes and with a smile he agreed, but when I had laced the brown Oxfords he smiled triumphantly and held up the twenty-dollar bill I'd secreted under the sole.

But I'd jibbed at the passport. I told the gallant Captain that I'd face up to being turned out on the street without luggage or money but not without a passport.

'How am I to leave Italy, Captain?'

He was a fat little fellow who looked a bit like an overfed schoolboy growing out of his uniform. He tapped his desk and tried to appear important. Obviously he didn't give a damn what happened to me but if I were picked up as a penniless vagrant and the British Consul were informed he might lose his spoils or at the best have to share them. He pulled the passport from the pile of my possessions.

As I reached for it he spotted the jade cuff-links, a present from a Chinese lady. He didn't bother to ask for them – he merely snapped his fingers. I took them off and exchanged them for the passport and, as he was trying to see if the gold was real, I casually picked up my wallet. Fortunately it was old and shabby and the hundred thousand lire, of course, was long gone but it contained things I could use. He made no objection as I pocketed it.

'You will be taken back to your cell, Colonel,' he said, 'and after about five minutes you may open the door. Turn left, walk outside and do not speak to anyone. Do not linger outside and don't ever come back here.'

Shortly afterwards I pushed my cell door open, and as it creaked the gaoler at the end of the corridor disappeared into the lavatory. In the main hall the duty officer carefully kept his eyes on his day book. At the street entrance the policeman on duty, the same bastard who had nearly twisted my left arm out of its socket the day before, glanced at me as though he had never seen me in his life.

I felt elated at being free again and lost no time in getting away from the ugly police station. I walked away, turning at the first corner, which I remembered led to the market place. I had to get right out of town, but without a penny in my pocket it wasn't going to be easy. I don't want to walk and I am a bit beyond the age for hitch-hiking, especially in Italy.

I toyed with the idea of going back to Maria-Luisa and throwing myself on her mercy, asking for just a few thousand lire for 'bus fare', but I remembered how spitting angry she'd been when she handed me over to her Captain Nicolo. She hadn't shown much mercy then and if, as I thought likely, she didn't know that he'd let me go, all I could expect from her was an attempt to have me put back behind bars.

In the couple of days that I'd spent in the town living with her I'd come to know a few people, at least superficially. I'm good at getting on friendly terms with people quickly – God knows I've had enough practice. I ran through them in my mind but decided I didn't know any of them well enough to borrow even a small sum.

But there was a local entrepreneur who bought vegetables from the farmers and took them to the central market in Milan. I knew him only as Ulrico and that he had been a friend of Maria-Luisa's mother during the war and did favours for Maria-Lusia from time to time. We'd drunk a litre of wine with him.

I knew the early morning café he used at the market place and I was glad to see that he was there, having just bought a load of mixed vegetables. The bargain was being sealed with an espresso and a glass of grappa even though it was not yet seven o'clock in the morning.

I waited until the transaction had been completed and then walked over and greeted him. He looked surprised to see me at that early hour.

'Are you going to Milan, Ulrico?'

He nodded, indicating the loaded farm cart which his assistant and the farmer were beginning to transfer into his truck.

'Can I come with you?'

He looked surprised. 'Sure, you can come okay, but you gotta ride outside. It's not allowed for three in the cab.'

'That's all right. I'll give you a hand loading up.'

It took about twenty minutes and then he and his helper climbed into the cab.

'Can you let me off at Milan Central Station?'

'Okay. What's the matter – you in trouble?'

I saw that he hadn't yet heard of my arrest, which was surprising in such a small town. He would, of course, as soon as he returned that afternoon.

'Yes – a misunderstanding with the signora and the police. I can clear it up but now I have to get away.'

He nodded sympathetically – trouble with the authorities is regarded by most Italians as one of the inevitabilities of life – and got into the driver's cab with his not too bright partner.

6

Bouncing along the dusty road which led to the main Monza to Milan highway and getting filthier every minute, I almost despaired at the thought of the long way up I had to climb. If I had been in England I think I might have given up, opted out and let the State take care of me, but there was absolutely no sense in thinking that way as a foreigner in Italy.

By the time I dropped off the truck my self-confidence, seldom more than surface deep, had almost disappeared. But less than half an hour later the bath, the shave and my clean hair had worked wonders. I was ready to start playing again.

If this is to be a truthful account, and I've decided that it only makes sense that way, I must try and give an objective description of myself, since what I look like has a lot to do with how I lead the life I do.

I'm five feet eight inches – all right, five feet seven and a bit – and my best working weight is a hundred and thirty-five pounds, nine stone nine, as I am small-boned. My hair is very black and perhaps a little too curly and I pull out the few white hairs. I get my olive complexion from my father and blue eyes from my mother. My teeth, which are naturally very white, are one of my best features and I have a straight nose, high cheekbones and rather full lips. I cultivate an English military-style moustache which is ginger coloured, probably from my mother's Irish ancestors. My hands are small and fragile-looking and I take only a $5\frac{1}{2}$ in shoes. I am stronger than I look although about the only exercise I take is swimming. I know that I look my best in white bathing trunks and a woman painter I posed for once told me that my body, though slight, had almost classic proportions but she may have been biased.

I realize that this must sound as though I am ridiculously conceited, but I don't think I am because I know that my physical make-up is an accident, a matter of luck, and only a fool takes credit for luck. But these assets are just about all I've got and so I have to be aware of them and to take care of them.

As I waited for the attendant to bring back my clothes I wondered what else I could get out of him, a cigarette at least, even perhaps a few lire so I could buy something to eat or a cup of strong black coffee. I opened the door a few inches but there was so sign of him. All I could do was to play it by ear when he brought back my clothes.

There was a rickety cane chair in one corner and I sat in it and put my feet up on the side of the bath, content to rest undisturbed for a little while. I badly needed a cigarette and a cup of coffee and, having had nothing in my stomach but water for the last twenty-four hours, I was damned hungry.

It wasn't the first time that I'd been rudely returned to square one but on those other occasions I'd lost the initiative as well, my future had been taken care of; board and lodging provided behind bars. I'd been given time in more than one sense to plan, to borrow enough to set up in business again. But now all the time I had was the minutes graciously granted by a public lavatory attendant. When he showed me the door I would be on my own, hungry and penniless. I'd never been in exactly that position before and had thought that, with all my advantages, such a disaster could never happen to me. Once it had all looked so easy; what the hell had gone wrong?

2

TWENTY-FIVE YEARS before, when I was in my teens, I'd escaped prison by a narrower margin than I'd realized. I'd been lucky and had guessed correctly: General Sir Wilfrith Rokesby-Gore had decided that what remained of his daughter's reputation was worth saving and had paid me fifty pounds. He had also turned me out of the room over the garage where I'd been allowed to live because I was Katy's bastard and Katy was his wife's beloved personal maid.

He'd warned me never to set foot on his property again but that hadn't worried me at all. I'd already discovered that the world was full of middle-aged, rich women in need of sex mixed with romance: I was sure that I could supply a good imitation of both. It had been demonstrated that my looks appealed to women; I found it easy to charm them and to get money out of them. I was bright, cunning and quite unscrupulous. Surely it would only be a matter of time before I seized a place far above the one into which I had so unluckily been born.

And yet here I was all those years later sitting on a rickety chair in a public bathroom dependent upon the charity of an old man who had none of my natural assets. Why had I never learned my lesson? Why hadn't I a friend in the world other than Peter the Barman? Why hadn't I found some other way to survive than by cheating women?

I'd always told myself that it was because of my lack of education, of training or of any skill, which had kept me from having a proper job and a wife and children. But I knew very well that it wasn't. Many boys had left inferior village schools and had still managed to achieve reasonably happy and fulfilled lives.

Admittedly the only subject I'd been any good at had been English, but I'd been quite good at that and the bored Careers Guidance Officer sent to talk to us before we left at fourteen had suggested that I try to get work at a printer's. But even at that age I had been determined to escape from the working class. I read a great deal, I was quick-witted, a natural mimic, and living at the Manor House had given me many chances of listening to and watching the upper classes in their world of ease and privilege. I knew I could pass myself off as one of them; all I needed was an introduction, and I could get that through a woman.

But it hadn't worked. Something always went wrong; nothing lasted. The cause wasn't that I hadn't been able to pass as a well-born, educated and cultured English gentleman, for I had – at least with foreigners. No, it was something else, some inner demon which had brought me to such utter desolation. I wasn't over the hill yet but in my early forties it was a probability I had to face.

I never knew the man who fathered me, Antonio Sacco the General's chauffeur, for he had been interned when Italy came into the war and afterwards sent back to the wife and children he'd left in Naples. The General and his young second wife had brought Antonio back from their honeymoon in Italy and his dark good looks and undisguised sensuality had caused quite a stir among the village girls, and among some who were no longer girls, even though it was known that he was married and a father.

My mother had only recently been promoted to lady's maid to Lady Liz, as the General's new wife was known below stairs, and she made sure that Tony kept his distance. As a poor Irish girl who had been taken on as a sixteen-year-old scullery maid only because her father had been the General's batman, she was well aware that her good name was practically her only asset, and she wasn't going to risk losing it. Knowing that she was very pretty and being in a good position she was in no hurry to get married. She was sure that she could do better than the local young men.

As I grew up I became bitter about my mother, particularly after starting at the village Church of England school where because she was a Roman Catholic I was treated as being outside the pale. When I was nine or ten someone called me an 'Eyetie bastard' and the name stuck until my teens when it was replaced by the less offensive 'Woppie'. I blamed my mother for my unhappiness; it never occurred to me that she might be unhappy too. When I left, or rather when the General kicked me out, I hadn't been sorry for many reasons to leave my mother. I was quite happy never to see her again.

But a dozen years later when I returned to England after a grim spell in a French prison I had her come up to London and we got drunk together. It was then that she told me about my father.

There had been a do at the village hall and most of the servants from the Manor House had gone. My mother had danced with several of the village young men and Tony Sacco with many of the young wives. One husband, a farm labourer, got the idea that the 'Wop' was being a bit too charming to his wife and called him outside. The news flashed round the room and my mother joined the crowd of spectators. She expected the fight to be a brawl like the ones which had often broken out on Saturday nights in Ireland, but when the aggrieved husband, having taken off his coat and rolled up his sleeves, turned with raised arms and clenched fists to face his opponent he saw to his astonishment that the Italian was crouched with a very wicked-looking knife in one hand and a scarf wrapped around his other forearm.

'Fight fair – with your fists, like a man,' growled the aggrieved husband, and the crowd agreed.

'You fight your way – I fight mine,' Tony answered. 'Come on – I'm going to cut your ear off.'

Instinctively the big man's hand went to his ear, which was fleshy and red.

'That's not how Englishmen fight,' he protested.

'It's how Neapolitans fight,' said Tony. 'The knife and the foot – see!' He demonstrated with a fast kick that was only inches short of the other man's face. 'Si, sometimes one dies – but not often.'

'I'm not fighting with bloody knives, but if you don't leave my missus alone I'll break your bloody arms one day when you haven't got that knife.'

'I always have it,' Tony said, shutting it with a click and somehow making it disappear, 'but don't worry – I don't want your wife.'

'That's all right then,' said the husband and they all returned to the dance, honour having been satisfied.

'I know it seems daft, but I think that was when I fell in love with Tony,' my mother said. 'He seemed so lonely somehow, not one of them and never could be. I felt a bit like that too, being Irish and Catholic living among damned English Protestants. They were Ireland's enemies and I knew I could never be one of them. And then Tony was, well, you know, a man I couldn't help thinking about that way even though I knew it was wrong.' She looked at me pleadingly.

'That's all right, ma. I'm not a lad any more. God knows I'm not. Go on.'

'I knew he was married and the first time he tried it on I gave him what for. I knew adultery was a terrible sin but by the Holy Virgin I couldn't help myself. He knew, of course – you bloody men always know – and he crept into my room a few nights later. I tried to stop him, I kept saying no, but he got into bed naked and I didn't dare cry out because I thought we'd both get the sack. I crossed my legs and locked my feet, George, I swear to God I did.'

'I know you did, ma, I know. And that's how I came to be born, eh?'

'Not that night, no. I was a virgin you see and – anyway it was the wrong time. I'd just finished bleeding and he said it was a safe time.'

I patted her hand. 'Go on.'

'Tony was surprised. He was ever so gentle though. I was crying and he kissed me on the eyes and said he was sorry and promised to take care of me.' She sniffed. 'And he would, I know he would, only there was his wife in Italy – but he didn't love her, George, he loved me and I loved him and that's why I wouldn't do nothing about it when I found out I was pregnant – not only because the Holy Church is against it, but because I loved him and I wanted to have his baby and I thought, you never know, maybe his wife would die – it's awful unhealthy in Naples – and then we could get married and if I had you I could keep him. Well it didn't work out that way, but I'm glad I had you.'

'I'm glad too.' We both laughed and had another drink.

'And when the war ended they sent him back to her,' my mother said bitterly. 'And I never heard from him no more. And when he was gone they wouldn't let me alone . . .'

'Who?'

'Men – all kinds of men who had always treated me decent but who thought that just because I'd had a – love child – I'd be easy. But I wasn't!'

'I know you weren't, ma.'

'I never let no man touch me while Tony was interned – not one, although enough of them tried – you'd be surprised if I told you some of the names.'

I didn't say anything; if she wanted to tell me she would, and such information could be valuable.

'Well I'll tell you one because he really did surprise me – Mr Dilkes.'

'Old Dizzy Dilkes the headmaster?'

'Yes, but he wasn't so old then and he wasn't the headmaster, only one of the teachers. It was when you started school. He asked me to come and see him to talk about you and I like a fool believed him. You could have knocked me over with a feather when he grabbed me.' She laughed. 'I gave him the old knee treatment in the – you know – and he fell and broke a chair and the other teacher came in to see what was wrong and although Mr Dilkes said he'd tripped it was obvious what had happened.'

Her telling me that solved a mystery for me. From the first the headmaster had disliked me and I'd never known why. He'd seen to it that I had a pretty rough time at school and there had been one experience which I had not needed the prison psychiatrist to tell me had been a traumatic one for me.

Even though I was known as that Kate Kelly's 'mistake' on the rare occasions when one of the other boys took me home, and was made to feel like something the cat dragged in, I knew in my secret mind that I was superior. When the red-faced country boys with large hands and feet called me 'Pretty Boy' or 'Dolly Face' I knew it was really because they were jealous. And when the not much smaller village girls joined in I had only to remember the number of valentines I found in my desk every year.

I didn't like games; I was afraid of getting hurt, especially by the rock-hard cricket ball. The only success I ever had was when I told stories of my adventures which were supposed to have taken place in London where I went every summer for a fortnight at my Aunt Colly's. Of course they didn't believe everything but they listened, even those who disliked me most and who always called me a bloody liar. But I noticed they always listened to the end before saying it.

Once when I was thirteen and on my way to school an Austin Seven stopped alongside me and a woman asked the way to the Portsmouth road. Without knowing why, I said I was trying to get there myself to see my father who was in a hospital, so they gave me a lift. During the ride I told them he was a sailor and had fallen from the crow's nest and broken his back and that although my mother had no money to give me I'd made up my mind to go and visit him somehow.

There actually was a hospital on the road as we entered Portsmouth and I said that was where my father was. The woman in the car was nearly in tears as they let me out.

'What about food?' she asked. 'And how will you get home tonight?'

'I'll be all right,' I said bravely. 'I don't need much food and I

13

expect my dad will give me the fare – even if he has to borrow it.'

She told her husband to give me ten shillings but he said that was too much so all I got was two half-crowns. I had six penn'orth of fish and tuppence of chips for lunch and then went to the pictures for ninepence. For tea I had egg and chips and an ice and I bought three books from a stall for a shilling. One was called *The Confessions of a Confidence Trickster*, and it seemed to me later, when I'd read it twice, that he really wasn't all that clever. That, I thought, was probably the reason he'd been caught and sent to prison and had to earn money by telling his story to the newspaper reporter who had written it down. I was pretty sure that I could do better at tricking money out of people.

I did not get home until after seven and my mother had already been to the village policeman's cottage. He'd laughed at her and said I'd just been playing truant and would be back when I got hungry. She was so angry when I walked in she grabbed me by the collar and slapped my face and sent me to bed without any supper.

The next day I was the centre of attention at school because everyone knew about my mother's going to the police. During the break I told them that a big black car had stopped with three men in it and one had got out and asked me in a foreign accent if I knew the road to Portsmouth and when I'd said that I did he'd grabbed me and pushed me into the car, which had driven off at high speed.

I had practically every boy in the playground hanging on every word.

I told them they'd asked me where the naval dockyard was and where the submarines were kept and that I'd refused to tell them – this brought cries of admiration from some – and that then one of them had threatened me with a huge knife so I'd pretended to take them to the submarines but had instead led them to the police station and had jumped out of the car and run inside, and although they'd driven off at high speed again the police had caught them.

The Navy had found out that they were Russian spies and a naval officer had given me five shillings reward. Then I told them about the picture I'd seen and the fish and chips and egg and chips and ice-cream and I showed them the two sixpences and two pennies I had left as proof that my story was true.

My moment of glory did not last very long, for it all got back to the teacher and I was sent for by the headmaster, Mr Dilkes, the next day. I tried to stick to my story but he tore it to shreds without difficulty and I was caned for playing truant.

I yelled at the top of my voice so he wouldn't hit so hard, but all that did was to earn his contempt.

'You're not only a slacker and an incorrigible liar, George Kelly, you're a snivelling coward,' he said when he'd finished and I was holding my swelling fingers in my mouth. 'Now you're going to wear this for the rest of the day.'

He picked up a piece of white cardboard on which he'd written 'I AM A LIAR' with a broad-nibbed fountain pen and he added underneath 'AND A COWARD'. He hung this around my neck and I had to bring it back to him when school ended.

I was only thirteen years old when that happened, but even though I'd hated the caning and the cruel gibes of the others I knew that I had tasted success. I'd got what everyone in the world wanted, money and respect, by telling a tale to two grown-ups and then I'd invented a completely different story for a crowd of boys and – for the time being at least – had made them believe that I was something more than Kate Kelly's Eyetie bastard who couldn't play games and didn't like to do any of the things they did. It was then that I got the name 'Woppie' and that it was accepted that although I would never be one of them I had earned a place in the local hierarchy.

But the important thing, the reason that I've remembered that incident all my life, is that when I was telling the couple in the car about my father lying in hospital it was all true; he was there and I was unhappy and on the edge of tears. And when I was describing the Russian spies that was true too and my heart raced as I remembered being threatened by a huge, sharp knife.

To make someone believe something, I had learned, you have to believe it yourself. It had since proved to be a useful lesson.

A double knock on the bathroom door scattered my memories.

3

THE ATTENDANT HELD out my suit brushed and pressed, my shirt washed and ironed dry and my shoes now shining. Before I could get out more than a 'Mille grazie' he'd thrust it all on me and shut the door.

I stood on the chair to put my trousers on so as not to spoil the crease; I carefully knotted my tie further down so as to conceal the old grease marks and I cleaned the front teeth which show with soap and a corner of the towel. I pulled my coat into place and smiled at my reflection in the flaking, full-length mirror. Despite the hint of a double chin and the lines on my face I could pass for thirty-five. I was back in business and there was still time to win my Snakes and Ladders.

I carried the soap, towel and razor back to the attendant in his little room. He stood back and inspected me and then nodded with satisfaction.

'You are yourself again – is it true?'

'It is true and I owe it to your kindness. I . . .'

'Coffee?' He pointed to a copper pot on an electric ring at the same time indicating his upholstered chair with a sweep of his arm. I sat down while he prepared the coffee in small, white cups.

I looked round his castle; crowded, snug, brightly lit, cooled by a noisy, standing electric fan, a room to be lived in. Next to his chair a small table held magazines in English as well as Italian and an open paperback copy of Moravia's *Woman of Rome*. Framed photographs of couples with children stood on a shelf with a vase holding two roses; on the walls were colour pictures carefully cut from magazines including, surprisingly, a reproduction of a painting by Magritte.

For a moment I found myself envying him his dry, safe cave and I wondered if that would be how I would spend the last years of my life – as a night porter in a small hotel perhaps.

He handed me my coffee and politely sat on a stool himself, knowing what was due to a guest. We chatted about the state of the world and the chances of the Communists coming to power, an outcome which he would deplore as he was sure that one of the comrades would get his job. I agreed that it would be a terrible thing to stifle free enterprise – it would certainly make life difficult for me.

It was very pleasant. All that was missing was a cigarette but as there was no sign of an ashtray I guessed that he didn't smoke. I got up to leave and he rose too.

'You have been very kind. Will you tell me your name and where I should send payment?'

He shook his head. 'Please do not think of such a thing. I too have known mala fortuna and poverty – I was not always a success and life was not always as comfortable as this. It would be sad if we could not hold out a hand when a fellow-traveller stumbles.'

I held out mine. 'I see you are a philosopher as well as a good Samaritan. Thank you then and arrivederla.'

'Arrivederla – some day when the sun is shining for you again you will no doubt pass through Milano. Come and pay me a visit, Onorevole.' The use of the honorific was deliberate, I was sure. I had moved up my first ladder.

'I will – you may depend on it.' We shook hands.

I meant it and perhaps one day I will go and see him – if I'm allowed to leave my 'last resort'.

I walked back into the station. The policeman, not recognizing me, looked almost respectful. The problem now was food; I'd been given nothing at all to eat in the police station during the whole of the preceding day and night – no doubt the cost of my food was another of the police chief's perks – and the coffee I'd just drunk had made my stomach expect something more substantial for its gastric juices to work on. I had to get food inside me somehow.

I walked out into the street and looked for a hotel, not a big one, for their security systems are too efficient; and not too small, for they know their guests by sight; not too expensive since I didn't look that prosperous; not too cheap because in those they are always suspicious.

Two streets from the station I found what I was looking for, a modern six-storey hotel catering to those who couldn't afford luxury but still had fairly high standards. I walked briskly in and made unhesitatingly for the main stairs, taking in, while not appearing to do so, the location of the desk, around which guests checking out were clustered. I registered the porter's desk, the lifts and the way to the lounge.

I carried on up the stairs to the second floor. Pausing for a look around, I stood in front of the lifts. As a couple came from one of the corridors I pressed the button. The lift arrived just as they reached me, the arrow showing it was going down. I beckoned them in.

'I'm going up,' I explained.

As soon as the doors shut I saw that someone had put out a breakfast tray and I walked towards it. There was an untouched roll and some jam but I was determined never to be reduced to scavenging. Two rooms along a door opened and a man came out carrying two suitcases. I walked on as though returning to my room, noticing that he left his door open as people often do on their departure. I turned the corner and waited until I heard the sound of the lift descending again. Then I hurried back and popped into the room, number 219, closing the door behind me.

He had, of course, left nothing of value, at least nothing he thought was of value, but on the floor next to the bed was a copy of the *Wall Street Journal* only a day old, which, as a badge of respectability, was valuable to me. I restored it carefully to its original folds. Then I emptied the waste-paper basket on to the floor.

There was a ballpoint pen not quite used up, the rejected drafts of two letters, and notes on a business interview which made no sense to me.

From the bathroom I pocketed a tablet of soap still in the hotel's wrapper and tore off about four feet of toilet paper which I carefully folded and put in my pocket. I would probably need it before I was settled again. I was tempted to take a face towel too, but I didn't. If I were caught in the hotel and discovered not to be a guest they would only show me to the street as long as I had nothing of theirs. If I had even a face towel they might well hand me over to the police. Anyway I am not a sneak thief.

With the *Wall Street Journal* tucked under my arm I opened the bedroom door, unfortunately just as a waiter passed carrying a breakfast tray. He looked surprised and I realized that he had probably served breakfast in that room.

'My friend has gone,' I said in Italian. We exchanged 'buongiornos' and as I walked towards the lifts I noticed that he took the tray into room 220, almost opposite the one I'd left.

At the ground floor I walked over to the desk. 'I have an appointment here, so I'll have a coffee – where is the dining-room?'

He pointed to it and I walked in and sat at a small double table and opened my *Wall Street Journal*. When the waitress came I ordered a hot chocolate, which has more food value than coffee, bread and sweet rolls, and then, almost as though it were an afterthought, a plate of prosciutto and cheese. From this she would assume that I was Dutch and I phrased my answer in a Dutch accent just in case she was brighter than she looked.

Everything went without a hitch, as I had been confident it would. The dining-room was full of busy people gobbling their breakfasts and as long as I was careful not to give the number of a room whose occupant was at another table there was no way the waitress could guess the truth, unless by some great bad luck she remembered the man or woman from room 220 from the day before, but I guessed that if he or she were having breakfast in the room that morning, as I had seen, it was probably a regular thing.

The hot, sweet chocolate, rolls and butter, cheese and delicious smoked ham quite put me back on the top line and I walked out of the hotel as though I were a major shareholder, smiling graciously at the young desk clerk. I made my way back into the station and walked past the cop and straight into the First Class Waiting-Room. One is always safer in First Class. I chose a seat by the window from which I could see passengers arriving. I was ready to stalk my prey: somewhere nearby, I was sure, was a middle-aged and lonely woman with more money than she needed. All I had to do was to contrive a meeting with her.

My best bet was to mingle with a largish group of English or Americans being shepherded around Italy on a guided tour. If I could inconspicuously join them and appear to be on chatty terms with one, the others would assume that I was a new member of their group.

There are many such parties all over Europe during the summer holidays, and it wasn't long before I spotted about a twenty-strong covey moving through the crowd and keeping close together. My experienced eye told me they were lower-middle-class British on a guided package tour, probably 'abroad' for the first time.

The men, sweating in ordinary business suits, their Sunday best, had bravely left off their neckties and, as a further concession to the informality of the holiday, were wearing sandals – with wool socks. The women, middle-aged and out of breath as their courier whipped them along at a trot, had done extraordinary things to their hair.

It takes time and trouble to get money out of hard-up people travelling on a tight budget. They have almost always spent more than they intended to and suspect everyone of having designs on their shallow purses and are not far wrong. I let them go.

About twenty minutes later a short, chubby Italian in a dark blue uniform bustled importantly into the station followed by porters pushing two trolleys piled high with luggage. He was wearing a huge black hat, around the brim of which I made out the words 'Art Appreciation Adventure Tour'. Behind the trolleys came a crocodile of prosperous-looking, middle-aged to elderly tourists. I slipped out of the waiting-room and moved in behind them. They were, as I had guessed, Americans. I recognized the subdivision too: fairly well-heeled, acquirers of instant culture after years of chasing more mundane goals.

I moved in, smiled at the last couple as though we'd met before, exchanged a casual phrase with the next clutch and kept my eyes open for an unaccompanied woman. The courier handed a wad of tickets to the man at the gate and we all trickled through as he tried to match the number with us. The train was a rapido to Venice. The porters unloaded the luggage on to the platform opposite a first-class carriage reserved for the AAA Tour and everyone sorted out their own.

With my hunter's instinct I picked out a lone middle-aged female struggling with two large bags.

'Here, let me give you a hand,' I said.

She turned, her face full of suspicion, but the British accent and the military moustache worked as they usually did.

'Well thank you – that's real nice of you.'

I followed her into a compartment and hoisted her overweight bags on to the luggage racks.

'Do you like to face the engine?' I asked.

'Huh?' She was puzzled. 'Oh, I see what you mean – well it doesn't really make any difference to me. How about you?'

'I like to sit with my back to it.' It wasn't true, but that way I could see who was coming and spot whether there was going to be a check of tickets against numbers. We sat by the window facing each other. She patted her blonde curls into place – not a wig I decided, but obviously dyed – and smoothed the wrinkles in her black and white checked slacks.

I knew she was surreptitiously summing me up, so I looked out on to the platform so she could enjoy my right profile which is by far my best, strong and distinguished. The left goes wrong somehow.

'Do you mind if I smoke?' I asked.

'No, you go right ahead,' she said graciously.

I reached into my pocket and looked dismayed. 'Damn! I've left my cigarettes and lighter in the hotel.'

'That's too bad. If you don't mind American cigarettes, have one of mine.'

'Thanks,' I said, taking a Winston. I'd have smoked old rope at that point.

Now I had to stalk my prey cautiously. Limited time and complete lack of money were serious handicaps. Women of a certain age with some money of their own are suspicious when an attractive man is attentive to them, unless he gives the impression of being fairly prosperous. If they conclude that he has more money than they do themselves and that he is a busy man of the world, then they are often ready to trust him completely.

With even a small amount of ready cash I can play that role convincingly, but with empty pockets it's most difficult. However, I had nothing to lose and I saw the stalk as a challenge to my skill.

Immediate tactics, I decided, would be to establish that so far my motives had been no more than to help a lady with her luggage and that I would probably slip out of her life as casually as I had entered it. I smiled at her, nodded slightly to indicate that we had finished our immediate business, and opened my *Wall Street Journal*. I turned to the London Stock Exchange quotations and, with the ballpoint pen I had scavenged, made one or two large calculations in the margin: I was glad to note that she looked slightly disappointed.

Suddenly the air was split by one of those American women's voices which have such remarkable carrying power.

'Hey! I got four places – right over here. Hi, Dora! – C'mon! – Hurry up!' There was a flash of lime green and a large woman spread herself over the two double seats across from our singles.

Moments later a smaller woman in bright orange slacks and a blue, polka-dot top joined her and each sat in the middle of a double seat, claiming possession with outstretched hands. After one or two frustrated passengers had been warned off, two panting men arrived laden down with suitcases like pack mules. One, a small dark man of forty or so, was dressed in a bright red and blue checked jacket – all these colours reminded me of Mardi Gras in Rio – and stacked the bags in the luggage racks as they were handed up to him by the other, a very large man of about the same age, dressed in a blue and white seersucker suit. He lifted up the heavy suitcases, one in each large hand.

When the bags were piled precariously on top of each other seersucker suit glanced over at us.

'Pushy huh, Dora – how'd ya get settled in so quick?'

My mark looked pleased with herself.

'Hi, Leonard, well you see this gentleman very kindly helped me with my bags.'

We exchanged 'hi's' and handshakes, the big man either feeling it necessary to show his strength or just not realizing the power in his fists. The smaller man, however, treated my mangled hand gently, which made me think that he was more intelligent. I associate fierce handclasps, at least after adolescence, with the not too bright. The smaller man's brown eyes looked straight into mine with friendliness, while at the same time I felt he was shrewdly assessing me.

The woman in green pushed between the two men. 'Say, that was real polite!' She nodded her approval and for a moment I was sure that she was going to pat me on the head, but she turned to the two men and silently pointed to their seats. They obeyed and she took the aisle seat and leaned across to me.

'We're the Harrises – Leonard and Marge.' She indicated seersucker suit who jerked his head and smiled pleasantly. 'And these love birds are the Angelinis, Gino and Catherina – they just got married.'

Checked Jacket and Orange Slacks were a couple in their forties who smiled happily at this introduction, apparently quite unembarrassed. They all looked at me expectantly.

'How d'you do. Rokesby-Gore, Colonel Rokesby-Gore, retired.'

'I bet you're English,' said Catherina. The others laughed. I admitted it.

'You haven't told me *your* name,' I said to my victim.

'Mrs Dora Bukovski.' She evidently felt this needed explanation. 'My husband was a hundred per cent American but he was of Polish descent. I'm of German descent myself.'

'And I'm of Irish descent,' Marge said, which explained the wearin' o' the green. 'And Leon's folks came from Lithuania – and their name wasn't exactly Harris.'

'But I'm a hundred per cent American too,' Leon said enthusiastically. 'We're all Yankee doodle dandies.'

'That's fine,' I said, taking up my *Wall Street Journal* again.

'What's the D.J. doing?' asked Leon.

'It's still stuck: this bull market hasn't really sparked off yet.'

It was a remark I'd overheard in the Ruhl bar in Nice, and they all looked suitably impressed.

'Would you like to see it? I'm afraid it's yesterday's though – probably too late to act on special situations – not that I've spotted any.'

He took it and I saw that he had noticed the calculations I'd made.

'I guess you play the market?' he asked.

I laughed deprecatingly. 'Oh, I have a flutter now and then when I get a tip I can trust.'

'Where there's a tip there's a tap,' he quoted, no doubt to let me know he wasn't an ordinary punter. I agreed and for the next ten or fifteen minutes he and I talked about shares which had shot up and fortunes which had been made and lost. Then I switched the subject to other opportunities to make a quick profit: stamps, coins, banknotes for instance. The rest became interested and I entertained them with anecdotes of remarkable finds in small shops in small towns, and was glad to find that none of them was a philatelist or a numismatist, a fact which opened possibilities for me.

The ice having been broken, we talked about ourselves, always an interesting subject and one in which the women joined.

By the time the train drew into Pescheria I knew that Dora was one of the ever-growing regiment of middle-aged widows who, because their husbands carried more insurance than they could really afford, are left on his death with more money to spend than they'd ever known.

'We were planning to see Europe when Jersey retired', she said, 'and I know he'd have wanted me to go, and I've always been interested in Art, so I signed up for this tour. I've learned a lot already.'

By Verona, Leonard had told me how he had sold his grocery store in the Bronx for several thousand dollars more than it was worth by falsifying the turnover.

'I gradually increased my orders from the wholesalers and passed what I didn't sell over to my brother who has a store in Newark. I had to mark it down ten per cent and I had to pay tax on profits I wasn't making, but I made the little decaying business look like a gold mine. I bet the sucker who bought it is still wondering where all the customers have gone.' He and the others laughed.

23

From Verona to Vicenza I heard the story of the Angelinis' lightning romance. Gino, who worked for the telephone company in the Los Angeles area, had met Catherina, whose real name was Kate, when he called to repair her telephone.

'We clicked right away,' he said, winking at me.

'It was our destiny,' Catherina said. 'I knew right away it was.'

A double divorce followed and their marriage in Reno took place in a beautiful white chapel made to look, they said, like the ice palace of the North Wind, whatever that is. That had been only two weeks earlier and they were now on their honeymoon in the country of Gino's parents.

'The telephone company gave me an extra two weeks,' Gino said. 'I guess I deserve it after sixteen years.'

The trip had been paid for out of Catherina's share from the sale of her marital home.

'Ninety-four thousand bucks,' she crowed. 'Split right down the middle – that's California community property law.'

From Vicenza to Padua it was my turn and they learned a great deal about Colonel Rokesby-Gore – I told them that they could call me 'Ronald' – who had lately buried his dear wife, Jane, and retired from the Army and was now travelling in Europe because Sussex was too full of sad memories. They were most sympathetic and when Dora patted my hand I saw there were tears in her eyes and I wondered just how much cash she was carrying.

As we pulled in to Venezia Mestre, which I had to explain to them was not yet Venice, I discovered that they were all booked to stay in the Gabrielli-Sandwirth Hotel facing the San Marco Canal. It is a very comfortable hotel and I was tempted to stay with them, but decided that without baggage it would be too risky. Instead we agreed to meet in the hotel's bar the following day for drinks before I took Dora to lunch.

As the train crossed the bridge leading to Venice I got up. 'My things are in the luggage van,' I explained. 'See you tomorrow then.'

'So long, Ronnie – see ya!' said Leonard jovially.

I made my way along the length of the train and locked myself in the lavatory in the last car, waited until the noise of departing passengers had died away. Then I dropped down on the tracks side of the carriage and crossed three sets of lines to a large, empty platform.

4

For a few moments I stood in the shadows to see if anyone had spotted me running across the track, but the whole area seemed deserted. I tried the nearest door; it was unlocked and I went through, closing it softly behind me. In a long, high-roofed, windowless shed there were hundreds of suitcases, trunks and boxes, presumably holiday-makers' luggage sent in advance.

Yet another of my rules is that I don't steal if there is even a slight chance of getting caught. A professional should compete seriously only in his own game and I am a specialized conman. On the other hand I wouldn't starve in a ripe apple orchard, and I had to be carrying a suitcase if I were to get into a hotel without being asked to pay in advance. If I looked respectable, was carrying at least one bag, and had a British passport, I could get a room in any good hotel merely by signing the register.

The only lighting was from a single large bulb hanging high above the luggage so that the edges and ends of the shed were in shadow. I stood stock still holding my breath and straining to hear any sound, but after a minute or so I was almost certain there was no one else within earshot. I looked over the suitcases in the nearest pile until I came to a heavy pigskin one secured with a wide strap. It must, I felt sure, belong to a man, which, of course, was essential.

There was a name tag but the light was too bad for me to read it – all I could make out was the word MAINZ in capital letters. I tore the tag off and stuffed it inside a basket so that no sharp-eyed porter would spot it and start looking for the piece of luggage it belonged to. If by some bad luck I was stopped and questioned it would be fatal for the bag I was carrrying to bear a name tag which didn't match my indentification.

I went back through the same door, trying to look cool and unconcerned in case there should be anyone there. There wasn't, so I walked down the platform towards where I guessed the way out should be. At a choice of three passageways I chose the largest, which ended at a double door, and found myself looking into what was obviously the staff canteen. It was full of railway employees talking, gesticulating, drinking wine or coffee and smoking in such numbers that the air was blue.

I froze, but no one took the slightest notice of me and I went back to where the passages met. Several people passed me without even a curious look; I might have been invisible. I tried both the other passages but each led only to offices. There was no way out into the street except over an open footbridge crossing the tracks to the main station. Besides being in full view of everyone, it would not help since I would still not be able to get out of the station without passing a ticket collector.

I decided to see if I could leave by the side of the station, guessing that there would probably be some kind of a gap from where I could make my way around to the front. I went around the long shed and scrambled across the railway lines with the suitcase, which seemed to get heavier by the minute. I hoped that whatever weighed so much was valuable and easy to sell.

At last I came to some broken and abandoned buildings and threaded my way through them, clambering over rubble and fallen beams until I found myself on the inside of a fence separating the railroad property from the Grand Canal. I found a bag of cement which had hardened and which enabled me to get high enough to drop my bag on to the other side. I started to climb over myself and just as I was carefully lifting my leg over without touching the dirty fence top, a crowded vaporetto, which must have just pulled away from the Ferrovia landing-stage towards the Piazzale Roma, passed within a few feet of me. The passengers stared with some surprise and a small boy pointed his finger at me. His mother slapped his hand down for being rude. Obviously, I thought, as I waved to him, they were not Italians.

I picked up the bag and walked along the canalside path only to come to a locked iron gate. I could see a couple of hundred feet away the crowded open space in front of the station. I scanned the people for police but spotted none, so I climbed up over the gate with the suitcase, which took a bit of doing. I dropped to the other side and looked to see if I'd been noticed, but if I had no one made any sign.

I tried, without much hope, to open the suitcase but it was firmly locked. I had taken pains not to get any dirt or stains on my suit, but my hands were filthy and that wouldn't do for signing in at a good hotel. I picked up the bag, walked up the station steps, into the front hall, and found the men's lavatory, where I got the worst of the dirt off with lukewarm water and my stolen bar of soap. I dried my hands with toilet paper and set off to find a hotel.

The bag was so heavy I soon wished I had chosen a lighter, smaller one, but I consoled myself that it surely must contain something I could turn into cash as soon as I could get the damned thing open. I hadn't gone very far along the Lista di Spagna before I passed a restaurant with a refrigerator window full of fish and shellfish, and realized that I was ravenously hungry. At the next such restaurant, the Gobbi, I looked through the window at a table piled with mouth-watering dishes; a plate of small artichokes in olive oil, another of mushrooms, a platter of crayfish and squid. I speculated on how to get a meal, but knew that it was no use. If I ate first and then said that I'd lost my wallet they would almost certainly call the police. I slogged on with my pigskin bag. It was not long before my right arm felt as though it were about to be dislocated at the elbow. I shifted to the left hand but soon had to put the case down and rest.

A boy offered to carry it for me and I was tempted to let him, but that would only lead to a row when we reached the hotel, and I couldn't tip him. A row about money was the last thing I wanted. I passed two or three hotels which would have done, but I wanted to be near enough to the Gabrielli Sandwirth on the Riva degli Schiavoni for Dora to be able to walk to mine.

Finally, after what seemed an age, I reached the Rialto, having crossed eight or nine of Venice's four hundred humpbacked bridges, and sat down on one of the benches until my arms stopped aching. Now I was not only hungry, but thirsty and tired as well; somehow I had to find shelter, food and drink or I would drop.

I struck off once more towards the church of Santa Maria Formosa, crossing two more bridges with steep steps and resting again. Now I was not more than three or four hundred yards north of their hotel and it was time to find one of my own. I picked up the damned bag again, crossed yet another bridge near the main library and came upon a small, elegant hotel backing on to a canal. It was called the Questura and seemed to be just right for me; not too big and not too small. I pushed open the door, said 'grazie' loudly to the non-existent man who had supposedly carried my bag, and walked confidently in and up to reception.

'Have you a single room with bath for two or three nights?' I asked in my English colonel's voice. The manager looked at me with half-closed eyes, either because he was too tired to keep them open or had drunk too much.

'Have you booked, sir?' I recognized the ploy – it was to give him time to size me up.

'No, I came on the spur of the moment – if you don't have a room it doesn't matter – I'll walk on to the Danieli where I usually stay.' The Danieli is one of the oldest and best of Venice's hotels and I made as though about to pick up my bag.

'We do have a room, sir, with bath. It's a quiet room on the first floor.'

'How much?'

'Eighty thousand lire with service and I.V.A.'

'What credit cards do you honour?'

'Most of them – Diners, American Express, Eurocard – which do you have?'

'All of them.'

He opened the register and turned it round for me to sign. I felt I'd won the first round on points as I signed Colonel Ronald Rokesby-Gore, Retd, giving my address as The Manor House, Norley, Brock-enhurst, Hants, guessing that he would know enough of England to be impressed. I handed over my passport and to show me to the room he whistled up a boy who placed the heavy suitcase on a stand and, after a hopeful pause, left me in possession.

The first thing I did, my standard procedure, was to see if the window opened easily and that there was a way out. It did and I saw that it looked on to an inner court with a tired tree and a couple of tables.

There was a ledge a few feet below from which I could get on to a flat roof and then to the ground.

Priority was to get the suitcase open and see what treasures it yielded. The locks were solid brass and I would need a hammer and chisel to force them, and I couldn't think of a reasonable way of asking for those. But a sharp knife might do the job. That gave me an idea. I picked up the phone and ordered a pot of coffee with milk, a selection of cakes and then, as though it were an afterthought, a bowl of mixed fruit. While I was waiting for these to come I undressed and went into the bathroom, turning on the shower when I heard the waiter at the door. I shouted for him to come in thus making it appear quite natural that I didn't tip him.

As soon as he'd left I wrapped a towel round my middle and had a look at what he'd brought. There was a large pot of coffee, a jug of milk, a plate of pastries and a bowl of apples, oranges, bananas and grapes with, I was glad to see, a stout little fruit knife.

First I tried to pick the locks with the point of the knife but they were well-made German ones and I had no success. I tried to cut round them but found that they were welded on to a strip of metal under the leather. As I've said I'm not a hotel sneak thief and I've never acquired the specialized skills of that profession. Finally I decided the only way to get at the contents was to cut the bottom of the case open. The leather was tough but the knife was sharp and I finally managed to cut two diagonals joining the corners. This allowed four triangular flaps to open outwards and I dumped everything out on the bed.

I saw immediately that the owner must have been a much bigger man than I am, for the waist of a very expensive pair of trousers was about eight inches too big and a beautiful pair of hand-made Italian shoes were size 11. His silk shirts were $17\frac{1}{2}$ collar and I am 14. I could have wept. However, I put on the silk pyjamas with legs and sleeves rolled up and wrapped the Paisley dressing-gown around me.

I then sat down and enjoyed my coffee and pastries plus an apple, a banana and some grapes, after which I felt much better and went back to the contents of the suitcase to see what I could turn into cash. I had hoped that there might have been some money, but there wasn't a penny. The only things I could sell quickly were an electric razor, four pairs of cuff-links and a dressing-case of alligator skin with silver fittings and the initials B.L. on the outside, also in silver. One pair of cuff-links was gold, two were silver and the fourth, jade.

I hung the clothes up in the wardrobe, put the shirts, socks, handkerchiefs and underwear in drawers, the pyjamas under my pillow, and left the dressing-gown on the bed. I put the suitcase on top of the wardrobe so the cuts couldn't be seen.

I pocketed the cuff-links and put the dressing-case inside my jacket under my left arm. I caught sight of the little fruit knife and took that too – it would be better than nothing. Although I am not a brave, tough man, I have discovered that few others are either, and a threat is often all that's necessary to discourage aggression.

I walked back to the station and went up to one of the touts wearing a cap with the name of a cheap hotel. He was a seedy-looking, fifty-year-old with bloodshot eyes.

'Yes, sir, you want a nice room – not 'spensive, twenty thousand?'

'No – I've got some things I want to sell and I need some advice.'

'What kind of things?'

'Well – this.' I showed him the dressing-case.

'Not here, not here – follow me.' He went out of the station, turned left, and then almost immediately left again into a narrow street and then into a dingy café-bar.

'You want a grappa and coffee?'

'Yes, but I've lost all my money – that's why I'm selling my things.'

'If I pay I take it out of what I get when I sell your things – okay?'

'Okay, but I'll only sell for a fair price – nobody robs me.'

'Don't worry – I got the best connections in Venezia.' He brought two thick white cups of steaming black coffee from the bar and then two equally thick little glasses of grappa. He took a sip of grappa and a gulp of coffee. 'Okay – let's see what you got there.'

I pushed over the dressing-case and put the cuff-links in a saucer. He examined them minutely.

'How much?'

I reckoned the gold ones – which were only fourteen carat – had probably cost about sixty dollars, the silver perhaps half that each, and the jade, which were modern, about forty dollars, and I thought if I got a quarter of all that I'd be doing well.

'Eighty thousand lire for the lot.'

'Lei scherza!'

'I'm not joking at all,' I said. 'That's the price.'

He shook his head. 'No chance – maybe fifty thousand.'

'Che ridicolo!'

He shrugged his shoulders and took up the dressing-case, peering at the brushes to see if they were silver or plated. I showed him the hallmark and he nodded. He pointed to the initials.

'Yours?'

'Si – Bernard Leach.' I didn't think he would have heard of the great potter.

'How much?'

The case could not have cost less than two hundred dollars new, probably more.

'A hundred thousand lire.'

He laughed. 'It's silver, not gold, signor. Maybe – a occhio e croce – I could get you forty-five thousand for both the case and the cuff-links.'

The bargaining went on for another quarter of an hour and another grappa before we agreed on seventy thousand. He wrapped the cuff-links in his handkerchief, put the case inside his coat and got up from the table. I started to rise.

'No – you have to wait here. They won't buy if anyone is with me.'

I gave him a long, steady look but he didn't drop his eyes. I took out the fruit knife and began to clean my finger nails with its sharp point.

'Don't forget to pay at the bar before you leave.'

He scowled. 'Don't you trust me?'

'Not yet – I don't know you. Don't be long.'

As he paid I heard the barman call him 'Giusepp'' which would make it less difficult to find him again if I'd been a mug, but he was back in less than a quarter of an hour. He sat down at the table and counted out a wad of one-thousand lire notes.

'Two t'ousan' t'ree hundred lire for the grappa,' he explained. 'Okay?'

'Okay.' I pocketed the money and we shook hands.

'You get any more you bring 'em to me – I get you the best price.'

'I'll do that.' I wondered how much he'd made on the deal. 'Ciao, Giuseppe.'

'Ciao – what's your real name?'

'Johnny.'

'Ciao, Johnny.'

With money in my pocket, even though it was only about twenty-five pounds, the world seemed a much less frightening place. Cigarettes were a necessity and I bought a packet of cheap Italian ones. The food I'd had at the hotel had made me less hungry but I wanted a substantial meal. I walked firmly past the expensive restaurants near the station since I had a lot to do with a small sum of money. I went along the Calle Priuli towards the Lista di Spagna where, I knew, there were cheaper places to eat.

The prices on the menus displayed outside came down steadily as I got into the workers' Venice. Spaghetti alle vongole dropped by a hundred lire a time until I saw it advertised for 3800 in a restaurant crowded with local people, always a good sign. I went in and took a seat, enjoying the familiar smell of Italian food. There wasn't exactly an overabundance of shellfish in the dish but I treated myself to a half litre of white wine as well and got through two baskets of bread. I refused coffee but did have cheese, and the bill, including service, was only 4950 lire, the 50-lire change being four boiled sweets.

Feeling that I had moved another few squares up towards the winning one, I strolled through the beautiful streets of Venice to the Piazza San Marco, which always gives me pleasure. I arrived just in time for the nightly lowering of the flag by a party of marines. As they marched off, the petty officer shouted an order every ten seconds or so at which they stamped down hard with the left foot, making a sound which rang the cobblestones and echoed off the stone walls. I may, I thought, be on my uppers but I'm free, thank God, and no one can make me stamp my foot if I don't want to.

To finish the evening pleasantly I walked to Cande della Giudecca and boarded a vaporetto. I was lucky to get a seat right up in the bow and so had a tour of the Grand Canal, sixteen stops for 400 lire, an even better travel bargain than the Staten Island ferry. Just as the pilot tucked the boat expertly into Rialto I saw Dora and the Angelinis in a gondola, one of the picture postcard ones, fast disappearing because of the high initial cost and because the sons of the traditional gondolier familes prefer to earn high wages in the factories of the mainland rather than poling tourists through the Venetian canals while doing a bad imitation of an opera singer. The one vigorously poling Dora, Gino and Catherina was actually belting out *Santa Lucia*, a performance which his passengers completely ignored as they shouted witticisms to Leonard and Marge Harris in another gondola a few yards behind.

Their gondolas would have set them back at least ten thousand lire a head; obviously they were not short of a bob or two. Dora must be carrying at least a thousand dollars, and I decided to go for about half. I pulled back from the rail since my travelling on the public water bus would not fit in with my role as a rich English traveller.

Fatigue hit me like a blow when I got back to my room. It had been an exhausting day since walking out of the police cell just after sunrise, riding in Ulrico's truck to Milan and the long train ride to Venice, followed by the considerable walking I'd done since, and I wanted nothing more than to crawl between clean sheets and to sleep for nine or ten hours.

But I forced myself to wash my drip-dry shirt in the basin with the hotel soap and to hang it in the shower and to fold my trousers and put them under the mattress. Then I got into bed and fell asleep almost immediately, but only to wake suddenly an hour or two later with a sensation of fear and distress. It was a condition I had grown to know well and there was no use trying to get back to sleep or lying in bed in the dark getting more and more depressed.

Instead I got up, put on B.L.'s silk dressing-gown, lit a cigarette and sat in a chair, determined to reason myself out of the threatening mood of black depression and loss of confidence.

After all, I told myself, I'd made a pretty good recovery very quickly; twenty-four hours earlier I'd been lying awake on a lumpy mattress in a police cell with all my plans smashed. Now I was in a comfortable hotel room with money, not much but enough to enable me to get more since I had already found my next mark and was pretty sure of success – if I couldn't take Dora Bukovski I'd better give up and try and make an honest living.

No, I didn't want to think about that, not even jokingly, for it reminded me that in my forties without qualifications or references no one would employ me, except perhaps as a kitchen porter. I put the whole picture firmly out of my mind, determined to think of something else: Maria-Luisa, who was seldom out of my mind for long.

It had been an enterprise which I had thought was going to bring me many millions of lire but which had resulted in stripping me of everything.

5

M Y MISTAKE HAD been in ignoring one of my own basic rules: never try to con a woman under forty. It's not only much more difficult to overcome her suspicions, but she takes being swindled as a personal insult, gets angry and turns vicious.

When a middle-aged spinster or a widow wakes up to the realization that both I and a chunk of her money have disappeared she is unhappy, furious and humiliated. But as long as the loss of money is not catastrophic she usually has a good cry and then makes no fuss, not wanting her family and friends to find out what a fool she's been.

I try within reason to give value for money and I like to think that once the pain and anger have abated my victims may even have a soft spot for the charming rogue who brought them romance and sexual pleasure long after they had ceased to expect it.

But when a young, attractive woman discovers that the man she thought was at her feet really had his hand in her purse her rage is quite frightening and in her desire for revenge she doesn't care if she herself gets hurt. I'd learnt this lesson in my twenties at the cost of my first prison sentence and I'd made it a rule ever since to pick marks over forty and, preferably, plain ones.

Maria-Luisa was certainly younger than that and to make it even more dangerous was intelligent, a divorcée with a good deal of worldly experience and with powerful friends. Also, being beautiful in a ripe, well-upholstered sort of way, she was used to being desired as a woman so that when she discovered that it was her money that I wanted, her hurt pride made her want to kill me.

The ridiculous thing was that she was wrong, for I'd broken another one of my cardinal rules: I'd become emotionally involved with one of my victims. Not that I was willing to admit that I'd fallen in love, for after some twenty years of perfecting a technique of living off women I was sure that I would never be trapped by that delusion.

But I had forgotten to act like a professional; I'd lowered my guard, dropped some of my screens and at one time had almost taken off my mask, which would, of course, have made it impossible to con her. In short I'd allowed myself to regard a mark as a fellow human being, which was a bit like a lion trying to befriend the antelope he is about to eat.

I suppose the difficulties came about because when we first met I hadn't thought of her as a victim at all. I was in Cannes, 'resting', as actors say, after an arduous but most rewarding six weeks with a wholesale grocer's widow in Glasgow on whom I'd unloaded just over 5000 shares of a bankrupt company at 62p each.

With all that money in my pocket I'd gone to London on a buying spree, renewing my clothes from socks and underwear to Yves Saint Laurent ties, a silk suit and a cashmere overcoat. I'd told myself that it was all an investment like redecorating an expensive night-club but the truth is that I always spend money recklessly when I've had a successful con. A prison psychiatrist once told me I was trying to affirm a success in which I didn't really believe, but I'd lied to him so much about my childhood he couldn't have known anything about me really.

Anyway I'd also bought some beautiful new luggage and a ticket to Nice which is where I go when I'm not working and want to live like a normal human being for a little while. As far as I know, the Nice police – who are much respected in the criminal world – don't know of my existence. Interpol does though, so in these unfair days of linked computers it wouldn't take long for the local fuzz to get a complete story on me were I to attract their attention. So in Nice I keep my nose clean and ignore the easy marks who clutter up the hotels and the casino.

When I can afford it I stay at one of the fashionable hotels in Cannes where most of the film people live during the annual Festival. The bar is very famous and Peter the Barman is one of those international characters the jet set know and the would-be jet set want to know. Pietro Piedmonti is an old friend of mine, a classmate in fact since we did time together in Malabata Prison, Tangier; he for having helped himself out of the cash register in the bar in which he was working, and I because of a misunderstanding about the rate at which I'd exchanged five hundred dollars for a jolly Dutch woman who'd taken a fancy to me. It turned out that the owner of the bar was an ex-con himself who had forgotten more ways to milk the cash register than

Peter knew and my jolly Dutch woman was an economist when not enjoying herself in places like Tangier. Our both being inside through our own stupidity was a bond between us and since we were released within days of one another and had been required to leave Tangier I'd come back to Nice, Peter's home town, with him.

There his mother, a waitress, had a tiny flat in the poorer quarter. Peter told me that he had no father and I left it at that. We were both broke and couldn't find work and I slept on the sofa and he on a camp cot in the same room until I picked up a pair of English women in Menton and went off to Italy with them.

I always look Peter up when in the south of France, and if he steers a good mark my way and backs up my bogus identity in the subtle way a barman can, I pay him between ten and fifteen per cent of the take after I have coincidentally met the victim at her next stop.

But this time, I told him that first night, I really was taking time off – no matter what came my way. He then invited me to go back to Nice with him when he finished that evening. He now had a small house up on top of the hill in the Piedmontese district where he lived with his mother, wife and small son.

I was sitting in a corner of his bar reading *Paris Match* and sipping a local pastis before dinner when Maria-Luisa came in. She paused briefly in the doorway and surveyed the room, her eyes passing over a family at one table, an elderly couple at another, and stopping for not much longer than a second or two on me. I looked straight back at her and she moved with ease and grace to an empty table, half turning her back on me.

'Good evening, Mrs Neilson,' Peter smiled at her.

'Good evening, Peter, a Gibson please.' She had a low voice and an American accent but not, I thought, that of a native-born American.

She was dressed as though for an evening out with bare arms and shoulders, glossy black hair done up in a thick coil and emerald ear-rings which, if genuine, and I had a feeling they were, were worth a decent sum.

She was obviously not a tourist on holiday, for her skin, which was the colour of dark olive oil, showed no signs of having been quickly toasted in the sun and her long dark red dress was not at all what holiday-makers brought with them to Cannes in May.

She sipped her dry, dry martini and seemed quite content to do nothing else, not finding it necessary to read or turn out her bag, or to do any of those things which women do who cannot sit still. She had an air of repose which I guessed meant that she was used to being alone. I wondered, since she was so attractive, why that should be.

Perhaps I should say that I found her attractive although many men might not, for she was not at all like the young starlets or long-legged, slim-waisted, high-breasted photographers' models who fill the smart bars in Cannes and St Tropez. She was well-rounded, her neck flowing into sloping shoulders and arms which were not quite plump. Her breasts, held up by the strapless evening dress, were full but not large and when she got up to go I saw that her belly had that slight roundness found in classical statues. We did not exchange glances as she passed my chair but I watched her leave, admiring the full thighs and buttocks which had they been only slightly larger would have seemed gross but seemed to me to be perfectly proportioned.

I went over to the bar. 'Is there a Mr Neilson?' I asked Peter.

'No – not with her anyway. She's been here four days and keeps pretty much to herself. Probably divorced – she doesn't wear a wedding ring.'

I let a decent interval elapse and then followed her into the dining-room, choosing a table and seat from which she could see my strong right profile. I took care to finish before she did, so that she wouldn't guess that I had decided to scrape an acquaintance with her.

My motive was not an amorous adventure which, since I spend most of my time making love to women for money, would have been a busman's holiday, but to have someone attractive and, I guessed, intelligent and amusing with whom I could spend part of my next two weeks' leisure. I hate being alone and I would get to know this Mrs Neilson. If she turned out to be the kind of woman I thought she was then we would enjoy each other's company for a little while. If not then I was quite confident that I'd find someone else.

On the way back to Peter's flat later that night I questioned him further about Mrs Neilson, but he knew little.

'She's self-possessed and apparently not looking for any attachments – one or two guys have tried to pick her up but she's brushed them off easily. She's well fixed, always carries plenty of cash and has one of the most expensive rooms. She's phoned California twice – and not at the cheap time either.'

'She's from California, do you think?'

'Maybe but not originally. I'm pretty sure she's Italian – though not Piedmontese; from her accent I'd say she was from Lombardy.'

'Fix it for us to get talking tomorrow, will you?'

'Sure – she comes in for a drink before lunch every day – about one. Business?'

'No – strictly pleasure; it might be fun to spend time with her during my little holiday, that's all.'

'Is that all?'

'Yes – why?'

'Nothing – only it strikes me that she's your type. You know who she looks like, don't you?'

'Who?'

'That actress you always rave about – Anna Magnani.'

'You're right,' I said, 'only about fifteen years younger.'

I knew there was no use trying to convince Peter that I really wasn't in hot pursuit of love-making, since from our earliest acquaintance he has been sure that I am some kind of satyr whose sexual appetite is insatiable. For some strange biological reason he is quite lacking in sex appeal himself, one of the reasons why he is such a good barman. Successful, free-spending men, usually no longer young, make the reputations of barmen and they do not like sexual competition, particularly since their companions, male or female, are often a generation or so younger.

Peter had watched me go to work many times and had seen the effect on the women I bedded, a cat that's been at the cream look which he didn't realize came from a cold-blooded effort on my part to give maximum satisfaction while seldom enjoying the exercise myself. Actually I am not at all highly sexed and sometimes think what a relief it would be if I didn't have to make love to a woman for six months or so. My admiration for Mrs Neilson had been something like an art collector must feel when he sees a particularly desirable painting. I looked forward to spending some time with her but I didn't want to possess her.

At half-past twelve the next afternoon I placed myself discreetly in the hotel lobby so that I could see the entrance to 'Peter's Bar' while remaining inconspicuous myself. At five to one she walked briskly in and I hurried so that we both arrived at the bar at the some moment.

'Good morning, Colonel – your usual? Good morning, Mrs Neilson.'

'Yes, but please serve the lady first,' I said without looking at her.

'Oh I can make two drinks at once – one of my Horse's Necks then, Colonel?'

'Please.' Now I turned to her and smiled in a friendly but completely impersonal way. 'Peter's Horse's Necks are famous in this part of the world.'

'They're famous all over the world,' Peter corrected.

She laughed, a deep, unrepressed laugh. 'In that case I'll have one too.' She turned to me and I saw that her eyes were blue, like my own, unusual in dark-skinned Mediterranean types like us. 'Thanks for the tip.'

Then it was easy for Peter to introduce us, thus establishing that I was to be trusted. It is really rather surprising that respectable women take seriously an introduction from a barman or a restaurateur, but the fact remains that they do – or at least American and English women do. French, Spanish and Italian women are much more on their guard. I later learned that Maria-Luisa had left Italy as a small girl and gone to live in America where she had become used to such informal introductions.

I excused myself, apparently to make a phone call to London, and was away for about five minutes, time enough for Peter to fill in some fascinating details about me which, as I could tell from the way she looked at me when I returned, he had done.

'Now I'm free,' I said. 'And I want another Horse's Neck – will you join me?'

'No, I limit myself to one drink before lunch,' she said, 'for dietary reasons only.'

I did not pay the invited compliment, judging that it was too early in our relationship.

'Do you like the food here?' I asked.

'It's all right – why?'

'I find there isn't a great deal of choice. Would you think it too pushy of me to ask you to have dinner elsewhere tonight?'

She gave me a long look and I thought that I'd misjudged my timing.

'I think I'd like that,' she said at last. 'But only on the strict understanding that I pay for myself.'

'If you insist.'

'I do.'

'All right then – shall we meet in here about seven-thirty?'

She agreed and left with a nod and a smile at Peter.

'I love to see you work,' he said, shaking his head. 'It's an education – what's it going to be this time, the unknown Van Gogh or the Mexican silver mine?'

'I told you this is strictly pleasure, Pietro, and I mean it. Besides you know I never work the Côte d'Azur.'

'There's always a first time – but don't forget my cut. I stuck my neck out this time.'

'Thanks, but I mean it. Pleasure, not business.'

I had a light lunch at a café, walked quickly a mile or two along the front as my daily exercise, and slept a couple of hours in the afternoon, still getting my strength back from my heavy duty with the Glaswegian widow.

I took Mrs Neilson to a Spanish restaurant just off the flower market in Nice and we discovered that we both liked gazpacho and roast suckling-pig and appreciated real flamenco, the first of many tastes we were to find we had in common. We exchanged first names and talked about a number of subjects, on most of which she seemed to have something interesting and original to say. We enjoyed being together, dancing together and bantering. In short we found that we liked each other in what, so far at least, seemed an almost sexless way.

We left at dawn, walking through the flower market just as the stalls were being opened. I bought Maria-Luisa a great bunch of flowers which the amused taxi driver carried up front with him. At the hotel I think fatigue overcame both of us – at least I know that I was very tired after a physically and mentally exhausting ten hours in her company. I slept without stirring for five or six hours, having agreed to meet her again later that afternoon.

This time we walked through the town to the older part, where in a café attached to a patisserie we told each other bits of our lives while eating deliciously rich mille-feuilles.

But, of course, I wasn't able to tell her any of the truth about myself even though I wanted to do so. I was wearing my Colonel Rokesby-Gore mask and I didn't dare take it off and reveal George Kelly, bastard son of a servant girl.

Instead I deepened the disguise by adding a decoration won in Aden as a Captain and an early retirement from the Army following rough treatment as a prisoner.

'And inheriting my father's estate at about that time made it possible for me to resign my commission and settle down in Sussex. I'd still be there if my wife hadn't died rather suddenly three months ago.' I choked up and her sympathy was immediate.

'I'm sorry, Ronald.' She put her hand over mine. 'Have you any children?'

40

'No – I'm afraid not.' That was not quite true, for although I've never stayed long enough with any woman to become a father – at least as far as I know – I do have a son in his twenties who doesn't know I fathered him.

I thought that within reason she told me the truth about herself, starting with her recent divorce of a conveniently unfaithful husband, and going sketchily back to a childhood in California where she'd been taken by her mother and American stepfather. Much of the background was in shadow but after all we had only just met and I respected a decent reticence.

What was obvious to me was that she had weathered some bad storms, which was something else we had in common and was part of the reason why we got on so well together. But it was only part, and a much larger part was that strange affinity which on rare occasions springs up between two human beings without apparent reason. It's not necessarily sexual and can happen between heterosexual men and, I suppose, women. It is a powerful force and long-lasting.

I suggested that we dine together again that evening, but she begged off, saying she needed an early night.

'All right,' I said. 'But look here: we're both on holiday and I expect you're as bored with this tourist-ridden, crowded coast as I am. Why don't we take a few days off and explore the countryside? We could stop in little villages wherever the fancy took us.'

'You mean hire a car?'

'Yes, I'll get a small one from Avis in Nice – we might even go up into the mountains and cross over to Italy and then down to Genoa and back along the coast through Menton to Nice. What do you say?'

'Well if it didn't sound too corny I'd say "Isn't this rather sudden?"'

'If I were propositioning you it would be,' I said, giving her my frank and open face. 'But I'm not – separate rooms and we'll each pay our own way. We're just sharing a holiday together.'

'Perhaps I'm crazy – but I accept.'

'Good – we're going to enjoy ourselves.'

We told the desk we'd be checking out the next morning and I phoned Avis and booked a Fiat 127 for up to a week.

I went into the bar early that evening, so that Peter would be alone, and told him what we were going to do.

'So you're going to take her after all?'

'No! damn it, I'm not – I just want to spend a few days with her and

41

that's all.'

'Don't blague me, George. If she's got money you'll con her – you can't help yourself. But when you do don't forget my cut.'

Before I could protest Maria-Luisa came in.

'Drinking already, Ronnie? All right, I'll join you – a Horse's Neck please, Peter.'

'Good evening, Mrs Neilson,' he replied in his barman's voice, and I didn't get a chance to talk to him again. I decided that I'd probably have to drop him something anyway.

We picked up the Fiat the next morning, putting it down on Maria-Luisa's American Express card which Avis preferred to cash. She seemed surprised that I had no credit cards but content with my saying that I disapproved of them on principle and giving her half in cash. Actually you can get a lot of things with a bogus identity, but not a Diners Club or American Express card.

'Now for supplies,' I said as we drove away. 'One of the great pleasures of a roving trip like this is to be able to stop anywhere you like for a picnic lunch.'

We bought paper plates and napkins, plastic cups, knives and forks, a tin-opener, corkscrew and two wine glasses. Then we stocked up with prepared food and a couple of bottles of wine and drove up into the hills behind Nice.

The sun shone and it got very warm in the little car. I was in a short-sleeved shirt and she wore a cotton blouse, and from time to time our bare arms touched or my hand brushed her leg as I changed gear, and I began to realize that the sexless friendship wasn't going to work after all.

Just after one we decided to find a picnic spot and I turned off the main road down a rutted narrow one which led to fields of flowers planted for the Grasse perfume industry. We stopped by the side of rows of severely pruned rose bushes planted in long, strictly geometric lines, tamed and regimented as a commercial crop. Their scent was almost too powerful to be enjoyable but we spread our things on the sparse dusty grass and soaked up the sun, watching the bees and other insects gorge themselves. Later, full of food and wine, we lay next to each other talking drowsily for a little while before we both dozed off. Some time later when I awoke I found that she had snuggled up to me. I put my hand over her warm breast and she immediately opened her eyes. We kissed for the first time and then lay quietly together for two or three minutes before breaking apart and sitting up. Her black, shiny hair, which she usually wore in two coils had become loose and I saw that it was much longer than I had supposed.

'We'd better be moving on,' I said, 'and find somewhere to stay tonight.'

We continued up into the hills towards Italy and an hour or so later came to a small auberge by the side of a stream. I went in and booked a double room for Colonel and Mrs Rokesby-Gore. Maria-Luisa made no comment when the porter, who was, I guessed, the proprietress's husband, left us standing by the large double bed. I crossed to the window and pulled the curtains aside.

Below was a small garden with tables and chairs while in the distance lay the foothills of the Alpes Maritimes, top-lit by the setting sun. Maria-Luisa joined me; I put my arm around her and we stood without talking as the hills turned from dark blue to black.

The meal was a simple one of soup, pasta and veal, more Italian than French, and we didn't wait for dessert but took a pear each and went up to our room.

But we didn't stop to eat our fruit, for the postponing had brought us both to a state of excitement which was most unusual for me. As soon as the bedroom door shut we felt for each other and within minutes lay clasped together in the bed, our clothes scattered on the floor.

Maria-Luisa had been without a man for over three months and her lovely rounded body felt as though she had a fever, making me feel almost young again. But from long practice I was able to delay my orgasm and to bring on hers several times before my own sexuality took command and I thrust deeper and faster until her orgasm brought a cry which must have been heard all through the small hotel.

Outside the light faded, a huge moon popped up behind the dark hills and shone full on us. For the first time in years I felt utterly relaxed, without worry or tension, not apprehensive of a knock on the door. My buzzing brain usually so full of schemes had blessedly switched to 'Low'.

For a little while after that the days were idyllic, the happiest, I think, I'd ever spent. Our route was lazy, unplanned, on minor roads, and we stopped often, treating the woods and fields as though we owned them, trespassing shamelessly. We chose small, old, family-run hotels, shabby but clean with large, light bedrooms, 'matrimonial' beds with sheets that had been dried in the sun and put away with lavender.

We talked, God! how we talked. We found each other endlessly interesting although, trapped inside my bogus identity, I had to be on my guard lest I contradict some earlier story. I grew to hate Colonel Rokesby-Gore: more than once I nearly jettisoned him and brought on George Kelly but my courage always failed. I believed that my caution was because I didn't want to lose the precious happiness, but one day Maria-Luisa said something which instantly made me realize why I had hung on to my retired-English-colonel identity.

Any reticences she had when we set out gradually disappeared and she abandoned those little pretences we use to camouflage our real selves in the early stages of an evolving relationship. I got a fairly clear picture of the road she had taken so far. She was originally Italian, but her life had changed when her mother, whose husband had died, married an Italian-American G.I. who took her and Maria-Luisa back to his home in Monterey, California, where she quickly learned English and, of course, went to school.

One balmy night in Aix-en-Provence, Maria-Luisa, a little squiffy from an extra bottle of wine, suddenly put her hand on mine and squeezed. I covered her hand and smiled.

'We're never gonna lie to each other, are we, Ronnie?'

'No, never.'

'Okay. Well – I didn't even finish high school,' she said sadly. 'I wanted to go to college, but I got married in my junior year and dropped out.'

'Why did you drop out – did your husband make you?'

'No – the baby made me. That's why I had to get married.'

'It didn't work out?'

'No, the guy was only nineteen – a year older than me. We stuck together until he graduated from college – his family supported us until then – but it was no good when he had to make a living. We fought all the time until we decided to call it quits. We got a divorce in Guadalajara, Mexico.'

'What happened to the baby? Was it a boy or a girl?'

'A girl – Nicoletta. Oh, I brought her home with me to Monterey and my mother took care of her while I was working in a hotel. I started as a maid but later I worked at the desk for a couple of years. Jesus, how I hated it.' She finished her coffee and I caught the waiter's eye. He refilled our cups and our glasses and she lit another cigarette.

'What then – a different job?'

44

She laughed. 'You could call it that – a lawyer from Chicago who was staying at the hotel propositioned me. It wasn't the first time, of course – a divorcée working in a hotel seems a set-up for most guys – but this time I decided "what the hell", why not?'

'Why – did the Chicago lawyer sweep you off your feet?'

She laughed. 'Good God, no, Morris was fat and fifty, married with four kids. No, it wasn't that, but he seemed a nice enough Joe. He promised to fix me up in an apartment of my own and to help me get a job. But that wasn't it either, really.' She sipped her cognac and looked off into the shadows under the trees across the street.

I waited quietly. I could see that she wasn't finding it easy.

'The thing is it was getting difficult at home. My stepfather is five years younger than my mother and he looks and acts even younger while my mother suddenly looked older than she was. I guess it wasn't easy for him having a young woman in the house who didn't have a man. Most guys are wolves and he thought it was up to him to fill the gap in my life.'

'I see,' I said. 'Tricky.'

'No, you don't see, but it could easily have turned out like that. He's an attractive guy and he was right – I did need a man but I wasn't that crazy – particularly with six-year-old Nicoletta in the house.' She stubbed out her cigarette, reducing it to shreds. 'That was another reason I felt I could go. Nicoletta was getting on fine at school, liked my mother and thought of Joe as her father – she even called him "Papa" – much to my mother's annoyance. I thought it was best for everyone all round if I just got out, so I did.'

'Have you ever been back?'

'No. I got married two years later – not to Morris but to a client of his in Detroit, Arthur Neilson. Morrie took me there on a business trip. The very first night when he was entertaining Morrie and me in the Detroit Athletic Club this old wolf started playing footsie with me.'

'How old?'

'Artie was sixty-one and had just divorced his third wife. He had a good business making TV cabinets on contract and he'd always treated his ex-wives generously. I'd had enough of the mistress routine: two nights a week and the occasional weekend, with Morrie worried in case one of his kids spotted us. And to be fair I think he was about ready to change partners too. Anyway Morrie was real nice about Artie, who came to Chicago to see me, and he gave me a thousand bucks for a wedding present. I sent Nicoletta a hundred for her birthday that year.

'And you moved to Detroit?'

'Yes – just outside Ypsilanti actually, but we didn't spend much time at home. Artie is a swinger and he says his old man made him work too hard when he was younger. We went to New York, Florida and once to Paris. For a while I thought it was great.'

'And then you didn't?'

'Well I knew my Artie. He'd started playing around within six or eight weeks of marrying me, and he didn't really try and keep it from me either. He even suggested a foursome with permutations – you know, man with man, woman with woman, and then cross over?'

'No,' I said. 'I've always been straight – never seem to have found time to try it with another man.' Which is true. It's not a question of morals but just that as I'm not turned on by men – or beautiful boys for that matter – I couldn't fake it as I can with women.

'Well, old Artie has tried just about everything, and it's like too much rich food – after a while nothing tastes good any more. Anyway he was good to me and generous so long as I played by his rules, which broadly were to leave him alone with his fun and games if I didn't want to join in – and I didn't. Then he didn't want any more kids – he'd had five – and I had to promise not to get pregnant, or to get rid of it if I did.'

'It doesn't sound deliriously happy.'

She laughed, but without joy. 'Maybe not, but it was as good as most people have – or at least that's how it seemed to me. Anyway we carried on like that for five God-damned years and then one day I was made to look at myself by someone I thought I'd fallen in love with. I'd ducked out and gone to him. Afterwards when I was feeling real good, he said: "God, if it wasn't for the difference in our ages I'd ask you to get a divorce so we could get married."

'He was twenty-eight and I was thirty-one; I was so angry I got the hell out of there and I didn't go back to him though God knows I wanted to. He was the only guy who had ever really got to me.'

'What did you do?' I felt myself getting annoyed and I didn't know why.

'I went back home and had a lousy, drunken week or two and then decided to get the divorce anyway.'

'Why?'

'Because I couldn't face a future of becoming middle-aged while I waited for Artie to die and leave me rich.'

'So you asked him for a divorce?'

'No. Maybe it sounds hard but I wanted the most I could get for the five years I'd given him. I got a private dick and told him I didn't give a shit about which of the women Artie was laying, he had to get Artie cold with one he'd have to pay to cover up. It took a little time but in the end I had colour photographs of him screwing his partner's wife.'

'So you took him to the cleaners?'

She looked quickly at me. 'Now you hate me – you think I'm a grasping bitch.'

'No I don't. I know it's a tough world. I don't blame you for getting what you could. How much did he cough up?'

'A thousand bucks a month – tax paid. And for life unless I remarry.'

'Not bad, not bad at all.'

'That's not all – I got a lump sum to cover what my smart lawyer called "displacement costs".'

'How much?'

'Thirty grand.'

'Jesus! Thirty thousand dollars?'

'Yeah – less five thousand for the lawyer, but that left me twenty-five big ones and I've got them safe on deposit with the Bank of America.'

'Now that's not smart,' I said, and it was then that I knew at last why I'd hung on to 'Colonel Rokesby-Gore'. Maria-Luisa was, after all, going to be another mark. Having her loot dangled in front of my face had been like putting a glass of whisky into an alcoholic's hand or taking a compulsive gambler to the track. I suddenly wanted that money so badly I could see and feel the notes.

Without my having worked for it Maria-Luisa had become an ideal mark, since she now trusted me completely and was convinced that I had no need of money. It would, I thought, be like cheating a child in a game of Snap.

But it hadn't turned out that way at all.

47

6

I STUBBED OUT MY last cigarette and went back to bed just as the sky
was lightening. The therapy of remembering the brief happiness of
the early part of Maria-Luisa's and my time together had worked, and
whatever it was that had been depressing me had gone away or at least
slipped back for the time being into wherever nightmares are stored. I
fell asleep and didn't wake until the sun was well up.

The elderly maid who brought the large pots of hot milk and coffee,
the plate of rolls and bread, butter and peach jam told me with I
thought a hint of disapproval that it was nearly half-past nine. But the
disapproval disappeared when I gave her a two-thousand lire note for
a packet of Italo's, the cheapest Italian cigarette I can smoke without
coughing my guts up, and told her to keep the change. After a wash
and shave and in my laundered shirt I went out into a bright, sunny
day, ready to go on with this Snakes and Ladders game.

In one of the narrow streets off the Piazza San Marco I found a
prosperous-looking stamp shop evidently catering for the serious
collector, of which there are many in Italy, as there always are in
countries where the people have suffered from seeing their own
currency devalued.

The dealer was young, which meant that he would probably co-
operate with me so long as he was not required to break the law
himself. Young dealers in the dog-eat-dog stamp business who still
have to attain a certain security are usually less scrupulous than older
ones who, having built up a clientele, have more to lose. We talked
stamps for a while and he finally asked me if I were a dealer.

'Not really, although I do buy and sell from time to time and advise
friends with money how to invest in stamps – if you see what I mean.'

He smiled. 'I think I see what you mean, signor. What can I do for
you?'

'I am looking for a collection which would do for a friend, an

48

American lady who is just beginning – something better than a schoolboy's album while not being a specialist's collection.'

'I have a number of albums which I think would meet those requirements. I'll get them for you.'

'Thank you, and at the same time would you show me what you have in early South American issues, which are my own speciality?' It was true that I do know quite a bit about Latin American stamps as one of my victims had been left a superb collection by her husband which I had sold for her to a friendly London dealer – friendly to me that is.

He brought back three albums and some loose pages of Argentina, Uruguay and Brazil. These I examined first, looking for a moderately priced variation of an expensive stamp. The dealer gave me a torch with a built-in magnifying glass but, I noticed, didn't let me out of his sight. He needn't have worried for I was neither bold enough nor so stupid as to try and steal from him.

I soon spotted what I was looking for and asked for a catalogue which confirmed the price. 'Would you like to sell me one stamp from this group of the Brazil 1844 imperfs? I'd like the 60 reis.'

It was catalogued at £6 in his Stanley Gibbons and I got it for 10,000 lire, a couple of pounds less. I then examined the albums. One had evidently been put together with loving expertise by a collector with limited funds, for while it contained no really rare stamps there were many examples of variations of colour, perforations and watermarks of nineteenth-century issues, the mark of a serious collector. I was glad to see that there were some first day covers as well. The catalogue value of the album, a note said, was over two hundred thousand lire and the price was a hundred thousand.

'This, I think, would do very nicely for my friend. I'll bring her in later.'

'I'll be very pleased to help the lady,' he said, handing me my stamp in a little transparent envelope. 'And, if the signor would like to come back after she has bought, I would be glad to offer him a complimentary choice from other Latin Americans I have.'

'That won't be necessary. I take it that as long as you get the high price you are asking, a hundred thousand, you will be satisfied? Regardless of what the lady thinks – do I make myself clear?'

'Perfectly, signor.'

'I'll see you later then.' We understood each other.

'Arrivederla, signor.'

I next had to find some white ink, and that gave me a little trouble, but I ran some down in a photographic supplies shop where I also bought a fine nib. Then on the way back to my hotel I kept an eye open for an out-of-the-way, modest restaurant to take Dora to. The Isola Bella seemed to fit the bill. From the menu posted outside I reckoned I could get away with twelve thousand lire top whack as long as I kept her off the expensive dishes.

I went inside and booked a table for two, casually mentioning that I was looking for somewhere I could bring a party of tourists for a good, inexpensive meal. Although the head waiter was polite to 'Colonel Gore', I could see that he was not going to offer me a complimentary meal as I had half hoped.

Back in my hotel room I set up a work table lit by the standard lamp with the shade taken away. I experimented with mixing the white ink with dust from the top of the cupboard until I could almost match the faded shade of the old stamp. Then, very carefully, I raised the figures from 60 reis to 600; the 600 reis was catalogued at £500. My forgery wouldn't deceive even a knowledgeable amateur, but I was banking on Dora Bukovski being completely ignorant of the strange world of stamp collecting. I put the stamp back in its little sachet and tucked it into the change slit in my jacket pocket where I could get at it inconspicuously.

Now I had my hook baited and had to decide when and where to cast it. It was tempting to strike quickly, say over lunch, and ten or fifteen years earlier I might have risked it, but experience increases not only cunning but also caution, and it would be folly to risk a failure when my funds wouldn't support a second attempt.

No, I should first have to win Dora's complete trust, and there was only one way to do that quickly. She would not be expecting a pass so early in our acquaintance and I thought that given the advantage of the circumstances – she was away from her respectable community, without a man and almost certainly still hoping secretly for romance – I could probably take her by storm.

If I could get her into bed I was confident of the result, for I have spent a good deal of time and effort in learning how best to give women maximum pleasure in love-making. I concluded long ago that one reason I can satisfy them so well is that sex is not really very important to me. Because it isn't I am able to remain quite detached while on the job, rather, I imagine, like a ballet dancer who has to convey emotion while he's really concentrating on his technique. It is very seldom that I am myself really aroused sexually. Even in my late teens, when other men have told me life is dominated by the need for a woman, I worried very little about it. Of course that may have been because very early on I was taken in hand by an older woman. Anyway, from an early age I had been able to stay in control when making love.

Being thus detached has meant that I have almost always been able to bring the woman on to her orgasm. More than one has told me that it was something they had never fully experienced before. It is a skill which I have consciously acquired and upon which I pride myself; I do take their money but I do give something in return.

Now age had never made much difference to me. I agree with Benjamin Franklin who pointed out that women age very little between the waist and the knees. Some I had made love to had been in their fifties and sixties and in one memorable case a huntin', shootin' English woman of sixty-two had nearly broken my back.

Her name, I remembered, was Prudence. We had been introduced at a Newmarket meeting where one of her horses was running – its jockey allowed himself to be caught on the run in and her language had reminded me of an unfriendly boatswain I'd once briefly worked under. To Prudence I'd been William Mackenzie, the self-made Canadian, as she would have seen through Colonel Rokesby-Gore in less than five minutes.

I was included in a general invitation to drinks at her house where she made all the going, dismissing the other guests and ordering me to stay behind. She didn't actually order me to 'get up them stairs', but we went to bed very early. After a long hard climb she came with a whoop, at the same time slapping my bottom hard as though I were a hunter which had just gone particularly well.

In the week that followed I certainly earned the hundred quid she gave me to bet for her on the same horse. Of course I stuck the bet and the bloody animal won at 5 to 1, odds resulting from its fading a week earlier, and not for the first time I realized what a wicked world this is. I suppose I could have confessed and worked off the debt, but I didn't think I had enough strength, so I caught the train to Nice and took a week to recover. After that I looked at older women with new respect, particularly some English upper-class women, who are not only free from bourgeois morality but are quite unrestrained in bed.

Anyway I was pretty sure that after a romp with me, Dora'd be eating out of my hand. It was getting late, so I set out to walk the comparatively short distance to the Gabrielli-Sandwirth.

On the way I had a florist make up some cheap flowers into a nosegay. It cost only a couple of thousand lire but still brought my capital down dangerously; I decided it was worth it as I am a great believer in flower power.

I could manage the modest lunch I'd planned but not much else and I'd have to be careful not to get stuck for a round of drinks at the hotel. On the other hand it would be fatal for Dora to suspect that I was short of money.

In the hotel I moved inconspicuously to where I could see into the America Bar; Dora and the other four were talking at a table, or rather Leon was talking and gesticulating and they were listening. I was glad to see that their glasses were empty which meant that they would soon order more drinks. I had to wait a full five minutes though, during which I saw Dora take a surreptitious look at her watch. At last Gino caught the barman's eye and as soon as they were served I walked in, paused to locate them and then presented Dora with the flowers.

'Oh, say they're beautiful, really beautiful!' She actually blushed. 'I'll take them right up to my room and put them in water.'

'Oh, the waiter will see to that,' I said calling one over. 'What's your room number?'

'Careful, Dora!' Leon wagged a finger. 'This guy's a fast worker.'

'Oh go on, Leon!' she protested. 'I'm in 415.'

I handed the flowers to the waiter and then, as an afterthought, I asked them what they were drinking.

'We've just got fresh ones in,' Leon said. 'But you go ahead,' he added generously.

'No, I think we'd better go – I'm sorry I'm a bit late: I got hung up on a telephone call from London – I ordered a table for one-fifteen and it must be almost that now.'

'Where are we going?' Dora asked.

'A little restaurant I know used almost exclusively by the Venetians and unknown to tourists – I think you'll like it.'

'It sounds a real fun thing – is it very far?'

'No, it's only a short walk, but we'd better get started.' Out of habit I looked at where my wrist-watch should have been.

'It's ten past,' said Gino. 'You lose your watch?'

'No – it's one of those electronic ones and it went crazy on me so I took it back to the shop in Milan. They promised to mail it to me.'

'I prefer the ones you wind up,' said Leon, indicating an enormous one on his wrist. 'I've had this ten years and it keeps real good time and tells you the date and phases of the moon.'

'That must be useful.'

When Dora stood up I saw that she was wearing high-heeled scarlet shoes which were too tight, stretched slacks, buttercup yellow and, unbelievably, a light blue blouse. All that was needed, I thought, was for an invisible orchestra to break into 'Enter the Gladiators'. Although the Isola Bella was only about a thousand yards I wondered if she could make it on her ridiculous shoes. However, there was no choice since there are no vehicles in Venice except boats.

She was limping when we got to the restaurant and puffing like a horse after a race.

'Goodness, I haven't walked that far for years and now I'm . . . er, perspiring. Do they have a little girls' room?'

'Over there in the corner – may I order for you?'

'Oh yes – surprise me.'

The waiter, who had greeted me as 'Colonel' as though we were old friends, showed me to a window table with, I was glad to see, fresh flowers. He handed me the menu with a flourish.

The fixed price lunch and a bottle of wine would, with service and taxes, take almost half of my working capital, but I couldn't settle for less.

'Due pranzi a prezzo fisso', I ordered. He made a note, not bothering to conceal his disapproval of my cheapness.

'Minestrone o pastasciutta?' he asked in a quite different tone.

I rose as Dora came sailing back having made repairs.

'Are you ordering something exciting?'

'Yes – something they do rather well here.' I turned to the waiter. 'Pastasciutta e vitello arrosto.' I hoped that as a good American she had so far stuck to steak or chicken and had not had the ubiquitous Italian veal.

'E da beve, signor?' the waiter asked in a tone which implied that he wouldn't be surprised if I settled for tap water.

'Un fiasco di Chianti.' The straw-covered bottle was, I felt, a necessary touch to enforce the idea that we were eating in a 'real' Italian restaurant.

During the meal I made sure that she drank about two-thirds of the wine, and this, added to the stiff drinks she'd already had with her friends, soon had its effect.

The veal was tough and tasteless and the salad was made from left-over vegetables, but she shoved the food into her mouth without comment. I talked a little sadly about my dear, lately departed wife and she told me how much she missed 'Jersey', her husband, whose name was spelled 'Jerzy' but who had given up the Polish pronunciation before he met her.

'We never had a cross word in twenty-three years of marriage,' she lied. 'We were just like love birds.' Her eyes filled with tears.

'It was like that between me and Lady Jane,' I said, deciding to promote my fictitious wife to an earl's daughter. 'A real love match . . . and now I'm terribly lonely.'

That did it. The eyes overflowed, smearing her make-up. I put my hand over hers.

'Be brave – we must learn to live with our loneliness.'

She gave a series of quick little nods, got tissues out of her handbag, mopped her cheeks, making the smeared mascara worse, and blew her nose vigorously. Then she smiled bravely.

'I'm better now but I'll have to go back to that horrible bathroom and fix my face – I must look just terrible.'

'You don't at all. Look, my hotel isn't far from here – you can use my bathroom and we'll have our coffee there.'

'Well . . .' she said doubtfully. 'Wouldn't they mind you taking a lady to your room?'

'Goodness gracious, no,' I said in 'no nonsense' tones. 'The Italians are romantics. They'll think we're lovers and wish us well.'

'All right, then.' She giggled. Her suspicions were lulled and at the same time she was excited by the idea.

It was only a short walk to the hotel and I didn't hurry her. As I picked up my key the hotel clerk gave me back my passport, something which was necessary to my plans. I ordered coffee and brandy for two to be sent up to the room.

It came while Dora was still in my bathroom and I set it out on one of the bedside tables and drew up the chair, which I took so that when she came out there was only the bed for her to sit on. We lit cigarettes.

'I'm sorry about crying like that', she said, 'but it suddenly came over me when you said you were lonely too.'

'It's not only the loneliness', I said, putting the coffee and brandy next to her, 'and the loss of companionship, but one misses other things too.'

'Other things?'

'Come, Dora, we're not children – you know perfectly well what I mean – sex.'

'Sex?' she said, catching her breath. 'You mean – sex?'

'Of course I mean sex – God, you're still young, as I am, you must miss it too, don't you?'

'Well', she said weakly, 'to tell the truth Jersey wasn't too interested in that side of things for his last two or three years.'

'Then he must have lost his sight,' I said gruffly. 'Dammit Dora, you're a very desirable woman.'

'Well he didn't think so – anyways not recently. Do you really think I am?' She gave me what she no doubt thought was a wicked smile.

'I find it hard to keep my hands off you.' I felt the time had come for direct attack, and I'm seldom wrong.

'Well, you are a fast worker and no mistake!'

'There you're wrong. I never do this sort of thing. There's been nobody since Jane died. I haven't wanted anybody, but . . .' I stood up and she tensed. 'Drink up your brandy, Dora. Let's get out of here before I make a fool of myself.' It was pretty basic stuff but I've long since learned that most women are vulnerable to dialogue straight out of a romantic novel.

'I don't do this sort of thing either and I can hardly believe it's happening, but perhaps I'd like you to make a fool of yourself, Ronald.' She stretched out a hand. 'Perhaps I want to be a fool too.'

She certainly knew her soap opera and I played my part: I took her hand gently, kept my eyes gazing into hers with a solemn look which could mean what she wanted it to mean, and bent down and kissed her. Then I crossed to the window and darkened the room with the venetian blind; I hung up my jacket and took off my tie, put out the DO NOT DISTURB sign, and locked the door. I returned to where she was still sitting on the side of the bed, put my hands on her shoulders, and pushed her firmly but not roughly down on the bed, at the same time leaning forward and pressing my lips against hers. She shut her eyes and I ran my fingers over her breasts, or rather her very solid brassière, and down her body, encased, as I had guessed, in an armour-like girdle, until I could feel the flesh inside her thighs, into which I pressed my fingers meaningfully.

She grabbed my ears and pulled my face down on to her breast, giving my nose a painful bang on her metal-cupped bra which brought tears to my eyes. I released myself and with considerable effort hoisted her legs on to the bed and prised off her shoes. Then I kicked off my own, lay down beside her and pulled her on to her side.

55

'Oh Ronald! Do you think we ought to?'

It was, I assumed, a rhetorical question so I set about the cumbersome and exhausting task of peeling off her yellow slacks and unlocking her armour-plating. I then covered her naked body with the sheet and got out of the rest of my clothes, which I dropped on the floor. We had reached a point where, as they say in contracts, time was of the essence.

As I've said, I take good care of my assets and I knew my deeply tanned, wiry body (particularly with my belly pulled firmly in) and white skin where the shorts had been would help to keep her aroused. I hoped that she wouldn't notice that I didn't have an erection, but after all nobody is perfect.

Enough light found its way around the shutters for me to see that what the manufacturers cleverly call 'foundation garments' had camouflaged her real shape most skilfully. There was an inches-thick roll of fat around her middle and her breasts hung like toy balloons two-thirds full of water. Her thighs and buttocks reminded me of a Japanese wrestler I'd seen in Tokyo. She looked anxiously at me but I kept my expression under control and smiled tenderly at her.

'I had a beautiful body once,' she said.

I kissed her nipples, which hardened, and ran my hand down over her belly and between her thighs, which she was keeping pressed tightly together. Although the alcohol she had drunk had helped to overcome her scruples, it had also made her slow to rouse and I had to use all my skill. I was careful not to hurry, for while a passionate assault sometimes succeeds in unlocking the dam, it can frighten and thus increase resistance. I slowly eased my fingers down into the space between her legs and worked them up to her bush. She gasped, squeezed me close to her with considerable strength and began to breathe heavily with her eyes firmly shut.

I knew if I now went down on her that a minute or so's work with my tongue would undo her completely but I didn't think it was necessary. Instead I first massaged her according to a routine taught to me by a Thai lady and when she began to thrash about and utter little groans I masturbated her vigorously until she had reached the right state for me to enter her and bring her to a climax. It was a clinical exercise for me and I did not have an orgasm, a fact which I'm sure my well-timed and dramatic collapse concealed. She was gasping as though she'd just run a mile and I was tempted to tell her that she may have been perspiring earlier but she was in a right muck sweat now.

After a barely decent interval I rolled off the bed, scooped my clothes off the floor and went into the bathroom. The face that looked back at me from the cabinet mirror was not only showing signs of age but also had new worry lines across the forehead and around the eyes. I bared my teeth and saw that the superficial brushing had allowed them to become dull and that plaque was already forming at their base. I resolved to get another electric toothbrush as soon as possible.

My penis and testicles were aching, due I supposed to my not having had an orgasm. I bathed them in cold water, which gave me some relief, but one ball went on aching for hours and I decided to ask the next doctor I met whether an incomplete copulation were dangerous. I can't help worrying about cancer whenever I have a nagging pain. I had a shower, finishing off with cold water and a hard rub down. I was glad to see that the face in the mirror had improved a little.

I went back into the bedroom and saw that Dora had got her girdle and bra back on as I had guessed she would. She gave me a little smile, embarrassed and uncertain, so I kissed her tenderly, almost reverently, on the forehead and smiled reassuringly. She gathered up the rest of her clothes and went into the bathroom.

I opened the curtains, letting in the afternoon sunshine, and pulled the counterpane up over the wrecked bed. Dora came out fully dressed and I took her in my arms and held her close, thus assuring her that she was not despised.

'Are you sorry?' she whispered, still quoting.

'Of course not – and thank you,' I said humbly, knowing my lines too. I squeezed her arm affectionately.

'Do I look all right?'

'Like the cat that's been at the cream.'

She laughed. 'I feel *good*. But what can we tell the others we've been doing?'

'Oh that's easy – we can say we've been looking over the local stamp dealers, searching for bargains,' I said casually. 'As a matter of fact I did pop into one on my way to meet you. It looked interesting but I needed more time. Let's go back there so you'll be able to tell them a convincing story.'

On the way to the shop I chatted about rare stamps and told a few stories of fortunate finds I'd made at out-of-the-way dealers, explaining that most of them were very knowledgeable about their own country and those connected with it but often surprisingly ignorant of the countries less popular with their collectors. By the time we arrived she was sure that I was an expert on rare stamps.

The dealer greeted me deferentially and produced three albums; I leafed through the first, then took up the second, the one upon which I had already decided. When I got to the page with the first day covers of the 1900 'Discovery of Brazil' I lifted them up and did an obvious imitation of a double take, hastily putting the envelope down again and closing the book.

'And the price is one million lire?' I asked him.

He didn't show the slightest sign of surprise at my multiplying his price by ten.

'Si, signor.'

'I don't have that much with me but I will return. Meanwhile I wonder if I might borrow your Gibbons Overseas Catalogue while we have a coffee at the café opposite?'

For a moment he looked suspicious but then he glanced at Dora, who could only be an American tourist, and was reassured. He handed me the catalogue.

'I know you found something, what is it?' Dora asked excitedly as we sat outside the café.

'Underneath one of the envelopes in that album is a very valuable stamp,' I said. 'Here I'll show you.' I opened the catalogue to Brazil and showed her the 600 reis black 1844. 'Take a good look at that. Now the one in the album is a perfect specimen and it's worth a thousand dollars, more or less. He's only asking for the whole album a million lire, which is six hundred dollars, and the catalogue value of all the stamps in the album is over two million lire. I could take out the Brazilian stamp and easily sell the album to another dealer for say, seven hundred and fifty thousand lire. I'll just about double my outlay.' A golden rule is not to make it sound too good: an enormous profit arouses suspicion.

'Is that honest?'

'Certainly it is. It wouldn't be ethical if he were a private person, but he's a stamp dealer and it's his job to know what he's offering for sale.'

'So, you're going to do it?'

'Unfortunately I don't have that much cash with me. I've arranged with my bankers in London to send a draft here but it won't arrive for a couple of days and I'm afraid he'll find the stamp before then. I think he was a bit suspicious – the trouble with me is I can't conceal my excitement.'

'I certainly knew you'd found something,' she admitted. 'But how do you know you can sell it for the price in the catalogue? Isn't that the price anyone could buy it for right now?'

'Of course,' I said, realizing that she wasn't as stupid as she seemed, 'but I know a collector of South Americans in England who would jump at the chance of buying a superb specimen for, say, a hundred dollars under catalogue, and that still leaves a very nice profit.' I stood up and sighed. 'I'll take the catalogue back and ask him to hold the album for me until Saturday though that's an open invitation for him to examine it minutely.'

'Wait a minute,' she said. 'I've got five hundred dollars in bills as well as some more in traveller's cheques.'

'No, no, I can't borrow from you – I mean you've only just met me,' I said. 'I suppose we could be partners though.'

'Partners?'

'Yes – you put up the money and we'll divide the profit equally.'

'Well – I don't see why not. But aren't you giving me too much?'

'I'm not greedy. But *you* must hold the stamp until I get the money from my chap in England.'

'Oh, you don't have to do that. I trust you, Ronald.'

'Nevertheless I insist.'

'Well, okay then. Now I'd better go back to the hotel and get the money, hadn't I?'

'Yes, I'll get you a water taxi and I'll tell the boatman to wait for you.' I returned the catalogue and told the dealer I'd be back to buy the album and, having found out where the nearest motorboats were, walked Dora to them. 'I'll wait here for you. I think that's better, don't you?' Actually I didn't have enough money left to pay the fare, and also I felt that she wouldn't change her mind if she knew I was waiting.

It was nearly an hour before she came back, flushed and puffed. She paid off the water taxi and we walked back to the shop.

'Will you come in or will you wait for me in the café?'

She hesitated but was too embarrassed to suggest that she didn't trust me out of her sight. 'I'll wait for you in the café. Please order an ice-cream for me, one of those with three flavours.'

I sat her at a pavement table and ordered. As soon as the waiter had gone she opened her bag and handed me a wad of notes, crisp new American twenty-dollar bills. I felt the excitement I always feel when I am about to get hold of a large sum of money and I had difficulty in controlling the trembling of my hand as I took them from her. My mouth was full of saliva and I had to swallow but I don't think she noticed. As I put the money in my pocket I realized that now I did have an erection.

'There's five hundred in twenties,' she said. 'And here's three fifty-dollar traveller's cheques. I've already signed them.'

In the shop I gave the dealer two of the traveller's cheques, got nearly eighty thousand lire in change and the album and bought a packet of stamp hinges. Lastly I asked him if he would be good enough to change another fifty-dollar traveller's cheque. While he was doing so I got out a hinge and opened the album to Brazil and, lifting up one of the first day covers, I stuck down the 60 reis stamp which I had earlier raised to 600 reis.

From the money he gave me I extracted fifty thousand lire to give Dora as change and added the rest to my lire, keeping it in a separate pocket from the beautiful wad of twenties.

He wrapped up the album neatly and handed it to me, saying, poker-faced, that he hoped we would do business again some day.

Dora was scraping the plate with the spoon when I returned. I patted the packet.

'We've got it!'

'Are you sure it's still there?' She obviously hadn't forgotten that she was going to hold the security.

'We'll soon see.' I sat down and unwrapped the album and, simulating trembling excitement, opened it to Brazil and lifted the first day cover. 'There – see, it's exactly right.'

'Goodness! To think that little old piece of paper is worth a thousand dollars!'

'Well, nine hundred anyway. Here, you keep it until we get the money. Have you got an old envelope?'

'Yes, right here in my purse.'

'Well tear off the corner and put the stamp in that and then keep it with your credit cards.'

'All right. When do you think you'll hear?'

'Oh, by tomorrow morning, I suppose. Shall I pick you up for lunch again? Afterwards we'll go to the post office and mail him the stamp, registered, of course.'

'But not *right* after lunch, Ronnie.'

'Perhaps we will find something else to do right after lunch.' I kissed her and she pushed me away coyly.

'Now we'd better get you back or your friends will think I've kidnapped you.'

'Oh, that's all right. I saw Gino and Catherina when I went back for the money.'

'Oh? Did you tell them about our little deal?'

'No, I just said I needed some extra dough to buy something I'd seen; they wanted to hear about you but I said I'd tell them later but, of course, I won't really. I will brag a little when we've made our profit. That smart ass Gino thinks I'm a *Dumb* Dora.'

I paid for the ice-cream and insisted upon paying for the water taxi back to the Rialto. At the entrance to her hotel I offered the album to her.

'Oh no, Ronald, you keep it.'

'All right. We'll find another dealer tomorrow and sell it for what we can get.' I watched without a twinge of sympathy as her large yellow bottom disappeared into the revolving doors. The money she'd lost wouldn't break her and she might even come to think of it as well spent. I knew I'd damned well earned it.

I felt the ache in the small of my back that always comes at the end of a successful con. It has something to do with adrenalin, I think, and is accompanied by a fierce exultation at having vanquished the enemy once again. Ever since my teens I seem to have been fighting a running battle with women, on which despite occasional local victories I can never win. The feeling of triumph disappears as quickly as it came and with that the realization that the war goes on. Even as I am forced to look for the next victim I know that my eventual defeat is inevitable. I didn't think so when I was younger; then I was confident that through women I would get all the good things of life, for to the victor belongs the spoils. Now I knew that I would never be the real victor; women's weakness was an illusion. Even when I'd seemed to vanquish them it was really they who had been strong and I who had been weak. It wasn't Dora who had been 'dumb'; it was I.

I supposed the psychiatrists were right; the answer must lie buried in the past, in my childhood and adolescence.

7

WHEN I LEFT school I asked my mother to get Lady Liz to persuade the General to let me work for him. If some day I was to live in his world there were many things I had to learn. I told my mother that I didn't want any pay, just to do something towards my board and keep. A few days later he sent for me.

'What sort of things d'ye think you could do for me, eh, boy?'

'The sort of things my grandfather did for you: clean your boots, look after your clothes, take messages,'

'I see. Well I hope you're a bit soberer than Corporal Kelly.' He leaned back in his big revolving chair, which had been a forbidden plaything when I was a small boy, and assessed me. 'Not that your grandfather wasn't a good batman; he did for me for over twenty years. You're not very big but I don't suppose that matters,'

'I'll get bigger.'

He laughed. 'I expect you will. All right, you can report to me tomorrow morning at ten and I'll see what I can find for you to do. Tidying up in here to begin with; I don't let the damnfool maids touch anything. I understand you don't want any pay.'

'No, I don't.'

'Can't have that – slavery's been abolished in England. Right. Tomorrow here at ten, then.'

'Right-o, thanks.' I turned to go.

'Boy! What's your name! Oh, yes, George. Well, George, if you're going to be my batman you must call me "sir".'

'Yes, sir.'

Of course the other servants said I was sucking up but my mother defended me and the two girls from the village who kept the house clean welcomed my taking some of the work off them. One taught me how to get his laundry ready, to iron his shirts and press his trousers. I tidied up his bedroom, dressing-room and study and after a few blow-ups learned what not to touch.

Apart from serving on one or two committees he spent most of his time at his desk with his investments. He took both of the financial papers as well as the *Telegraph* and the *Stock Exchange Gazette* and he spent at least an hour each day, sometimes longer, in writing on filing cards and marking up charts.

Gradually as he got to trust me he let me do more for him in this field. He would cut out things like buying or selling tips or forecasts of profits and leave them for me to file for him, either by writing them on to an existing card (he made me print in small capital letters because my writing was so bad) or in manila folders in a metal cabinet.

Occasionally he would talk to me about stocks and shares.

'Pure gambling, young George,' he said once. 'But there's scope for skill and you don't often lose the lot.'

He had a large post and I learned about 'rights' issues and 'bonus' issues and option dealing.

'You know how to remember which option is which, George? No? Well, just remember this: you call *up* your stockbroker and you put *down* the money. Got that? Buy call options if you think the share's going up; put options if you think it'll go down.'

He had a lot of Stock Exchange sayings, the meanings of which he would explain to me, sometimes in unnecessary detail. I learned a good deal about the world of stocks and shares, knowledge which I was later able to put to good use.

I think I half expected the General to do something about finding me a job but he didn't. I would have jumped at the chance of working as an office boy in a stockbroker's but I'm sure such a thing never occurred to him. He probably expected me to go into service but that never occurred to me as I was convinced even then that I was destined for better things.

Soon after my sixteenth birthday Lady Liz received a telegram which caused her to hurry up to London. She came back with Emmeline, the General's daughter, whom she had rescued from a home for alcoholics. Emmeline was Mrs Hugo Dunne but she hated to hear the name of the man who had divorced her during the war in a most ungentlemanly fashion, citing no less than three R.A.F. officers.

Not wanting to give up the gay life of wartime London she had taken over a run-down drinking club and turned it into the place for young officers to drink in the afternoons when the pubs were shut.

She became the mistress of a captain on Eisenhower's staff who promised to divorce his wife and marry her when the war finished. In 1946 he did indeed get a divorce but he married someone five years younger than Emmeline.

It was then that she crossed the line from being a heavy social drinker to an alcoholic, but she must have had an iron constitution, for although she was drunk most of the time it took over ten years for alcohol to bring her down.

Lady Liz and Miss Emmy had met in the 'thirties when Emmeline, whose mother had died when she was sixteen, had come back to England from her finishing school in Switzerland. The General had allowed her to live in London, acknowledging that the Manor was a dull place for a lively nineteen-year-old girl. Late in 1938 Emmeline had brought Elizabeth Coggeshall, an Eton-cropped, chain-smoking, cocktail-drinking divorcée of twenty-seven, home for the first of many weekends.

My mother, who had just moved up from scullery maid to house-maid, had been shocked at the state of Mrs Coggeshall's bed after a Saturday night's heavy drinking when the only man sleeping in the house had been the sixty-year-old General. But a few months later he married her and so they became respectable.

My grandfather, the General's batman, had known his first wife, Lucille Rokesby, when the General had been simply Lieutenant Wilfrith Gore. Lucille, the only daughter of a Midlands industrialist, had been sent to stay with a cousin whose husband commanded the regiment in which Lieutenant Gore served. She was then twenty-five which in 1899 meant that she was in serious danger of being left on the shelf. My grandfather told my mother, who later told me, that old Mr Rokesby had bluntly offered Lieutenant Gore fifty thousand pounds if he would change his name to Rokesby-Gore when he married Lucille. After the marriage, which occurred very soon after this offer, the old man promised a further twenty-five thousand in trust for a grandson. Lucille dutifully produced one the following year, shortly after Captain Rokesby-Gore had left for the war in South Africa.

I knew a little about the son, Ronald Gordon Rokesby-Gore, whose name I had stolen. Over the fireplace in the library hung a large oil painting of a very young man in uniform and one of my jobs was to polish the brass plate: 2nd-Lt R. G. Rokesby-Gore 9 March 1900–23 March 1918, and underneath DULCE ET DECORUM EST PRO PATRIA MORI. Although the General never spoke of him I sometimes thought that his kindness to me arose from my being about the age he remembered his son.

Miss Emmy was nearly twenty years younger than her brother. Her return in 1957 made a great difference to my life because she took an interest in me. She called me 'Georgie' which no one else did and sent me on errands for which she sometimes gave me sixpence. She questioned me about my ambitions and because I couldn't think of anything I said I'd like to be a photographer; that was why she'd got me a camera. She also questioned me about my love life and refused to believe that it was non-existent.

She was strictly rationed for drink, being allowed one cocktail before dinner and exactly a glass and a half of wine. The General had forbidden the stores or the village pubs to sell her any alcohol and because he was their landlord they obeyed.

One day she called me into her dressing-room and asked me if I would go to the next village and bring her back a bottle of gin from the pub's off-licence. I agreed although I knew the General would be furious if he found out. The gin cost thirty-seven shillings and I wondered how much of the three shillings change she'd let me keep. I was surprised when she let me have it all until I realized that I was being paid for being discreet as well.

Miss Emmy kept her secret gin supply locked in one of the drawers of her dressing-table and I glimpsed other things in there on the occasions when she still had some left and put the new bottle away. Knowledge, I had read, was power and I wanted to know what else she had hidden, but she kept the key on her key ring so that it was always with her when she was out. Then I remembered that Lady Liz had a similar dressing-table in her bedroom and when both were out I tried her keys in Miss Emmy's and found one worked. There was a bottle of gin wrapped in black silk underwear, a pink garter embroidered with roses, a packet of letters tied with ribbon and three books: *The Karma Sutra*, *Fanny Hill* and one by Krafft-Ebing called *Psychopathia Sexualis*. There was also an envelope containing photographs of naked men and women, and women with women, in complicated positions rather like circus contortionists. Finally there was an electric vibrator.

I put everything back in its original place and decided to read through the letters and the books when it was safe. The letters from Hugo Dunne, her ex-husband, were love letters, a dead bore, but the others were from different men with whom she'd had it off during the war and the mugs each thought he was the only one she was sleeping

65

with. Some of them went into considerable detail about what they'd done with her and what they were going to do and I guessed that was why she kept them. I read the books, even the one about case histories, and began to understand how powerful sex can be. Krafft-Ebing and the Indian manual opened possibilities to me.

But what I needed most was money and the next time Miss Emmy gave me an empty gin bottle to get rid of I took it to my room instead and from time to time poured a little from the one in her drawer into mine. I never took too much and I always rewrapped her bottle in the lace panties as I had found it. After about a month, instead of going to the off-licence in the next village I took her the bottle I had filled. I'd stuck on the paper seal from her last new bottle and I put a little glue inside the cap so it wouldn't unscrew too easily.

I took it to her, my heart thumping. She was lying on her bed with the curtains drawn. I offered to open it for her but she took it from me, twisted the cap off without noticing anything and told me to get her some water. She poured about a third of a tumbler of gin and added about the same amount of water. She took a long drink, closed her eyes and carefully put the glass on her bedside table.

'God, I needed that! Don't ever drink, Georgie, it's hell if you can't get it.'

'Yes, ma'am. Is there anything else?'

'No. You're putting on a bit of flesh at last I'm glad to see. How old are you now?'

'Sixteen.'

'You look older, very like your father and that's a compliment. I hope you're not so wicked though.' She laughed. 'I suppose you've got a full growth of hair now, eh?'

I put my hand up to my head and she laughed again. 'Not there, you innocent boy! Never mind, you can go now – and thanks.'

'Any time, Miss Emmy.'

'And you'll keep our little secret won't you?'

I nodded and went out elated; I'd made thirty-seven shillings at one blow and I knew I could do it again, perhaps as often as every four or five weeks. Also I'd known full well what she'd meant about my hair and from the way she'd laughed I thought she'd probably had my father when she was a girl and now she fancied me. If I played my cards well I could be making more than thirty-seven shillings out of her.

She seemed terribly old to me at thirty-eight, several years older than my mother whom I thought of as middle-aged. She didn't really look any older though because she had the time and the money to look after herself. I knew she dyed her hair because at one time it had been the same colour as Marilyn Monroe's but now it was brown. I remembered some years earlier when she had played tennis and rode regularly that she'd been a beautiful woman, but that was before her drinking turned muscles to fat. Now her large breasts were beginning to droop and her hips were spreading. Still, when she took the time and trouble she could look most attractive.

I hadn't been unaware of her as a woman but I know now that I was a good deal less randy than most boys of my age. My craving was for money and status and it was not until I realized what folly sex can lead men – and women – into that I became really interested in it.

Then the General went off for a fortnight's fishing and I didn't have to be so careful sneaking the gin into Miss Emmy's room, which was just down the hall from his suite. Lady Liz's room was in the other wing so there was little fear of her catching me. Both she and the General were pleased with what they imagined was Miss Emmy's reform.

I brought her a new bottle one very hot afternoon and was surprised that she was wearing only a bra and knickers, for I had knocked on the door as usual and in the past she had often told me to wait while, I had assumed, she put something on.

'Hand me my dressing-gown, Georgie, there's a pet. It's on my bathroom door.'

I put the gin down and brought her the dressing-gown which was so thin I could still see the underwear. There was a half-full glass next to her bed and I wondered if she were tight. She had also just put down a book: it was *Lady Chatterley's Lover*. She saw me looking at it and asked if I'd read it.

'No, ma'am.'

'Just as well – it might give you ideas.'

I knew something about the book because I'd heard the General say once to a couple of his men friends that there was no harm in letting your children read *Lady Chatterley* but it should be kept away from gamekeepers. I hadn't understood the laughter until it was explained to me later in the kitchen.

'You're not busy now, are you, Georgie? Well, sit down, I won't bite you. No, not there, on the end of the bed.'

I sat down thinking it best to say nothing.

67

'I don't suppose you drink, do you?'

'No. I tried beer but I didn't like it; sometimes I have a glass of sweet cider but I don't like that much either.'

'Try this.' She handed me the glass and I took a sip. I swallowed it but I shook my head and she took it back with a laugh.

She put her hand on my thigh. 'What do you do to keep fit? You never seem to play any games but you're obviously quite strong.'

'I don't do anything.'

'Nothing? Nothing at all? Not even an occasional romp with one of the village girls?'

'I haven't had the chance.'

'You must make chances, Georgie. You're a very attractive boy. It shouldn't to too difficult.' She took another long swallow. 'What time does the sun rise?'

'The sun?' I was bewildered.

'Yes, I want to see it. Find out the time and then come along and wake me about a quarter of an hour before. Do you understand?'

'I think so. You want me to come and wake you up just before dawn.'

'Got it in one. Now I'm a heavy sleeper and I don't want you disturbing anyone by knocking, so just come quietly in and give me a shake – gently so you don't startle me – and don't leave until you're quite sure that I'm wide awake.'

I borrowed an alarm clock but woke every couple of hours during the night, at last getting up and turning it off before it rang. I had a quick cat wash, untangled my hair, and walked quietly to her room. When I opened her door the light from the hall shone on the bed.

She had thrown off the bedclothes and kicked them down the bed so they were entangled in her feet. She was lying on her side with her mouth slightly open and an arm half across her face. Her nightdress had ridden up almost to her waist so I found myself staring at a large white buttock with the line of suntanned thigh making it appear that she was wearing light-brown stockings.

I found it hard to breathe naturally; my mouth was suddenly very dry and my penis was so hard it hurt. Not daring to wake her I tried to loosen the sheet and to pull it up to cover her without disturbing her. Bending down meant bringing my face to within a foot or so of her buttock, and as I very gently tried to pull the sheet loose she exhaled deeply and rolled over on her back, exposing what seemed to me a quite enormous bush of brown silky hair. I gulped and tugged a little harder and then something made me look up at her.

Her eyes were wide open and she was looking at me with a half-smile. I knew suddenly that she had been awake all the time. Before I could move or say anything she reached forward, grabbed my ears and pushed my face down on to her hairy mound.

'Oh you wicked boy!' she said. The smell was strong but not unpleasant but I grabbed her hand and freed my ears, which were burning painfully, and pulled my face away. She half sat up and kissed me, swallowing my mouth in hers. I could smell gin and tobacco on her breath and saw by the ashtray that she must have stubbed out a cigarette when she heard me coming.

She loosened my belt, unbuttoned my fly and pushed off my trousers in a practically unbroken series of movements. She tried to make me wait but I was inside her and having an orgasm almost immediately.

'Damn!' she said. 'Well – the best-laid plans of mice and women . . .' She pushed me off her, my trousers around my ankles and my shoes still on. 'Never mind – next time it will get better. Now pull your trousers up, make yourself decent and go back to bed.'

'Don't you want to see the sunrise?'

'Bugger the sunrise!'

That is how it all started and, of course, it continued: at first we were very cautious, always keeping to five o'clock in the morning, because I could leave my room and go to hers without running the risk of being seen, and as long as I left her at half-past five it was still pretty safe, but once or twice we both fell asleep. Once I only just had time to shoot out of bed and into her bathroom, grabbing my clothes, before my mother brought her the early-morning tea tray.

'Good morning, Kathleen – don't draw my bath just yet,' I heard Miss Emmy say calmly. 'I'm going to have a lie-in today.'

After that she turned me out as soon as I had satisfied her, but that in time took longer. Our love-making grew more and more strenuous as she taught me how to give her maximum pleasure, explaining about female orgasms and the importance of preliminary love play. She liked to hear me read from her secret books and corrected my pronunciation and told me the meanings of unfamiliar words.

We would read a description of a way of making love and then follow the directions – almost like learning a new, intricate dance step from a manual. She was mad about cunnilingus and I got quite expert at bringing her to the point of orgasm and then quickly finishing her off, sometimes provoking loud cries from her which I thought must wake the General. I got little pleasure from going down on her but I enjoyed the feeling of power. The morning sessions were exhausting because of the different positions she insisted upon, saying that at her age she needed the spice of variety. She was no featherweight and sometimes I felt she was going to suffocate me, but though small I was strong and healthy and learned how to satisfy her desire to be physically dominated.

I had wondered at first whether she would offer me money but I realize now that to do so would have lowered her self-esteem, for she was still an attractive woman and had there been any other man available she would not have bothered with me.

She did repay me, however, by taking me in hand, correcting my mistakes and telling me about the language used in her class, which was no more correct than mine but different, a signal, one of the ways they recognized each other. She ruled out a lot of words and phrases: I wasn't to say 'serviette', 'toilet' and many other words; not 'pleased to meet you' but a clipped 'how d'ye do', not 'ta' for 'thank you' and never 'bye bye' or 'bye for now'.

'Rather vulgarity than gentility, Georgie,' she said. She told me one day that I was a quick learner. 'I'm proud of you, you're my Eliza Doolittle.' When I didn't understand she bought me a paperback copy of Shaw's *Pygmalion*.

Reading that play was a turning point in my life. I suddenly realized that what I wanted more than anything else was actually possible: I could escape the prison of poverty and illegitimacy to which a malevolent fate had condemned me. I didn't have to be Kate Kelly's 'Eyetie bastard' for the rest of my life; I could learn to pass myself off as someone quite different. Women would be the means I'd use, sex would be the weapon, sex which I would always keep strictly under control.

8

I LOVE VENICE at any time but particularly when I have money in my pocket. I patted the bulge the notes made and wished that I could stay, move to one of the great hotels and resume my role as one of the world's privileged. But, obviously, I couldn't; I'd have to get out of this beautiful city before Dora had time to think about how she'd handed such a sum over to a man she'd only just met. I knew from long experience how easily suspicion is aroused.

I made my way to the Alitalia office to see about a flight to somewhere else in Italy leaving later that afternoon or evening. There was one to Rome in a little over two hours, just time to get back to the hotel, get rid of B.L.'s damning suitcase and pay my bill.

I did toy with the idea of not going back to the hotel and not paying the bill, since as soon as Dora discovered she had been swindled she would probably go to the police, who would then be looking for 'Colonel Rokesby-Gore' anyway, but I decided against that because there was a good chance that she wouldn't go to the police, wouldn't even tell her friends because she wouldn't want their contemptuous pity. Besides, I had long since learned not to get on the wrong side of hotels, who exchange black lists. Also, if I skipped they'd inform the police, who would then discover the suitcase and I'd be wanted for stealing as well.

No – I had to go back to the hotel and somehow I had to get the suitcase, with its bottom cut away, safely out.

As I was waiting impatiently at the Alitalia counter to pay for my ticket I felt a tap on my arm and could not stop myself from jumping. I turned to see Gino Angelini smiling at me.

'Hey, what's the matter with you?' he asked. 'You murdered somebody or somethin'?'

'Not yet,' I laughed. 'I don't like someone sneaking up on me, I guess it's from the Army – terrorists, you know.'

'Oh, sure. I'm sorry. I saw you through the window; you leaving us?' He nodded at the new twenty-dollar bills I was clutching.

'No. I mean, that is, yes, temporarily. I'm just making a quick trip to Rome.'

'You are? Dora just told me she's having lunch with you again tomorrow.'

'Oh I'm not going until after lunch tomorrow . . .' At that moment the girl returned with my ticket and change.

'The motor boat for the airport leaves in one hour, at seven o'clock, signor. From the Piazza San Marco.'

'Thanks.' I turned to Gino who was looking most unfriendly. I shrugged my shoulders. 'Well, you've discovered my secret. I have to see a lady in Rome tonight, but I will be back in Venice in time to take Dora to lunch tomorrow.'

He nodded his head slowly. 'Okay, if you say so, I guess. Dora seemed kinda happy just now and I wouldn't want to see her get hurt, you know? She's a nice lady.'

'I think so too,' I said sincerely. 'And I don't want to see her get hurt either. Now I have to get back to my hotel and pack an overnight bag.' I eased my way around him and hurried to the Rialto, where I got a water taxi back to my hotel. In the room I made an assessment of the state of the game. I'd climbed a long ladder and moved well up the board, but the way ahead was full of snakes and the next throw of the dice was a dangerous one. It was obvious that Gino was now suspicious, and if he were suspicious enough to tell Dora that I was flying to Rome it was very probable that she'd tell him about the valuable stamp we'd invested in, might even show it to him.

And then? I tried to put myself in their shoes. They'd probably get an expert opinion; ask the hotel manager for the nearest stamp dealer, who would, of course, spot my inexpert alteration at once.

Still, that would take time. No, I mustn't fool myself. Gino would have been back in the hotel while I was still in my water taxi, and could even now be on his way with Dora to a dealer. Or perhaps his telling her that I had bought an air ticket to Rome with new twenties would have been enough to make her come looking for me with him, and, perhaps, Leon. Suddenly I felt very precarious.

I got the suitcase down and the bottom opened out in four triangles; it was obvious that I couldn't carry it out of the hotel like that, and equally obvious that I didn't dare leave it behind. I went to the window to see if perhaps I could throw it far enough from the hotel grounds for there to be a good chance of someone picking it up and taking it away, but my room opened on to an interior courtyard.

I wondered what time it was; I should have bought a watch but I'd been in a bit of a panic since running into Gino. I supposed that must have been about thirty minutes ago, which meant that I'd very little time to catch the water bus from San Marco to the airport, say ten or fifteen minutes.

I stared at the mutilated suitcase; if there were only some way I could get it and its contents out of the hotel I could then leave it outside a shop confident that it would be stolen. If I had some of this modern glue, I thought stupidly, I could glue the edges together, but I knew that that was quite impossible.

Wait a minute, though! If I had a piece of plywood the same size as the bottom of the suitcase I could smear it with glue, put it inside and stick down the bottom. Would it then hold all the contents? No, but it wasn't necessary to take them all, only those things like the suits which could be identified. I could leave all the rest of the clothing in the drawers.

But where in the next ten minutes could I get plywood and glue? There was not time to go out and odd bits of plywood are not usually found in hotel bedrooms. And then I saw the empty coffee cups and glasses still sitting on their tray, which was rectangular and made of very thin sheet metal. Thank God for the lax Italians; almost anywhere else the tray would have been cleared away.

I put the open suitcase on the bed with the cut flaps in their original position and placed the tray on top of them. Unfortunately it covered no more than about half the area, but with a good glue it ought to hold at least until I'd paid my bill and got out of sight.

I ran down the stairs to the hall porter, thinking that surely I was due for a little luck, and so it turned out, for he did have a pot of glue he used for sticking hotel labels on guests' luggage. I smeared this all over the bottom of the tray, put the suitcase on the bathroom floor, pressed the tray down and then put one of the Italian leather shoes at either end and laid two coat hangers across them to carry some of the weight.

I thrust B.L.'s suit jackets in the case, put the electric shaver into my pocket and picked up the stamp album. The other clothes and the trousers would be found as soon as the maid did the room, but as long as I had paid my bill all the management would do would be to parcel up my belongings until I got in touch with them.

73

Gingerly I picked up the suitcase. The bottom bulged and the paste oozed from the cuts, making a white cross which I wiped clean with a wet towel. I made sure I had my dollars and passport in my pocket and the key of my room, not wanting any delay while they checked that. Then I picked up the suitcase, holding it underneath, and carried it like a baby out of the room and down the main stairs. But then I had to hold it by the handle so as not to attract attention. I walked to the desk and put it down with the glued back against the wall.

I told the clerk that I had just received a message which made it necessary for me to go immediately to Rome. He looked surprised, no doubt wondering who had given me the message, but said nothing except that as it was now half-past six I would have to pay for an extra day. I agreed and asked him to hurry as I didn't have much time to get to the airport.

As he turned to make up my bill I glanced through the long glass windows of the hotel's front and to my horror saw Dora, Leon and Gino just about to cross the street.

In a panic I grabbed the suitcase and started to run. The bottom burst open, dumping the contents on the floor. I flung it from me and bolted into the empty dining-room, through the service door and into the kitchens, past an old woman who was scrubbing the chef's wooden work table, and out of the back door into an alley stacked with overflowing garbage bins. I could hear shouts behind me, so I kept on running.

The alley stopped at a narrow canalside path and for no good reason I turned right and, luck sometimes being on my side, came almost immediately to a landing stage where a water taxi had just disembarked a passenger. I jumped in.

'Al aeroporto,' I gasped. 'Quickly. I'll pay double.'

It was an almost new water taxi and its owner loved an excuse to let it all out. Ignoring the strict speed laws, he roared along the narrow canals making a wash which rocked the tethered gondolas and earned us a few angry shouts. We sped across the lagoon and arrived at the landing stage for the airport with a dramatic last-minute ninety-degree turn. I thrust bills for the double fare at him and ran for the airport.

As I was on an internal flight, I didn't have to worry about customs or immigration but went straight to the Alitalia desk and checked in for the Rome flight. It was five past seven, which meant that I had a wait of some fifty minutes.

I guessed that when they discovered I had run, Gino and the others would have gone back to the Piazzetta where the regular motor-boat service to the airport leaves, expecting to find me there since Gino knew that I was supposed to take the seven o'clock airport boat. If I were lucky, they would have let it go when I didn't show and would be wasting time looking for me, but it was more likely that they would take it themselves and try to catch me as I boarded the plane. In that case they would be arriving at about half past seven, which meant that I would have to hide somewhere for another half hour.

It wasn't the first time I'd had to avoid being seen while waiting to take off from an airport. I'd hidden myself in a number of places in the past: once in a broom cupboard in the gents, once lying curled up on the floor of a telephone booth; I'd even walked into a canteen kitchen and passed myself off as a health inspector for a critical quarter of an hour.

I headed straight for the men's lavatories, knowing there was one sure place where I could be alone and unobserved. I sat on the W.C. and tried to think calmly about my plight. It was not a large building and it wouldn't take Gino and Leon long to search the place thoroughly, starting, I was pretty sure, with the gents as soon as they had satisfied themselves I wasn't in the waiting-room.

I'd glimpsed the single-counter canteen on my way to the lavatories. Everything was prepared at it; there was no kitchen, so that was no good. There'd been a few doors leading to administrative offices and, I supposed, the police and airport security staff. I toyed with the idea of going to them with a long story of having had my luggage stolen, but there was a strong possibility that Gino and the others would go there themselves when they didn't find me.

I sat and stared at the graffiti, the usual crude drawings of sexual organs, male and female, I'd seen all over the world. I realized that I was in danger of just sitting there until Gino and Leon came in. I am sometimes tempted to react to danger with complete inactivity. Come on! Come on! I urged myself, *think*, as they say in I.B.M., THINK!

I went back into the waiting area, which was full of passengers arriving, departing or waiting. It was 7.18 by the big airport clock and I reckoned that the water bus would arrive in ten minutes or so. There would then be a further twenty-five minutes before the Rome flight was called, and it was quite impossible for me to keep out of sight that long. I was getting desperate as I racked my brain for somewhere to go.

The only way of leaving the airport was either to take a motor boat back to Venice or the Lido or one of the smaller islands, or to take the mainland bus back to Venezia Mestre and then to get a bus from the terminus to another town and, by repeating that once or twice more, destroying my trail completely.

That, I decided, was the best plan. I had noticed the bus waiting by the main entrance as I came in. I hurried outside only to see it disappearing down the road. The next one, the inspector told me, was in half an hour. Now it was too late: I was trapped.

I went over to the big board which listed flight departures just in case there were a delay on my Rome flight, and noticed that a flight to Vienna with a stop at Trieste left in ten minutes. I ran to the Alitalia desk and, pushing my way to the front of the queue with an apology, demanded a ticket to Trieste, saying that I had just had a phone call telling me my wife was dangerously ill.

It worked beautifully: the ticket was issued on the spot and a girl rushed me through the gate to join the group walking towards the aircraft. I looked over towards the jetty and saw, among the passengers disembarking from the airline's motor boat three figures detach themselves from the rest and half run towards the airport building.

As I was on an internal flight I hadn't had to produce a passport or any identification. I'd called myself Antonio Bergonzoli and as Gino would discover that Colonel Rokesby-Gore was still booked on the Rome flight they would spend some time searching the building for him.

As the plane climbed above the lagoon and headed east I felt a sense of triumph. It had been a close-run thing but here I was, only hours or so after walking out of a cell with practically nothing, flying to Trieste with nearly five hundred dollars and about a hundred thousand lire. Admittedly I would have to find another mark soon, but my tail was up and I was sure there was a middle-aged woman with spare cash not far away in whose hundrum life a handsome dark stranger was about to appear. In my relief I laughed out loud, which earned a disapproving look from the man in the next seat, an Englishman struggling with the serious problem of *The Times* crossword puzzle.

At Trieste airport there were no problems as we didn't have to go through the international part. Having no baggage, I was outside a few minutes after the plane touched down. There were the usual representatives of the bigger hotels but as I was not carrying a suitcase none approached me.

I went up to the elderly one from the Bristol, that monument to pre-war respectability, and told him to take me there in their Fiat bus.

'You have no bag, sir.'

'No, but don't worry about that.' He seemed doubtful but drove me to the Bristol nevertheless.

The desk clerk also looked doubtful as I explained that I had been summoned to Trieste on business at such short notice that I'd not had time to pack even an overnight bag.

'I'll buy what I need tomorrow.'

He said that he understood the situation perfectly but that it was unusual for guests to arrive without luggage and he was sure that I, in my turn, would understand . . . ?

'That I have to pay in advance? Of course.' I took the roll of twenties out and peeled off five. 'First would you be good enough to change a hundred dollars for me?'

His attitude changed in a flash from suspicion to servility. He handed me lire from the safe and I gave him back thirty-five thousand for one night. Minutes later I was shown to my room. As the boy left, I locked the door and felt safe for the first time since I had been startled by finding Gino standing by my side in the Alitalia office.

But I had an unpleasant feeling that I wasn't well.

My head was hot and throbbing, I had a horrible taste in my mouth and my tiredness was more than physical. I loosened my tie, undid the collar of my shirt, pulled off my shoes, lay back on top of the bed and lit a cigarette. My body was protesting – I hadn't had a decent sleep for days – and the draining of adrenalin caused by the precipitate flight in Venice and my fear of being caught and perhaps hit by one of Leon's large fists.

I realized that I was hungry, not only because it was getting on for eight hours since I'd had anything to eat but also as part of the reaction to a long and exhausting day. The room service menu was an extensive one, but I contented myself with ordering an American hamburger, hot chocolate and a cream-filled pastry. I also asked for some aspirin or codeine.

The bath was scalding hot and I soon got the grime off my hands and face and managed to clean my nails by digging them into the hotel soap and getting it out with the corner of a piece of folded toilet paper. The hotel also provided a toothbrush already impregnated with toothpaste and after brushing my teeth until the gums bled and gargling with warm water I felt much better.

The waiter brought four aspirins in metal foil with the tray and I gave him a thousand-lire note, thus assuring myself of excellent service. After I had eaten and drunk the sweet hot chocolate I felt a little better, but I knew something was wrong.

I took off my suit, which was once again looking shabby, beat the dust off with a towel and slightly dampened the jacket, which I then hung in the bathroom, letting a little hot water into the bath which steamed up the looking-glass. By morning most of the wrinkles in the jacket would be gone. I dampened the crease in my trousers and put them under the mattress and again washed my drip-dry shirt and wiped my shoes with one of the hotel's small face towels.

Then I got into bed in my underwear – I don't like sleeping naked – turned out the bedside lamp and was confident that I'd be asleep in a matter of minutes.

I was wrong. There was something the matter with me, for I was sweating badly, my joints were aching and my mind was jumping from one sequence to another; now an incident from the past, a flash of Malabata prison – that had been a tough one; the dash across the lagoon in Venice; Maria-Luisa – always these days Maria-Luisa. Dammit, I told myself, you're in control, remember? Now, forget everything and go to sleep.

I tried a trick I'd learned from an Indian I'd shared a cell with briefly in Delhi. It is to conjure up a blackboard in the mind's eye and to think of nothing else but the bare blackboard and an eraser. The moment anything at all appears on it you wipe it off. The trick is to concentrate solely on keeping the blackboard blank; if you can do that sleep usually comes quickly.

But before it could work this time I found myself shivering and then, of course, I knew what was wrong with me, an attack of recurrent malaria. I'd picked that up in India too, along with jaundice.

I knew from experience, although it had been years since the last one, that there wasn't anything I could do about it. Paludrine would help but I'd long since thrown the last away.

I found an extra blanket in the cupboard and put that on the bed, knowing that when the next bout of fever succeeded the chills I'd probably throw all the bedclothes off. The attacks lasted two or three days, seldom more. One thing was quite certain: I would not be able to go on the next morning, I'd need at least a day's rest; if I didn't give my body a chance to fight back I could be helpless for a week or more.

And yet staying on in a hotel where I was registered as Rokesby-Gore was dangerous: the dropping of the stolen suitcase in Venice had been a disaster and it was damned bad luck that I hadn't had time to pay my bill, because it had made it inevitable that the management would inform the police. My unusual name would certainly be on the police circular and there was a chance that it would trigger a memory at the station which would get the fiche I had filled in. I had carried my Canadian 'William Mackenzie' passport for just such emergencies, but as that was the identity I'd used when selling the valueless shares to my Glasgow widow I'd destroyed it. I hadn't got another when I went to Cannes because that had been intended as a holiday.

Now, undoubtedly, Colonel Rokesby-Gore had to disappear; I could probably risk one more day as him in this small hotel but I'd get out the following day and become myself for a change, George Kelly, British tourist who'd lost or mislaid his passport. But it was too risky to go to the British Consul in Trieste; I'd have to keep my Rokesby-Gore passport to get through the controls at the nearby frontier with Yugoslavia. Once in that country, which I knew well, I'd report a lost passport to the nearest British Counsul who could easily check that one had indeed been issued to a George Kelly, born in Hampshire on 7 February 1941, and I was confident that I could convince him that I was he.

I didn't think there was much chance of Dora and her friends tracking me down. When they had found that I wasn't on the Rome flight nor anywhere in the small airport they would assume that I had doubled back into Venice. Even if, by some remote chance, they had deduced that the man who had made a last-minute booking for Trieste was me they wouldn't be able to find me.

Unless they went to the police. Damn. Obviously the sensible course was to get out of the hotel early the next morning, but it wasn't possible; if I tried I'd almost certainly collapse in the street, be taken to hospital and draw the attention of the authorities to me. I decided to take a chance and stay in the room all the next day and night hoping to be able to start running again the following day, Friday.

9

I SELDOM SLEEP LATE in the morning, since almost any sudden noise startles me awake, probably because I can never forget all the people who are on the lookout for me. This sense of being hunted means that I am always ready to flee.

But it was nearly nine when I came out of the latest feverish nightmare in which Maria-Luisa had been riding me bareback wearing spurs. The sun was pouring into the room. I was hot, my bones ached where the spurs had dug in and I had a headache.

I ordered coffee, orange juice, a jug of water and *La Stampa* and when these came I told the maid that I wasn't well and would stay in bed that day. She needn't make up the room but I would appreciate some aspirins. She brought me eight and as I only rarely take any kind of painkiller the first two soon dulled my headache.

The newspaper had nothing to interest me, as elections, the Cold War, floods, earthquakes or other catastrophes don't somehow seem to have much to do with my world. I tried to think of the future, to make plans, but I was still in an attack of malaria and couldn't concentrate.

All my mind seemed to want to do was to remember Maria-Luisa. Wearily I lit a cigarette and gave in to its urgings. I let the memory come.

As soon as I told Maria-Luisa that it was not smart for her to leave her twenty-five thousand dollars on deposit in an American bank my mind started to buzz.

I began by saying that I really ought to go down to the coast to buy the financial papers and to get in touch with London.

'There's something I have to check on with my brokers,' I said. 'It's no use trying to phone through from up here – I know, I've tried it. It's hopeless and besides I'll have to phone New York – and probably Kuwait too.' I don't know why I added Kuwait – it just popped into my head, but it started a train of thought.

'You some kind of financier, Ron?'

'Well – not exactly. I was part of a small group dealing in the shares of international property companies for private investors once, but I sold out last year. However, part of the deal was that my ex-partners let me into a good thing when they've invested all they want to themselves.'

'So what's a good thing?'

'A chance to make a quick profit by prior knowledge of a coming bid either for a specific property or the shares of a company.'

'So how do they get this inside dope?'

'Usually because it is they who are instructed to do the negotiating. They have to watch their step because any large buying before the news breaks can lead to an investigation by the Stock Exchange Council.'

'It's illegal then?'

'Well, yes, technically. It's called "insider trading" and there is legislation against it in Britain and America, but in my opinion it's not immoral and as long as there's no chance of getting my fingers burnt I go in for my share.'

'How does it work?'

'It's usually a question of buying in my own and in nominees' names, holding for an account or two and selling when the news breaks, though sometimes with one of the big companies it's possible to deal in call options and make a real killing.'

She laughed. 'It sounds exciting but I don't know what the hell you're talking about.'

'Well don't worry about it. The thing is my old pals are acting for an Arab consortium looking to invest up to a hundred million dollars in prime commercial property in London and New York, and they also have among their clients a number of Americans who don't like paying capital gains tax. My friends are working on a deal to make both sides happy.'

I was rather proud of this, which came right off the top of my head. Maria-Luisa looked impressed.

'And you're in on this big deal?'

'In a modest sort of way. Nothing earth-shattering, but where the cake is in millions no one bothers about crumbs involving tens of thousands. Anyway I have to check on how things are going and also make sure I'm liquid. I'll have to go to Marseilles tomorrow; it's only about three hours' drive, and from one of the big hotels there I can make international phone calls.'

'How long will you be?'

'Two days – three at the most. Will you stay here or drive back to Nice? I'll come back there if you do.'

'If it's okay with you I'd like to string along.' She'd bit, but I didn't strike yet.

'I'd love that but I'm afraid you'll find it rather boring.'

'No I won't – there's plenty to do in Marseilles. I'll be out looking around while you're making like an international financier.'

That was exactly the reaction I had hoped for, as I was confident that once I gave the impression of making money by slightly illegal insider dealing she would want to get in on it. Another golden rule is to persuade the mark that the deal is a little shady; most people have larceny in their hearts.

We got to Marseilles by late afternoon and booked a bedroom and sitting-room in a large hotel in the Canebière, near the Old Port.

I bought a *Financial Times* and an *Investors' Chronicle* and while she was ordering tea got out my notebooks and made a few impressively large calculations. I had left my conning gear back in Nice with the rest of my luggage, being convinced that I wouldn't have need of it. It consisted of a selection of stock certificates in bankrupt companies, Chinese bonds and South American railways and blank contract notes, plus a number of letters on stockbrokers' stationery I'd acquired in various ways. I also had an investor's record book intended to be seen by anyone curious enough to want to check up on me – it showed buying and selling of shares and options in very large amounts. But I'd left all those with Peter in Nice and now had to try and create the same impression from scratch. I did have my address book and from this I chose Harrods' telephone number, after noting that with the time difference they were sure to be closed.

I picked up the phone and asked the operator to get me the number. A minute or so later she rang to say that it was ringing for me. Maria-Luisa was lying on the bed reading *Cosmopolitan*, but, I was sure, taking all this in.

Harrods' answering machine came on; I held the phone by the ear microphone so that nothing could be heard.

'Sir Thomas Lawrence, please . . . Colonel Rokesby-Gore . . . I see . . . well . . . please tell him I called and will try him again this evening at home. Thank you.'

I glanced at Maria-Luisa but she showed no sign of having been interested.

'Let's walk down to the Old Port and have a real bouillabaisse,' I said. 'I'll phone again when we come in.'

'Right on – hey, wasn't there a painter called Sir Thomas Lawrence?'

'Yes, an eighteenth-century portrait painter, an ancestor of Tom's.'

I kicked myself. I bet that on Interpol's file on me under M.O. is 'a tendency to use the names of real persons, usually famous'. I would really have to watch myself.

We had a magnificent bouillabaisse, prepared as only the Marseillais really know how, and then walked around the Old Port. We decided to take the boat the next day out to the Château d'If to see the cell where the Man in the Iron Mask spent twenty years – that is if my business affairs allowed me the time, of course.

I phoned the Harrods number again about eleven and this time pretended to be told that Sir Thomas wouldn't be back until midnight. I would, I said into the Harrods recording, phone him at this hour.

'Sorry about all this,' I said. 'There's no need for you to stay up though – I'll take it on the phone in the sitting-room.'

'Can't you phone him in the morning?'

'I could but I've left the message now and he'll wait up for the call.'

She then got into bed and I apparently busied myself with calculations, while actually working out the details of the con by which I hoped to detach most if not all of her capital. An item in the *Investors' Chronicle* about a possible take-over of the Savoy Hotel gave me the basic idea.

I had invented the business about calling at midnight because I knew that Peter would have arrived home by then and I needed his help.

At ten to twelve I asked the operator for an outside line, saying that I wished to dial direct myself. I spoke in a low voice as though I were trying not to wake Maria-Luisa, although I was fairly certain that she was listening.

I held the telephone release keys down with my left hand while I dialled the first five numbers of the London dialling code, and then I released them and dialled the eight numbers of Peter's home phone in Nice.

'Pietro Piedmonti.'

'It's Colonel Rokesby-Gore here – has Sir Thomas Lawrence returned home?'

'Is that you, George?' Peter was puzzled.

'Yes – I phoned earlier in the evening. I am in Marseilles and want to speak to Sir Thomas rather urgently.'

'So you *are* on a con – I knew damn well you would. That's it isn't it?'

'Yes. Is that you, Tom? Ronnie here, Rokesby-Gore. Fine thanks – and you? Good. I'm phoning to find out if there's anything new on that proposition we discussed last week.'

'What am I supposed to say to that? – I don't know what the hell you're talking about.'

'There is? That's great. Who did you say? Trafalgar House?' I whistled and Peter shouted.

'That nearly deafened me, damn you!'

'They're pretty big – how much will the bid be? Two fifty-five? Are you sure – I mean that's fifty per cent more than the closing price last night.'

'I'll just talk when you stop,' Peter said. 'Once upon a time there was a wooden marionette called Pinocchio . . . '

'Well I must say you've never been wrong, Tom. How much can I come in for?'

' . . . whose nose kept growing and growing . . . '

'If you're that sure, I'd like to go for call options – that way I'd really clean up. All right then – you call me tomorrow about ten and tell me the latest position.' I gave him the phone number and my room, spelling it out slowly.

'George – you really want me to phone you there at ten tomorrow?'

'I most certainly do – it's very important.'

'All right – I'll ring from the hotel as soon as I get in, but I don't have a clue about what you want me to say . . . '

'That doesn't matter – I'll take care of all that this end.'

'Okay, but watch your step, George. The cops in Marseilles are clever bastards.'

'Yes I know – so am I. Good night, Tom, and thanks for letting me in on this one.'

'Good night, George.'

I hung up and went into the bedroom. Maria-Luisa was awake and I apologized for having woken her.

'That's all right. Successful business?'

'Amazingly so – it looks like a big one; a battle between the Arab consortium Tom acts for and Trafalgar House Investments for control of the Savoy Hotel.'

'Who or what is Trafalgar House?'

'A big and very live-wire mixed investment group who have had remarkable success breathing new life into sleeping giants – they already own Cunard, the Ritz Hotel and Beaverbrook Newspapers. They make a bomb out of the Q.E.11 in the summer; bringing well-heeled Americans to London, putting them up in the Ritz and then flying them back. They've been after the Savoy for years, but everyone thought they'd given up when they sold a large block of stock.'

'Now they're after it again?'

'Yes – at a cheaper price. The shares are £1.55 and they've been buying them up as they come on the market. But what they don't know is that Tom's Arabs are also buying. Another Arab group already own the Dorchester, and his want the Savoy.'

'So the price is bound to rise?'

'Oh it's better than that. According to English company law an intending bidder has to come out in the open as soon as he controls a certain percentage of the voting stock, and Tom's bunch are very near that.'

'So?'

'Well Tom is pretty sure that Trafalgar House are preparing a take-over bid at about £1.90 and this will be countered by one from his group at £2.20 and they are prepared to go to £2.55. Most share-holders sit tight when there are two strong bidders around and let them outbid each other.'

'So you're going to buy Savoy Hotel shares and accept the highest bid?'

'If I did that I'd make something like fifty per cent after expenses and interest charges, but if I stick my neck out and buy for the call I can probably treble or quadruple my money.'

She sat up in bed and switched on her reading lamp. Then she lit a cigarette. Meanwhile I had put on my pyjamas and got into bed too.

'I'm tired, love,' I said. 'Good night.'

'Just a minute, Ronnie – say that again.'

'Say what again?'

'About trebling or quadrupling your money. How can you do that if the price is only going to go up from £1.50 to £2.55?'

85

'By option dealing.'

'What's that?'

'Well to put it at its simplest: I pay about fifteen or twenty pence a share for the right to buy them in three months at today's price – they're call options. If I thought they were going down then I'd buy put options – the right to sell at today's price in three months.'

'You mean you pay twenty pence down and the rest in three months?'

'No,' I laughed. 'That would be too good to be true. No, the twenty pence is what I pay for the right to buy the shares in three months at today's price – if they haven't gone up by at least twenty pence then I've lost the difference.'

'Oh.' She sounded disappointed.

'Yes, but in this case I know they are going up by a hundred pence. The first twenty-pence rise gets me my option money back and every twenty pence after that doubles my original outlay – or more if I can get the options for less than twenty pence.'

'It all sounds too easy – aren't there any snags?'

'Of course there are. If I bought the shares outright and there were no take-over, then I could sell them again, losing probably between ten and twenty per cent of my outlay. But with options I'd lose the lot if the price didn't go up in three months.'

'I see. How sure are you that they will go up?'

'It seems foolproof to me. Tom acts for an Arab group with at least five hundred million pounds behind them who want to put some in prime London property and they've instructed him to bid up to £2.55 for Savoy Hotel shares. I'm just waiting for him to confirm the details and then I'll scrape up as much cash as I can.'

'You mean you have to pay in pound notes?'

'No, of course not. It's just that if I were to give a straight buying order to my stockbrokers I wouldn't have to pay until the end of the account. But you've got to pay for options immediately. I'll have to start raising cash tomorrow.'

'How much?'

'As much as I can – I think about twenty thousand pounds, enough to buy the call on a hundred thousand shares.'

'And when the Arabs bid £2.55 you'll sell and make a hundred thousand pounds profit?'

'No, not as much as that. First of all I'm effectively buying at about £1.75 since I have to add the twenty pence a share option money to the price; there's the buying and selling expenses, which will be about five thousand pounds, plus the interest on the money I shall borrow at two per cent per month. Lastly, part of the deal is that I pay ten per cent of my net profit into Sir Thomas's numbered Swiss bank account, and that will be about five thousand – perhaps a little more. So I'll come out of it about fifty thousand pounds to the good.' Never make a con sound too good, especially if the mark is intelligent, and I knew Maria-Luisa was.

'How long will all this take?'

'A month or, at the most, two.'

'Good God!' She stubbed out her cigarette, turned out the bedside light and slid down in the bed. 'Have you done this before?'

'Yes – but never in such a big way. I've made the odd thousand or so, five grand once, but I've never had a chance like this.' I switched off the light. 'I'm dead tired and I've got a lot to do tomorrow so please let me sleep.' I kissed her firmly. 'Good night.'

'Good night.'

We lay quietly in the dark and I made my breathing deep and regular. I could almost hear the wheels turning in her busy little brain, and waited for her to speak.

'Ronnie?'

'Mmm?' I murmured sleepily.

'Ronnie – wake up a minute . . . '

I rolled over. 'Yes – what's the matter?'

'Can I have some?'

'Some what?'

'Of those option things?'

'Yes – of course you can. How much money have you got with you, a thousand dollars or so?'

'No, I mean a lot, say twenty thousand dollars' worth.'

'Well,' I said slowly, 'I suppose there's no reason why I couldn't increase my order to a hundred and fifty thousand or so, but how can you raise that amount of cash quickly?'

'I'd have to call Chase Manhattan to transfer it by cable and we'd have to go to Italy where I've got an external bank account. I could get a cashier's cheque in twenty-four hours.'

'Well – are you sure you want to do it?'

'Yes – it's quite safe, isn't it?'

'Nothing is a hundred per cent safe: the Third World War could start or at least the Savoy could burn down.'

87

'I mean apart from things like that.'

'Yes, I guess so, as safe as anything I've ever gone in for.'

'Then I'll do it! I've always wanted lots of money. We'll go first thing in the morning.'

'No – I've got to wait for Tom to call confirming everything and then I've got to make arrangements with my money-lenders. I shan't be able to leave until the afternoon. You'd better get the plane from here to Milan in the morning and I'll come on the next day and pick up the money and take it to London.'

'All right – and I'll come with you.'

'Marvellous – we'll have a wonderful time in London while we're waiting for our fortune to be made.' Once I'd got my hands on her twenty thousand dollars I'd get rid of Ronald Rokesby-Gore for ever and go to Mexico where, with that amount of money, I could buy a share in a small hotel on a beach and become George Kelly at last – it would be the top square of my Snakes and Ladders game.

At last life was going to be all right for me, even if I would be settling for a lot less than I had at one time hoped for. Of course it was a shame that Maria-Luisa was going to lose most of her nest egg, but she was still young and beautiful enough to get herself another rich husband. I was sorry that we'd never see each other again but she shouldn't have told me about all that lovely money; after all, opportunities like that don't come along very often – I'd never had a chance to lay my hands on so much and I'd be a mug to let sentiment stand in my way now.

I made up my mind to get rid of the heaviness I felt in my heart. I damn well would be happy at the great good fortune that was about to come my way. I'd be happy no matter how difficult it was.

I was jerked back into the present by the smell of burning – my cigarette was smouldering on the blanket. I put it out and remade the bed so the burn was at the bottom.

It seemed incredible that all that I had been remembering had been only a week ago. So much had happened in so short a time. It was now early on Thursday morning; less than a week ago Maria-Luisa had flown back to Italy and I had driven to Cannes and picked up my luggage, confident that I was about to make my biggest killing.

When I thought of how it had all gone wrong I was filled with sadness and disgust at my own ineptitude. Deliberately I once again pushed the whole unhappy episode out of my mind. Why should I feel so miserable? It wasn't as though no con had ever gone wrong before; many had, so many that I sometimes wondered if I'd chosen the right profession.

As soon as I'd thrown off this damned recurrent malaria I'd be ready to coninue playing my never-ending game of Snakes and Ladders. Not right from the bottom this time either, for although I possessed only the clothes I was wearing, an electric shaver, a stamp album and an Alitalia ticket from Venice to Rome I also had a small stake: eighteen twenty-dollar bills and over a hundred thousand lire. It was enough to get started again.

10

I SLEPT ON AND off most of that Thursday, eating nothing, only drinking bottles of gassy mineral water; I'd hoped to be on the mend by nightfall but I wasn't. Hours of high fever drained my strength and the optimism of the previous night gave way to the conviction that I never would win my Snakes and Ladders game. I'd come unstuck again as I had with Maria-Luisa, and even though bad luck had played a part in Venice I wasn't exactly proud of the stamp con. I knew it had been pretty crude with little of the ingenuity and finesse on which I prided myself. Perhaps I was over the top or, if not quite, well on the way. I went on wobbly legs into the bathroom for a pee and looked carefully at myself in the illuminated cabinet mirror.

I saw a blotched, puffy face which I could blame on the malaria, but it also seemed to me that my hair was thinning and when I took hold of my teeth they seemed to be loose. My looks were my main asset. What would I do when they were gone?

'Why is it that you never married one of these rich women?' a prison psychiatrist had once asked me. I'd told him it was because I didn't want to be tied down but to be free to roam.

'Perhaps,' he'd said. 'But perhaps it's because you don't do what you do for money at all but because you enjoy it.'

This was in a Californian prison for first offenders which, as far as they knew, I was. It was the most civilized one I've ever been in with opportunities for study and the stress on rehabilitation rather than revenge. In my two years there I took High School English, History and Psychology 1. I didn't pass in any of them because, largely thanks to the psychiatrist, I got early probation, my sentence having been five years as my victim, an attorney, had influence.

I think it was taking Psych. 1 that made me decide to let the psychiatrist have a real go at me; in other prisons I'd amused myself by inventing horrifying childhoods full of the drunken parents and

90

savage beatings the trick cyclist wanted to hear. But I'd been impressed with this one at the first regulation interview. He was dressed in faded jeans and sandals over bare feet and he didn't wear glasses. He was about my age, late twenties, and, though not as good-looking as I am, had a pleasant face. He didn't give me a list of questions or a test, as least not for some time, and he didn't take notes although he did tape, after asking me if it was all right. That in itself was unusual enough for me to think he was out of the ordinary.

We chatted casually, a bit like you talk to someone you spend a few hours with in a train or a bus if you happen to click with them and know you're never going to see them again.

After that first session, which lasted over an hour, he asked me if I'd like to see him on a regular basis.

'You don't have to, you know,' he said, smiling.

'Then I won't,' I said, wanting to surprise him and also to let him know that he hadn't charmed me. My shields were still in place.

'Okay. You can change your mind at any time.'

Perhaps I decided to start the Psych. I course because of him, or maybe it was getting interested in the subject that changed my mind. Anyway we settled down to a weekly hour of casual, or seemingly casual, chat and for most of the time I did tell him the truth.

I described some of my cons, trying to get him to express disapproval but he wouldn't do so, not even when I talked about the misery I'd caused. He did once ask me if I ever regretted that part of it.

'No, never,' I'd said positively. 'They had it coming.'

He gave me his half-smile and raised his eyebrows.

'Everybody thinks that men use women but it's really the other way round. They're ruthless. Women don't really give a shit for men except as meal tickets or to screw them when they feel like it and only when they feel like it.' I could feel myself getting angry.

'When did you reach this conclusion, George?'

'When I was a kid, a nobody living in that big house I told you about. I was sixteen and the General's daughter was pushing forty. She used me like she used her vibrator or a douche.' I spat on his floor but he didn't react.

'And your opinion of women comes from that experience only?'

'Hell, no. That same year I went up to London to spend two weeks with my Aunt Colly, my mother's younger sister. She was married to a gas fitter about ten years older, a decent bloke who slogged his guts out working overtime so she could have a nice home. I'd grown a lot in the year since I'd last stayed with them and he'd no sooner left for work on the Monday than she came and crawled into my bed. It was weird.'

'How, weird?'

'Well she wasn't ashamed that it was incest. Just the opposite. She made me call her "Auntie" all the time we were doing it. At the end she begged me to shout "I'm fucking you, Aunt Colly; I'm fucking my auntie".'

'And did you?'

'Yes. I did whatever she wanted but I made her pay. I practically drained her post office savings.'

'You left home when you were sixteen; did you continue the affair with your aunt?'

'No. The bitch set her husband on to me. Uncle Tom.'

'Tell me about that.'

'She used to get the condoms and once one burst, only once but it was enough. She got pregnant and Tom knew it couldn't be him so she told him it was me and she told him about giving me the money out of the post office, too.'

'What did he do?'

'He came down from London and took me into the woods and beat me nearly senseless. I was terrified; I thought he was going to castrate me.'

'So you're a father?'

'I suppose so but I don't think of the boy being my son and, of course, he thinks Tom's his father.'

'Any more?'

'Any more what?'

'Women, older women, who let you down, caused you pain, humiliated you?'

Oh yes, yes indeed but I'd never spoken to anyone about that, I'd kept it locked up tight inside. For a moment I thought about dropping my last shield but if I did I'd be completely vulnerable; I'd put all my trust in another person and I'd trained myself never to do that. So instead I told him about Mrs Shaughnessy, knowing that experience would supply him with an important piece of the jigsaw puzzle.

It had all come about when my mother quite unexpectedly told me that she'd come into some money and wanted to be taken out in London by her handsome son. Funnily enough I wasn't at all suspicious about where she'd got the money although I must have known that it couldn't have come from any of her family. This was after I'd been to bed with her sister Colleen, whom I didn't want to see, and I hesitated. She must have read my mind.

'We won't go to Colly's and Tom's. I want this to be a treat for just you and me, George. I've got the feeling lately that you're growing away from me.'

After that there wasn't much I could say and we went up on a cheap day return. I took her to an Italian restaurant in Soho and although she didn't like the food she was thrilled by the exotic surroundings. In the afternoon we went to the zoo.

After walking our legs off we made our way to the café for tea and were lucky to get a table as it was very full. An expensively dressed, middle-aged woman stopped near us obviously looking for a seat. I stood up.

'Won't you sit at our table?' I put on my newly learnt accent and saw my mother look astonished.

'Why thank you; it's most kind.' She smiled at my mother and I was going to pull out a chair but I thought that might be overdoing it, 'good manners don't mean being servile' Miss Emmy had told me.

My mother and I talked in a strained, artificial way, me trying to keep up a B.B.C. accent and she toning down her brogue. She wasn't very successful and her attempts at genteel conversation were pitiful. I wished she weren't there so I could invent an intriguing, exciting background; as it was I couldn't even open a conversation. Fortunately I didn't have to. The woman ordered her tea with the brisk pleasantness of one who had always been waited upon and then turned to us.

'Do you live in London or are you visitors?'

'We're just up for the day,' I replied. 'We live in Hampshire.'

'Oh, Hampshire, some parts are very pretty.'

'We're in a very pretty part,' my mother said. 'Aren't we, George?'

'Yes, in the south-west, not far from the New Forest.'

'Beautiful! I envy you. Living in Town one misses the real country.' She took out a packet of cigarettes and offered them: we both refused. As she lit up I got an ashtray from a nearby table.

'Thank you. I really should introduce myself: Mrs Shaughnessy.'

'Pleased to meet you,' my mother said. I, remembering Miss Emmy's lesson, said 'How d'ye do. I'm George Kelly and this is my mother.'

'That's a fine old Irish name like mine. My husband was a Dublin

93

man. Perhaps your family comes from there?'

'No, ma'am. I was born in Hampshire; I've never been to Ireland.' I wondered how much I could invent without my mother giving the game away.

But without seeming to be nosy Mrs Shaughnessy found out in a few minutes that I was not up at university – she obviously thought I was two or three years older – that I knew no one, that in short I was a nobody.

'May I ask what you want to be? I hope you don't think I'm being impertinent; if so you must forgive me. You see I have a son whom you rather resemble or rather you look a bit like he did a few years ago.'

'What does he do?'

'He's a pilot with B.O.A.C. In fact he's about halfway to India at this moment.'

'That's funny. It's what I've always wanted to be.'

My mother was about to express her surprise but I gave her a warning look.

'It's terribly difficult. But I expect you know that. It took Tony years and it was awfully expensive.'

'I know it's going to be a long pull,' I said in my most manly voice. 'But I'm determined. I'm starting night school in September to get the basic qualifications and I'm saving my money to pay for the training.'

My mother's amazement was so obvious that I was sure Mrs Shaughnessy would notice it, but she didn't seem to.

'Good for you! I'm afraid it will prove to be a long and arduous task, though. Can your father help you?'

'I have no father.' If only my mother hadn't been there I should have been the orphan of a war hero in the R.A.F., one of 'the few'.

'I'm very sorry.' She gave my mother a look of sympathy and I wondered if she had noticed the absence of a wedding ring. I had begged my mother many times to wear one but she'd always refused. 'Please don't think I'm pushy but I may be able to help – if only with advice.' She opened her bag and took out a leather case. 'Here's my card. If you'd like to give me a ring you could come and see me. There are one or two subsidized training schemes and I do know the ropes.'

She nodded to my mother and as she left I remembered to rise.

'Well! Did you ever!' exclaimed my mother. 'Here, let me see.'

I handed her the card. 'Mrs Isobel Shaughnessy – so she's a widow – or divorced. She's certainly taken a fancy to you, George. I hardly

94

recognized you, you talked so posh. You don't really expect to become a pilot, do you? Jobs like that are not for the likes of you.'

'You never know what can happen.' I took the card from her. The address was Cheyne Walk, Chelsea. Yes, I'd call on Mrs Shaughnessy but not to talk about becoming a pilot. Unless I were much mistaken we'd find other interests.

A week later, when I was tidying up the General's study and he'd gone out with Lady Liz and Miss Emmy, I decided to telephone Mrs Shaughnessy. The General always checked the telephone bill carefully; he had forbidden Miss Emmy to make trunk calls because the bill for the first quarter after her return had listed so many of them. But I reckoned I'd be gone before the next one came in so I didn't worry.

I had to repeat my name twice before she remembered who I was, unless, as I suspected, she was pretending. I said that if she really meant what she'd said I could come up the next day.

'All right. You'd better come to tea, about four-thirty, no, better make it four. I've got people coming for cocktails later and that will give us plenty of time.' I liked the sound of that.

When the General came back I told him that I'd asked at the Regent Palace Hotel, when I'd been in London with my mother, if there were any chance of a job. They'd told me the name of the man to see when he came back from holiday. I asked the General if I could go up the next day. He wished me luck, said he'd be sorry to lose his batman and gave me a quid.

I got the Underground to Sloane Square and walked towards the Embankment past the Chelsea Pensioners' Home. Several of them were sitting in their bright red coats enjoying the sun, waiting to die. I thought that most had probably started off poor, perhaps illegitimate like me. But whatever happened, I told myself, I was going to do better than they had.

Mrs Shaughnessy's house was a three-storeyed one with tall windows on the ground floor, window boxes and steps leading up to a shiny black door. I pulled a knob above the letter slot and heard a deep ring. I was quite expecting the door to be opened by a maid and had composed what I would say, but it was Mrs Shaughnessy herself who let me in.

She was dressed, rather strangely I thought, in a full-length robe of dull yellow silk which buttoned down the front from a collar which covered her neck right down to the hem. It had a bird like a heron embroidered on the back. I thought from the way her buttocks moved as I followed her down a corridor lined with Chinese water-colours that she probably didn't have anything on underneath. If that were so she was remarkably well preserved for her age.

I followed her into a large room which I realized took up one corner of the house. There were books everywhere, a blue and white vase of roses on a table under the window, photographs of various people, one in a silver frame of a large man who seemed to have taken a dislike to the photographer and whom I guessed to be her late husband, and another, obviously of her son, in the uniform of a B.O.A.C. pilot with his wife and two children. A dragon made of china or porcelain squatted in one corner and I was pretty sure the carpet was Chinese too. But the sofa was English, as were the two armchairs, one of dark green leather into which she beckoned me, seating herself on the long and comfortable sofa. She crossed her legs and I saw that the garment was slit to just above the knee. I wondered whether we'd finish up on the sofa or in her bedroom.

'I've got out some information about training schemes for commercial pilots.' She pointed to a desk on which there was a typewriter and a pile of papers. 'Actually I'm on the board of a Borstal and we try to give career advice to those of the boys we think may have potential. But first you must have some tea. Here – you can be looking at this while I get it.' She gave me a copy of *Flight* magazine.

I flicked through it, not really interested since I knew there was about as much chance of my becoming a professional pilot as of being a concert violinist. I contemplated tactics: I could use this occasion to lay the groundwork for another meeting but there was no reason to suppose that if she weren't ready for a tumble now she would be in a week or so. Instead the interval might give her time for second thoughts. No, if I were to succeed I would have to try and make love to her that afternoon, and soon, since she had people coming for cocktails, which I supposed would be about five-thirty or six. I wasn't sure how to start, not having been in a similar situation before, so I decided just to plunge in.

She called me from somewhere – for a moment I thought it might be her bedroom, thus solving my problem, but it was the kitchen and she wanted me to carry a long oval tray with a silver teapot, hot-water jug and spoons. There was a cake, scones, jam, bread and butter, and, of course, cups, saucers, plates, milk, lemon and sugar. It weighed a ton.

I had three cups of tea and even then it wasn't as much as one of the mugs in my aunt's house. I ate a good number of slices of thin bread and butter, followed by scones and jam, followed by cake.

'I'm glad to see you've got a good appetite. I like to see a boy – a man – enjoy his food.' She smiled at me in what I thought was a very suggestive way.

I got up and crossed over to her and put my hands on her shoulders and pushed her back, at the same time bending down to kiss her on the lips, but she turned her face violently at the last moment and I got a mouthful of hair and, almost at the same instant, a stinging slap on my cheek.

'You little tyke!' she said furiously, pushing me away and getting to her feet. 'You conceited little guttersnipe! Oh God!' She began to laugh. 'Did you really think I'd invited you because of your pretty face?'

'Yes.' I couldn't think of anything else to say.

'It's unbelievable! For God's sake, whatever put such a ridiculous idea in your head? Oh, never mind, don't tell me, I don't want to know, you're probably a male prostitute, common scum. Now get out of my house! Come on – out!'

She pushed me into the hall and held open the front door. I mumbled something about being sorry and almost ran down the steps.

Her words had not only hurt, they had badly shaken my confidence in my sex appeal. I'd done so well with Miss Emmy and my Aunt Colly I'd begun to think that I was irresistible which, I now realized, was stupid and that was something I could not afford to be. It had also been stupid of me to think that Miss Emmy's efforts to teach me how middle-class boys of my age behaved had been successful. I obviously hadn't fooled Mrs Shaughnessy for a moment. She'd called me a guttersnipe and a tyke and I found it hard to convince myself that I wasn't.

As I had guessed, the psychiatrist in California had thought this experience most significant.

'I think we're getting somewhere, George. Think about it during the week and see if you can't work out for yourself why you've been at war with women ever since you left home.'

Well of course I knew what he meant; I'm not thick. But he'd over-simplified because despite all his knowledge and his sensitivity he couldn't know what it had been like to be a half-educated, untrained, illegitimate son of a servant in southern England. I suppose if it hadn't been for Miss Emmy and my Aunt Colly it wouldn't have occurred to me to cheat older women but I would have cheated someone because the ability to make people believe my story was the only asset I had. It was the way the cards had been dealt; he'd got the trumps, mine were all losers.

Although it would never occur to him, we were really very alike: given his cards I too could have been a psychiatrist. I didn't know how he would have played mine. It was this realization that decided me to tell him after all.

I think he guessed that I had come to an important decision as soon as I came in and sat down, for he handed me a cigarette and got up to pour me a cup of coffee from a fancy device he had.

'You've come to a conclusion, George, haven't you?'

'Yes, but not what you think. I haven't told you everything and now I'm going to because I think you really do want to help me.'

'Thank you. I'm glad.' He tipped his chair back and we both smoked in silence. And then, haltingly at first but quickly losing all reticence, I released what I had for so long kept locked up.

It had happened a week or so after the experience with Mrs Shaughnessy. I'd got up in the night to go outside for a pee and then, as I often did, I let myself into the kitchen to see if any pudding had been left over from dinner; the General had a sweet tooth and so did I but that night there wasn't any so I crept through to the dining-room and helped myself to some chocolate mints. I knew that there was a big box of glacé fruit in the drawing-room. Just as I was crossing the passage I heard loud gasping noises and a moan.

They had come from Lady Liz's own bedroom which was on the other side of the narrow passage along which dishes from the kitchen came. I tiptoed to the back and listened at her door. Someone almost shouted 'Oh, oh, *oh*, oh!' and someone else said 'Shhhh!' Obviously Lady Liz had a lover with her.

The only men around were the gardener in his sixties and Joe, his grandson, who was practically a moron, and the General himself but it was well known that Lady Liz and he had 'ceased marital relations' as the cook put it. I had to find out who was with Lady Liz; such knowledge could be profitable.

Her bedroom had a dressing-room next to it with a bathroom which also opened out to the main hall. I turned the knob of this door slowly and noiselessly. The bathroom was unlit and the door opposite connecting to Lady Liz's bedroom was ajar. Leaving the bathroom door open as a line of retreat, I moved silently to the other one, through which came a low light. I waited to make sure they were still busy and then judged it safe to peek round the edge of the door.

The woman who was sitting up against the pillows, stark naked with her head tipped back, her eyes closed and her mouth open, was my mother. The other woman, also naked, and squatting on hands and knees on the bed with my mother's legs over her shoulders and her mouth working furiously, was Lady Liz. As I watched dumbfounded my mother gave one more strangled cry and, grabbing Lady Liz's hair, pulled her face away.

'Oh stop, my lady – you'll kill me!'

Lady Liz raised her wet, red face and laughed. She was panting as though she'd just had a hard run.

'You know you love it, Kathie,' she said, lifting the legs off her shoulders and letting them fall to the bed. My mother collapsed with exhaustion and Lady Liz got out of bed and crossed to the dressing-table. I had noticed before when I'd seen her in a bathing suit how well muscled she was but I saw now that she had the buttocks and thighs of a man while my mother's white body was full rounded. Lady Liz unlocked a drawer and took out something which I'd never seen before but which has since become part of my own working equipment. It was an abnormally large rubber penis fitted to a belt and elastic rings. She slipped these over my mother's legs, pulling them up to her crotch so that the penis was in the right place.

'Come on, Kathie.' She pulled my mother to her feet. 'Do your stuff, come on . . . ' She pulled the belt tight which fastened at the back just above where her buttocks met. The enormous artificial penis stuck out at a grotesque angle below my mother's rounded belly and large breasts, making her look like something out of a horror film. Lady Liz lay back on the bed and spread her legs wide.

'Be rough this time, Kathie, pretend you're an Irish labourer and call me dirty names.'

I moved back behind the door and let myself out of the dressing-room not letting the latch click. I sneaked back to my own bed and masturbated furiously, trying with my eyes shut to see Lady Liz's slim, hard body, but it was my mother's soft, round one which kept intruding.

The psychiatrist didn't say anything at first; I felt as though I'd put down a heavy box I'd been carrying for a long distance. Silently he handed me another cigarette.

'For Christ's sake don't tell me I've got an Oedipus complex.'

He laughed. 'Don't worry, I won't tell you that you've got any kind of a complex. That's not the name of the game; all I'm trying to do is to help you find out why you're so screwed up. Certainly what you've just told me is important, but perhaps not so important as you think it is, or rather as you've made it.'

'If I've made it important then it is to me, isn't it?'

'I can see you've been reading your textbooks, George, but remember that a little knowledge is dangerous. I think we've done enough for this week but next time I'd like you to tell me what you felt about your mother after that. Did you hate her? How soon afterwards did you leave home?'

I didn't need to think about it; I could remember clearly how I'd felt. It had certainly been a shock: I'd thought my mother was a naturally chaste woman who had been seduced by my father when she had been too inexperienced to resist. I'd concluded that she was too old for physical love – actually she was not yet thirty-six – and I knew there was no man in her life. When I found out that there was a woman I didn't blame her, or Lady Liz. As far as I could see they weren't doing anyone any harm by satisfying their sexual needs together and they were certainly discreet enough.

I think after I'd come to terms with what I'd seen it only confirmed a conclusion I'd already reached: the whole idea of sex being sacred, a precious gift from women to men, was the oldest confidence trick of all. The act of love means less emotionally to women, who are much more down to earth about it. Men in their conceit don't know that.

On the other hand I knew that women needed to be made love to and this made them vulnerable. I had Miss Emmy eating out of my hand and my Aunt Colly hadn't really needed any pressure to give me practically all her savings, and now there was Lady Liz running an appalling risk of getting caught and being turned out of the house – and in each case they had been led on by their need for sex. If I could give it to them without getting emotionally involved and if I could profit by it then I would have beaten them at their own con.

Somehow the special relationship which had been growing between the prison psychiatrist and me went wrong. I think I probably resented his having completely unmasked me and my having no more secrets made me less of a challenge. But though we progressed no further he did manage to get me paroled after only two years of my five-year sentence.

When they let me out into the California sunshine I walked with a springy step, convinced that given all I had learned from my courses, from the well-stocked library and from long talks with some of the professional men whose one slip had brought us together, I would not only be a better con man but I wouldn't get caught again.

Just before the sky lightened outside my window in the hotel in Trieste my fever broke. Before the next bout of chills came I fell into a deep sleep.

11

IT WASN'T THE bell on a police car, thank God, it was the phone and the pursuit had been just another angst dream.

Was I checking out today? Yes, what time was it? – eight-thirty? I'd be leaving in half an hour.

Although I knew I hadn't really thrown off the malaria and ought to rest for another day, I had a premonition of danger, perhaps arising from my dream; perhaps only the fear of the hunted. It didn't matter which, I had to take notice. I showered and dressed, paid for the second day, got my passport back and was out on the street before nine, feeling very rough indeed. I hadn't walked more than fifty yards when I saw the flashing lamp of a police car some five or six hundred yards away coming towards me. I stepped into a café and bought an espresso token. As the proprietor was drawing the coffee I watched the car stop outside my hotel and two policemen hurry in. It wasn't proof positive but I was glad not to be there still.

If they were looking for me it could be for leaving the hotel in Venice without paying the bill. Some alert young copper could have matched the name on the fiche I'd completed two nights earlier with one on the latest wanted list. Or perhaps after all Dora and Co. had described me to the Alitalia staff at the airport. The girl on the counter would certainly have remembered the passenger who had booked for Trieste at the last moment. I didn't think it likely but it was certainly possible; I ought to get out of Italy and into Yugoslavia without delay.

If I were not to attract attention as a traveller I must have at least one respectable piece of luggage and I also had to have a change of clothes from the skin out. I asked the cashier, almost certainly the proprietor's wife, for the best place to buy a suitcase and respectable clothes at a reasonable price. UPIM, she said, and added that they were having a sale.

By ten o'clock I had a large leather suitcase which had been a great bargain because it was faded from being so long in the window. It hadn't been sold because no one today wants to use up the air-travel allowance with heavy luggage. I'd also bought a drip-dry suit, a polo-neck, tight-fitting, red cotton shirt and a blue and white bathrobe of towelling. I added white swimming trunks, lightweight white shoes and socks, two handkerchiefs and underwear plus washing things. I changed into my new outfit in the store, putting my old clothes in the suitcase. I then telephoned the Metropole Hotel in Portoroz and made a reservation for George Kelly for three nights. In the shop's cambio I changed the rest of my lire into Yugoslav dinars.

Portoroz is a resort on the Adriatic coast only a few miles from Trieste. The Yugoslav authorities have spent a great deal of money there trying to attract tourists, especially from Austria and Italy. The Metropole is one of the new hotels and has a casino which does a fair business in the season.

A few years earlier I had picked up an Australian widow in 'gay Paree'. It hadn't been difficult, for she stopped me in Pigalle, asked if I were English and, reassured, had asked if I knew of a good restaurant for a lady by herself. When I heard her strong Sydney accent I abandoned the role of sophisticated man of the world and became a happy-go-lucky chum on his own like herself. We had dinner together and she insisted on paying for herself which, after a protest, I allowed. The next day we moved into a hotel as Mr and Mrs Coker, that being her name. She had been widowed three months before, left comfortably off, and had flown to London determined to have a little fun before it was too late. A London travel agent had sold her a European tour which included Paris, Rome and Vienna with a three-day stop after Rome at the new resort of Portoroz, where he had assured her all the celebrities spent their summers. But she was no fool so, on the 'softly softly catchee monkey' principle, I made sure that she paid only half of everything and from time to time I'd insist on buying the drinks before dinner or indulging her voracious appetite for chocolates. We were lovers and good pals and by the time we got to Vienna she was ripe for plucking. I have a contact there who makes a good living faking Roman antiquities. He sells them to dealers as replicas and they sell them to customers neglecting to mention that they are copies. I explained to Aggie that for a thousand dollars I could buy a replica of a Roman bronze which someone I knew in an American museum would buy for ten thousand.

'But surely he'd spot it as a replica, wouldn't he?'

'Yes, that's why I give him a receipt for ten thousand but he only gives me five, see?'

'Wicked!' she said admiringly. She handed over the thousand; I bought the bronze for a hundred and gave it to her to hold until we heard from my corrupt friend in Ohio – I think it was Ohio. I expect the bronze is sitting in her flat in Sydney to this day, much admired by her friends. I hope she agrees that the week's pleasure I gave her was worth what it cost her even if she did also have to pay the hotel bill in Vienna.

That was the last time I'd been at the Metropole, Portoroz, and I couldn't believe anyone there would remember me as Mr Coker, and as I hadn't pulled a con there no one would be looking for me.

At the bus station I got the last seat on the noonday departure. It was unbelievably cheap; I seemed to have more change than the ten-thousand-lire note I'd given. With a great show of British honesty I made sure there hadn't been a mistake; the last thing I wanted was to have attention drawn to me. In a café opposite I ordered a brunch of prosciutto, melon and an omelette and while I waited I assessed my position coolly and objectively.

I needed my Rokesby-Gore passport to get out of Italy but in Yugoslavia I'd use my own name and report my passport lost. They'd send me to the British Consul who, until he got authorization to issue me with a new passport, would give me a temporary identity document.

My genuine passport was safe in Pietro Piedmonti's keeping in Nice; all I had to do was to phone him at the hotel in Cannes and he would post it to me. Then I would report either that I had 'found' it or that it had been returned to me.

Yes, George Kelly would have to take care of himself, at least until he could afford to buy a new personality.

After my cappuccino and the table had been cleared I took everything out of my pockets so that this time I'd not be carrying any incriminating papers. I'd made sure that I had nothing on me with Colonel Rokesby-Gore's name on it – except, of course, the passport and as soon as I was in Yugoslavia I'd get rid of it – or perhaps I'd hide it in the lining of the suitcase. It seemed a shame just to throw away the Alitalia Venice/Rome ticket, but it was too obvious a link and the money just had to be written off. It hurt me, too, to destroy his driving licence and the post office savings book with thirty pence in it, but common sense told me that Rokesby-Gore had had his day. I tore everything into little squares and added the cards and other bits of paper. Then I went into the men's lavatory and flushed the evidence away.

In some ways I was sorry to have to kill off Ronald Rokesby-Gore whom I'd been on and off since the real General Rokesby-Gore had died in 1968 aged ninety. I'd pretty well grown into the part and I think I'd been fairly convincing – at least to anyone without experience of the British Army – and I'd been careful to steer clear of those who had.

It's always surprised me how a rank confers instant respectability – particularly in Europe. Americans, too, are impressed by titles; I am almost always a knight when in that country.

Even Maria-Luisa, a shrewd and experienced woman, had accepted Peter the Barman's story that I was a British Army colonel who had retired young. In our first days together she'd asked a few questions about my Army 'career' and I'd managed to imply that I'd had rather a bad time and didn't want to talk about it, and she'd been content with that.

After her departure from Marseilles everything had gone as smoothly as the Bolshoi Ballet. She'd cabled her New York bank to transfer twenty thousand dollars to her external account in Monza and I had told her that I'd increase my buying order by 55,000 call options at $21\frac{1}{2}$ pence.

'Hey – you know I'm all worked up,' she'd said, 'I've never done anything like this before.' I had told her there was still time to change her mind, but that only reassured her, and she'd caught the Marseilles–Milan plane. I was to drive the Fiat back to Nice that day and go on by train the next day to Monza where she would meet me.

When she'd gone I phoned Peter in Cannes and told him to forget about the ten o'clock phone call. 'It's no longer necessary – instead I'll drive back there to pick up my things – I'll get there some time tonight – probably quite late.'

'Will Mrs Neilson be with you?'

'No – she's gone back to Italy to pick up the money.'

'How much?'

'Never mind how much. You'll get your cut.'

'Okay. Your things are at my place – I'll wait up for you. Ciao, George.'

'Ciao, Peter.' I hung up. I wasn't sure how much, if any, of the twenty thousand dollars I'd send him since it wasn't likely we'd work together in future if this con worked as it should.

As soon as Maria-Luisa got the bank draft we'd hop on the first Milan–London plane, and if we arrived during banking hours I'd take it to her bank's London office and change the whole amount into sterling. If I knew Maria-Luisa she'd stick pretty close to me, but then I'd go to some other City bank where I'd already phoned ahead and made an appointment to see the assistant manager. I'd tell Maria-Luisa that this was where I banked and that I was going to pick up my cash to add to hers, and I'd see that she didn't come with me into the assistant manager's office. I'd explain to him that I wanted to put some money into gold and as I didn't know any bullion dealers I'd decided to ask his bank to get me as many krugerrands as about ten thousand pounds would buy. Krugerrands are coins of exactly one ounce of pure gold and fluctuate with the price of gold. They are untraceable, unlike banknotes. I'd show my passport so that he'd know he wasn't dealing with a crook and tell him that I'd be back to collect them the following morning. I was sure that any bank would jump at the chance of earning the commission on such an unexpected windfall.

Then I'd tell Maria-Luisa that instead of picking up my own cash the bank were going to buy the call options for me in the name of their nominees, thus concealing my identity, for, I would explain modestly, I was known in the City of London as a speculator who acted on inside information, and we didn't want to tip our hand. I could see no reason why she wouldn't accept that.

I'd have to entertain Maria-Luisa that night and I'd keep her out very late so that she'd want to lie in the following morning, which would give me time to buy a money belt and go to Cook's and book a cheap tourist holiday to New York leaving that night. Since I'd be carrying a lot of gold coins I didn't want to be stopped and searched, and the customs don't usually look for illegal exporters of gold among tourists on holiday flights – at least I hoped they didn't.

Then I'd take Maria-Luisa shopping or sightseeing until it was time to go to the bank and collect my gold, which I'd put into my money belt in the assistant manager's office. I'd go with her to the City, leave her having a coffee while I went into one of the big office blocks, telling her that I was finalizing the details of the deal. After chatting to someone in an office on some pretext or other I'd return to Maria-Luisa and say that I had to meet Tom Lawrence that evening at his club; I'd explain that women were not allowed in London Clubs. With a bit of luck she might then just let me go – I'd suggest that she went to a film – and if she did, I'd get the train from Victoria to Gatwick.

But if necessary I could let her accompany me along Pall Mall and watch me go into the Royal Automobile Club where, if the porters stopped me, which was unlikely, I could ask to see the Secretary – anything to use up the time it would take for her to have left the vicinity. I didn't really think it would come to all that but it was as well to have a plan for every contingency.

I'd travel to New York as Colonel Rokesby-Gore and I estimated that it would be one or two in the morning before Maria-Luisa was worried enough to start enquiring for me and probably, though not certainly, the next morning before she went to the police. It was just possible, if the worst came to the worst, that they could be checking at airports while I was still en route to New York, but I thought that very unlikely.

Anyway I wouldn't waste any time in New York; I'd get a bus from Kennedy into the city and then pick up a Greyhound to Washington and another as soon as possible to New Orleans, where I'd collect my George Kelly passport at the Poste Restante and make my way to Brownsville and so on to Mexico, where I knew I could lose myself.

I'd worked all this out while pushing the little Fiat at its top speed along the autoroute to Nice. It seemed foolproof at the time and I revelled in the thought that once in Mexico I could buy into a small hotel or even just a bar. I would have reached the winning square at last and I'd spend the next ten or fifteen years living quietly and comfortably in a pleasant climate – somewhere like Chapala in the mountains of Jalisco. I'd be safe in snug harbour; no more lying, no more worrying about the police, no more running, and no more pathetic middle-aged women. If I did need a woman – and I wasn't even sure that I would – I'd settle for a simple Mexican girl with a good mixture of Indian blood who'd be glad to cook and clean and be bedded occasionally in return for board and lodging and pocket money. Why damn it, I thought, we might even produce children – why not?

I stubbed out the cigarette and saw that there was still fifteen minutes before the bus went so I ordered another cappuccino and once again reflected on the bad luck which always seemed to upset my apple cart just as I was ready to push it away.

I'd got to Peter's flat about ten-thirty that evening and Marta, his wife, had given me some delicious fish soup and an omelette. Peter came home just before midnight and got down the box in which he kept the things I'd left with him.

In the little despatch case, which I always kept locked, I checked over my conning gear: worthless stock certificates, blank ones, a company seal I'd forgotten, the bogus investor's record book and another in which I'd recorded the particulars of my last year's cons, the latest being the 5000 shares of Rolls Razor I'd sold to Mrs McVean of Glasgow for 62p each. I keep a record for a few months in case I'm caught, for I can prove that the money I got was for the sale of shares – it then has a chance of being treated as a civil matter instead of a felony. I discarded most of my conning gear but I kept this little black book and some blank stationery that I'd 'acquired' from a stock-broker. I debated with myself about whether to take my George Kelly passport, my genuine one, and finally decided it was too dangerous to travel with two passports in different names and each bearing my photograph.

'If this one comes off, Peter,' I'd told him, 'I'm going to disappear in the States and I'll write and tell you where to send my passport.'

'Okay – and when do I get my share?'

'I'll send you five hundred dollars when I give you the address to send the passport and the rest when I get it.'

We joked a bit about honour among thieves and I accepted his offer of their sofa for what remained of the night. Before I went to sleep I looked through my little black book and was reminded of the last year or so's cons. Before the widow of the Glasgow grocer there'd been a greedy Hungarian lady I'd met in the London Hilton who jumped at the chance of passing off zircons as diamonds to silly Arab women, and before that there was a newly divorced woman in swinging Bournemouth. That was a childishly simple con involving the sale of an expired allotment letter for new shares which had so dropped in price the allotment wasn't worth taking up. I showed her the price on a page of a year-old *Financial Times*, which I'd inserted in that day's issue, and sold them to her for three-quarters of their apparent value – God knows how she could have believed my story of not wanting the sale to become known, but greed has the power to shut off common sense.

There were a number of blank pages left in my little black book and, telling myself that the Maria-Luisa con was a particularly complicated matter about which I couldn't afford to make a mistake, I wrote down the steps in detail and then locked the book in my despatch case.

I took back the Fiat the next morning and caught the train to Genoa, where I changed for one to Milan, and from there to Monza. Before leaving Nice I'd wired Maria-Luisa the time, and she met me in a large Lancia which, she told me gaily, belonged to an old friend, the captain of police of her little town.

The bank draft had not yet arrived as there was a weekend in between, so I just had to wait patiently. But it was very pleasant living in Maria-Luisa's little flat and having her cook for and generally look after me. When she collected all my dirty laundry out of my suitcase she found the despatch case. I told her it contained business papers and she seemed satisfied.

We met some of her friends when we dined out or sat outside the main café. One of them was the captain of police, who told us that Italy had gone steadily downhill since the fall of Mussolini. Maria-Luisa later apologized for him, but I said, truthfully, that I didn't give a damn – politics have never interested me, I suppose because to me any authority is on the other side.

Sunday was her birthday. I bought her a huge bunch of flowers and she gave me an Yves Saint Laurent tie, and we went out in the evening to an excellent restaurant, getting back late at night, having drunk rather a lot. Maria-Luisa had, I thought, questioned me rather closely about my Army career, but I'd done all right except a slip when I mentioned fighting the terrorists in Malaysia in 1970.

'I thought you were in Aden in 1970?'

'I was,' I said promptly. 'Much later though – after I'd come back from Malaysia.'

She hadn't said any more and we'd gone to bed and made love, which I was somehow surprised to find was still more satisfactory than it had ever been with any other woman. Full of good food and wine I rolled over and fell asleep.

I awoke with my head on fire as Maria-Luisa dragged me out of bed by my hair and, as I bumped to the floor, kicked me hard, aiming for my testicles but fortunately hitting the inside of my thigh, but with such force it numbed my leg.

'For Christ's sakes . . . ' I yelled, covering my face as she tried to scratch my eyes out.

She spat at me and screamed abuse in Italian, only a few words of which I recognized. I tried to grab her flailing arms.

'What *is* the matter, Maria?'

'You son of a bitch!' she said, switching to English. 'You dirty, lousy, lying, scheming son of a bitch – ' She got another kick in, my shin this time. She was barefooted thank God or she'd have broken my leg. 'You lied – you lied,' she panted. 'You pimp – you male whore – you shit – you thief.' She paused, her breasts heaving under her transparent nightgown, her lovely black hair loose over her shoulders, her blue eyes glistening with tears.

Behind her on the floor was my despatch case open, the key still in the lock, the share certificates and other papers spilled on the floor and the little black book in which I had so insanely given myself away open on her dressing-table.

'Maria,' I said, holding out my arms. 'I love you . . . '

'I hate you! You pig dog,' she screamed. 'I hope you go to prison for life – I hope you rot in prison.'

I didn't like the sound of that at all and I looked around for my clothes, determined to run for it, but she darted to the door and locked it.

'Give me that key, Maria,' I said sternly, or as sternly as I could standing stark naked.

She picked up a small pair of scissors and held them out like a knife fighter. 'Come near me and I'll kill you.'

I didn't think she could kill me – the blades were only about two inches long – but she could certainly scar my pretty face. I found my underpants and put them on, feeling a little less vulnerable. As I took my trousers from the chair, she picked up the phone.

'Maria – please.' I moved towards her but she still held the scissors over her head as though they were a dagger, and I stopped. She dialled the concierge and told her to call the police immediately.

I tried to reason with her while we were waiting for them, but she only cursed and spat at me like a wildcat. As I was getting dressed I put on the Yves Saint Laurent tie she'd given me. She darted forward, tore it out of my hand and cut it viciously with the scissors.

'I wish it was your balls!'

The police came, she made a formal complaint, and they took me and my belongings away. Two days later I was castaway like Robinson Crusoe with little but my wits to sustain me.

Sitting in the bus station in Trieste about noon that Friday, I could hardly believe that it had been less than five days since Maria-Luisa dragged me out of bed by my hair in the early hours of Monday morning. I'd lived those hours at a hectic pace and I was still running. Of course I was sorry that the con had come unstuck, but strangely enough I found that I regretted losing Maria-Luisa even more – and somehow I couldn't make sense of that at all. Not that it mattered, for I was sure I'd never see her again; I made up my mind then and there that I'd wipe her right out of my memory, right off my blackboard.

The Portoroz bus hissed into its place and, having collected my suitcase, I found my seat by the inside window on the back row. All the others were filled with Yugoslavs laden with baskets crammed with goods from Trieste shops. A little man with two enormous suitcases queezed in between me and a woman half buried under baskets and shopping bags. Annoyed, I balanced my own suitcase on my lap.

The bus moved off and turned left towards the nearby frontier post. 'Colonel Ronald Rokesby-Gore's Last Journey,' I thought to myself. We stopped at the lights in the main square; I glanced out of my window and gasped aloud, a cry of dismay.

There, at a sidewalk table outside a large restaurant, sat Gino, his wife Catherina, and Dora. I simply could not believe my eyes; it must be the fever, it could only be a delusion. But they weren't more than twenty feet from me and I knew they were real enough.

If only I hadn't moved I'm sure I wouldn't have been spotted, but just as the bus edged forward I put my hand up to screen my face and the movement caught Gino's eye. He stood up and pointed to the bus as we swung into the heavy traffic. I was sure that neither Dora nor Catherina, who had been talking animatedly to each other, could possibly have recognized me from the back of my head.

But it was only a matter of time before they got themselves together and came after me. What the hell, I asked myself miserably, was I going to do now?

12

THE BUS DRIVER, who obviously knew every yard of the route, drove with true Italian panache, weaving in and out of traffic as though he were driving a sports car. Although it was ridiculous I kept expecting to hear a police siren behind us.

We reached the Italian frontier post in about ten minutes and Italian immigration just waved me on when they saw the British passport.

At the Yugoslav frontier we were told to get out and carry our luggage through customs while the empty bus went through and waited for us on the Yugoslav side. I still felt feverish and decided to leave my suitcase on the seat, pleading ignorance if it were noticed. Since there was nothing in it which was dutiable I had no worries.

My neighbour with the two suitcases began to explain that it was necessary for me to carry my things personally through the customs, but I told him sharply to worry about his own luggage and leave me to deal with mine and he went off laden down with his huge and obviously heavy bags. The other passengers, all struggling with baskets, boxes and bags, formed a long queue.

I walked straight past them all and the customs men. They were obviously not feeling very conscientious, for they waved most people through, stopping only about one in ten for a desultory search. I was glad because the sooner we were on our way, the safer I would feel.

Yugoslav immigration hardly glanced at my passport. There didn't seem to be a notice out about me yet but we were still too near Italy for my liking. I climbed up on to a little hill and lay down with a vicious headache, while the rest of the passengers were going through the controls. When I propped my head up I had a good view of the Italian post; there was a queue of cars with buses being routed past them, and I saw a taxi approaching at speed. It tried to avoid the queue – I could imagine the shouts and protests from the other drivers. This quickly brought a carabiniere to the scene. I could see him pointing to the back of the queue and then one of the passengers got out. I would have recognized that checked jacket anywhere.

'Venga, signor!' the bus driver shouted to me. 'Andiamo.'

Back in my seat my neighbour smiled at me, suddenly happy.

'Today I pay nothing,' he said triumphantly. 'Transistors, calculators – I should have bought the little computer but how is one to know? Some days they take everything apart, every little thing, and other times, like today, you could smuggle an elephant.'

'Is that your business – smuggling?'

'Oh, don't call it that, my friend. I am an importer – I pay customs duty when it is demanded.'

'And hope that it won't be, eh?'

He laughed. 'Of course – the name of the game, as you Americans say, is profit.' It would do no harm, I decided, to let him think I was American. I generally pick up something of the accent of whomever I'm with and Dora had one of the thickest while Maria-Luisa's speech was also pure American.

'What about you?' My companion the 'importer' was evidently the talkative type. 'Nobody don't say nothing; they don't notice you leave your suitcase in the bus and walk past the customs?'

'Apparently not.'

'Is it possible! So simple! But then you were so cool, like Private Eye. Now I, I would have been sweating and they would know I was trying something.'

'There was nothing for me to sweat about as I don't have any dutiable goods.'

'No? What a waste – you could have brought anything in. Are you never tempted?'

'It doesn't make sense to me to run risks for a few dollars' duty.'

'Of course not – but for many dollars?'

'How many?' I asked, abandoning my holier-than-thou pose.

'Ten thousand, perhaps more.'

'That *is* a lot of money.'

'If you could do what you did today but carrying something small and very valuable we could share at least ten thousand dollars profit.'

'If you mean drugs I'm not interested.'

'Neither am I; it is not drugs.'

I didn't say anything; I'd let that ball go past me and see what he'd serve next.

'I think that in such a situation you would be just as cool, so dignified like today and you would not even be stopped, certainly not body-searched.'

I knew that the unconcern that had so impressed him had been due to my feeling so ill that I hadn't really cared if they stopped me or not, but I couldn't see any percentage in telling him that.

'Listen: I am too well known, I can never take chance of having something very valuable confiscated, especially when it don't belong to me but to some very hard men. Customs know I am small operator but sometimes they do strip me naked – once they give me enema. But they don't know you and it would only be one time. What do you say; you do it, fifty-fifty?'

I shook my head. 'Afraid not – I don't think I'd like a Yugoslav prison.'

'There's no danger of prison as long as we don't have no drugs or politics. No political pamphlets or anti-government propaganda – for that you *do* go to prison for long time. But for other goods only confiscation and fine. What do you say?'

'Sorry – not interested.'

'No? Well I don't think you are only a simple tourist. I am good at judging men and I am sure that you would not be afraid to take a chance for a lot of money. Am I right?'

'It would have to be more than five thousand dollars and the risk would have to be small.'

He laughed. 'More money more risk. I think maybe it could be more than five thousand. I will see my friends with the money and then maybe we make you a proposition. How long you stay in Portoroz, Colonel?'

That shook me. He'd been right behind me as we went through immigration and must have seen my name.

'I haven't decided; I am on holiday. I could well move on in a day or so. But I'm really not interested in your offer, thanks.'

He handed me a card: Andric Leskova, IMPORT/EXPORT. There was an address and a telephone number in Ljubljana. 'If you should change your mind – it could be most profit.'

At the first stop in Yugoslavia, a town called Muggia, he and most of the others who had boarded in Trieste go out. He stopped opposite my window and solemnly saluted as the bus moved off. There was a certain persistence about him which bothered me and I was glad to have seen the last of him. Such men are dangerous.

I knew that the Metropole Hotel was only about half a mile from where the bus let me off in Portoroz and I was tempted to walk, but it wouldn't do for me to arrive on foot carrying my own suitcase, particularly as I was going to report my passport lost. The taxi cost me nearly three times the bus fare from Trieste but the doorman opened the cab door and a bellhop carried my huge bag in so the investment had probably been worthwhile.

The reservation for George Kelly was confirmed and the standard fiche given to me. I then discovered that my passport was missing. I went through the motions of searching everywhere for it, making sure that the desk clerk saw that there was plenty of money in my wallet.

He phoned for someone with more authority to come and he soothed me down.

'It is quite all right, sir, perhaps you dropped your passport in the bus or the taxi, in which case it will be returned.'

'I certainly hope so!'

'Yes, but in the mean time it is necessary to report the loss to the police.' He wrote down an address. 'You should go there without delay, Mr Kelly – it is important and they will tell you how to go about getting a new passport.'

'Thanks – I'll go there as soon as I've had a wash and unpacked.'

My third-floor room was identical with half the rooms at the hotel; the other half were mirror images. There was a separate W.C. on the left of a little entrance hall, on the right of which were hanging cupboards. The room itself had twin beds, a dressing-table, two chairs, radio and television, and one wall was a huge picture window with a door which led to a balcony with deck chairs and table. On the opposite wall a door led to a small, well-designed bathroom.

The balcony looked over the gardens to the sea and was separated from other balconies on either side by a wall of open brickwork. Every side of the hotel was covered with similar balconies. It would, I saw, be a comparatively simple matter to climb around the wall to the next balcony, and so on to the next and the next and, although it would be more dangerous, it was quite possible to drop to a lower balcony since the space from floor to ceiling was only about nine feet.

I hoped that I wouldn't have cause to start climbing around outside the balconies but it is always just as well to have an escape route planned.

From a printed card on the wall by the door I saw that the room cost fifty dollars a day, but that included a continental breakfast, and the

Yugoslav version of a continental breakfast is a substantial meal of cold meats, cheese and boiled egg rather than the coffee, roll, butter and jam of Italy. If I were careful and bought some food outside my money would last about five days, and I was pretty confident of my ability to find another source before then. But it was important not to hurry things – I am apt to work too fast and although it sometimes comes off, as with Dora in Venice, it also sometimes frightens the bird into flying away.

Nevertheless, the sooner I got started the sooner the moment of plucking would come. The best place to examine the field and to be seen myself at this hour, mid-afternoon, was in the hotel's swimming pool, so I took my new white trunks and a bath towel and made my way there, first having washed out my shirt and hung it in the bathroom. I rang for the maid and handed over my English suit which had been through so much during the past week or so. It was promised for six o'clock, dry-cleaned and pressed.

The pool was shielded from the wind by high glass walls, but open to the sky so that the guests could get on with the serious task of turning their skins from white to rosy red.

But I noticed that one corner was in shade and there four young people, a boy and three girls, were settled nicely away from the crowd. They, like me, were tanned all over, and the girls must at some time have sunbathed without bras although they were wearing them now.

I chose a spot a few feet from them and got friendly smiles from the girls in reply to my 'good afternoon' and a cold nod from the boy, who reacted like a young male at the approach of an old bull. I made myself comfortable and half closed my eyes.

Soon the boy got up and dived expertly into the pool, breaking into a fast crawl as soon as he surfaced. After a few minutes I walked to the edge of the pool and went gingerly down the steps into the water. The boy was floating on his back and kicking up spray, but I knew that he had seen me. I swam over to him with a sedate breaststroke.

'I wish I could swim like you do,' I said.

He gave me a long look and I guessed that he was wondering if I were gay and making a sexual advance. He was a good-looking youngster of about eighteen or nineteen and was undoubtedly used to such approaches. I gave him my manliest smile – the one with closed teeth in which one side of my mouth goes up more than the other.

'It's really not difficult,' he said, evidently reassured.

'I suppose not if you learn it when young, but I was taught the breaststroke and find it very difficult to do the crawl. I suppose I don't like putting my head in the water.'

'Oh, you have to do that.'

'I know – my wife is very good but she has given up trying to teach me.' That, I thought, ought to allay any suspicions, not because there aren't plenty of married homosexuals, but because they would not immediately mention a wife.

'And Madame – she is with you 'ere?'

I guessed that he was French and that he had learned to speak English in England.

'No, she is making a film in Spain. She will join me next week.'

'She is an actress – a film star, perhaps?'

I have found that young people are almost always interested in anything to do with film-making; I expect they all think they could succeed in that world and talking of it is a sure-fire way of getting their attention.

'No – she's a continuity girl.'

'Ah! And you – do you also work in films?'

'I rewrite scripts – "Only a few people can write film scripts, but everyone can rewrite them".'

'Pardon?'

'It's just a saying in the business.' I nodded my head in a goodbye gesture and swam off, fairly sure that the next approach would be from him.

And so it proved. I went back to my towel and stretched out, and a few minutes later he called the waiter to order drinks. I sat up to do the same thing and he caught my eye.

'Will you join us, Monsieur?'

'Thank you – I'll have a Radenska, please.' I walked over to them.

'You must have been here before', one of the girls said, 'to know our local mineral water.'

'Yes, I have – once or twice.'

'Perhaps when they were making that English film in Piran?' she asked.

I realized that I would have to go carefully. 'No – I've never been on location in Yugoslavia. I was here for a holiday just as I am now.'

At that point the boy introduced himself, Alex de Crespigny, and the other three, Sonya, Anna and Michèle, who was his sister. I replied with my name, my real one for a change. The waiter arrived with the drinks and, the ice being broken, I was questioned about the making of films. How did one break in? Was it possible just to turn up on the set and get taken on as an extra? Was it difficult to write film scripts? Which famous actors did I know?

I replied as best I could, although the only contact with film-making I had ever had was when an episode of a TV series had been made in Tangier while I was living there and some of my Arab friends who hung around the Zocco Chico had been used as extras. I had once been to Hollywood and taken a tour of a studio and a tourist bus past the 'homes of the stars', so with ample use of the imagination and a good deal of boldness I managed to give the impression of one who had been in the film world for years. They were intrigued.

'And what is the name of the film on which your wife is working at the moment?' the second girl, also a Yugoslav, asked me.

I hadn't seen that one coming and was not prepared.

'Oh it's only a low-budget horror film – they're in great demand these days, you know.'

'Tell us the name so we can look out for it.'

'*The Mysteries of Udolpho*,' I said, that being a title I'd read somewhere. 'It takes place during the Spanish Inquisition and they're shooting it in Granada.'

That seemed to satisfy them and shortly afterwards I left, having promised to meet them for drinks before dinner in the cellar bar where there was a juke-box and fruit-machines. I was pleased with the afternoon's work because it meant that I would appear to be part of a group of young and attractive people, a situation in which it would be much easier to start chatting to an older woman on her own without putting her on her guard.

As I walked across the lobby towards the lifts I heard someone call 'Meestair Kelly?' and it was so long since I had used my real name I nearly ignored it, but remembered just in time and turned round. It was the official at the desk who had told me to report the loss of my passport to the police, and standing beside him was a policeman.

I walked quickly over to the desk. 'You've found my passport?'

'No, it has not been turned in, but I had to report the matter to the police, of course, and this is Inspector Kovaks who would like to get some information – to help them to find your passport, you understand?'

'Yes, of course. What would you like to know, Inspector?' I looked straight into his eyes which were very dark blue and very shrewd. He was about the mid-fifties or perhaps even older, but hard and fit-looking. He had probably been a soldier; of course at his age and in that position he had almost certainly been a young partisan. He was not the kind of man to be easily fooled or to fool around with, and Yugoslavia is not a country to be on the wrong side of the authorities. I began to be rather sorry that I'd killed off Colonel Rokesby-Gore, who would, I felt, have been better able to handle Inspector Kovaks than George Kelly, except that the Colonel was a fraud while George Kelly was a real person. On the other hand Interpol had a file on both of them.

'It would be best for you to come to my office, Mr Kelly,' he said quietly. 'We have all the necessary forms there.'

'Right,' I said cheerfully. 'I'll just go to my room and get dressed.'

'Certainly. Please don't be long. I have a car waiting.'

'Right-o. I won't be a tick.' I hurried to the lift and went to my room. My heart was beating fast and my instinct was to run like hell, but that would be fatal.

No matter how hard I try I can't help being nervous, frightened even, whenever I find myself in a police car, and an old experienced cop could always sense it; Inspector Kovaks was old and experienced.

He could, I thought, already be suspicious; perhaps Colonel Rokesby-Gore's description had been circulated. The hotel in Venice would have immediately called the police. Why hadn't I thought of shaving off my moustache before checking in at the Metropole? Oh well, it was too late for that now.

I would not have been so worried if it hadn't been for seeing Dora and her friends in Trieste; I wouldn't be surprised if they were waiting for me at the police station.

I put on my new drip-dry suit and the polo-neck and went downstairs trying to look calm and bored with the necessity of the paperwork.

The doorman signalled and a waiting police car drove quickly to the main entrance. The inspector opened the door for me, following very closely himself. He sat down rather heavily, his gun holster banging my hip. He grunted an apology as the car moved off.

13

'REALLY, INSPECTOR, THIS is a bit much!' I tried the note of irritation in my voice which would come from any wholly innocent tourist after being questioned for over an hour about a lost passport. 'I hope you're not going to take much longer.'

We were seated opposite each other at a plain wooden table at the end of which sat a young policeman who wrote down everying that was said, or at least that the Inspector translated into Slovenian, which he did after each question and answer. My irritation didn't seem to worry him, for he took his time in answering.

'Not much longer. Why don't you join me in a coffee while I just check through the record?'

'Thank you. Your English is exceptionally good, Inspector. Have you been in England?' I decided a spot of graciousness was needed on my part.

'Yes – I worked for a year at Scotland Yard.' He nodded to the police stenographer, who left the room through the door with the spy hole. That and the very bright light overhead reminded me unpleasantly of a number of such rooms I'd sat in during the last twenty-odd years.

The Inspector picked up the policeman's notebook and turned it back to the first page.

'Now you know you had your passport this morning because you showed it at the frontier, but when you got to the hotel you couldn't find it and it wasn't found on the bus – we've checked that – nor in the taxi – we know the driver and he's very reliable. Nor has it been found in the road – at least no one has turned it in. So far, so good.' He sounded quite cheerful as he turned the page. 'You can't remember the number on your passport and you say you didn't stop at an Italian hotel last night which would have a note of the details – why didn't you?'

'I told you – because I'd come from Austria.'

'Ah, yes – how stupid of me, here it is written down. You'd been given a lift from Klagenfurt – that's certainly in Austria. But apparently you didn't stay at a hotel there either – ?'

I had been caught napping when he'd asked me the name of the last hotel I'd stayed in and all I could think of was that I mustn't mention the Bristol in Trieste, so in a panic I dredged the name of an Austrian town out of my memory. That lie, of course, had forced me to start weaving a complicated web of supporting evidence. I hoped to God I could remember everything that was written in the damned notebook. The Inspector was waiting for an answer.

'No, I didn't stay in Klagenfurt – I just had lunch at the hotel there.'

'Yes – that's what you said. You'd been staying with friends in . . .' he looked again at the notebook, quite unnecessarily I was sure, '. . . in Graz.'

'That's right.' I'd kept my cool so far and was determined not to notice that I was being treated more like a suspect than an unlucky tourist.

'And they drove you to Klagenfurt – why?'

'Isn't it there, Inspector? I'm sure I told you – they drove over to visit their married daughter and as I thought it was about time I moved on I packed my things and went with them. I planned to get a train to Trieste.'

'But you didn't?'

'No – I got talking to this English couple at the next table . . . but I've told you all this once.'

'Yes, I know. You met these nice fellow-countrymen and learned they were driving over the mountains to Trieste and when they heard that was where you wanted to go too they offered you a lift in their – what was the car?'

'A Bentley.' Why on earth had I made it such a conspicuous car?

'Yes – a green Bently and they dropped you off near the station in Trieste. What did you say their name was?'

'Grenville – Dick and Frances.'

'Mmm – and the name of your Austrian friends?'

'Jannings.'

'Like the famous old actor in *The Blue Angel* – Emil Jannings?'

'That was a bit before my time I'm afraid, Inspector.' God damn it, I simply must break myself of the habit of using well-known names.

'I suppose so – of course we didn't get Hollywood films until some time after they were made. I suppose your friend's first name wasn't Emil, was it?'

He was, I knew, baiting me, but better men than he had tried that and failed. I was not going to get rattled.

'No – it's Karl, but really what has this to do with my lost passport? Shouldn't I now see the nearest British Consul and get some sort of an identity document from him?'

'Yes, of course. You can do that tomorrow. He is at Rijeka, which is rather a roundabout bus ride I'm afraid. But what I find a little puzzling is that if you had decided to come here, why didn't you go from Graz to Ljubljana and then to here?'

'I hadn't made up my mind *where* I wanted to go, and when my friends said they were going to Klagenfurt I decided on the spur of the moment to accompany them and then, as I said, while we were all having lunch we got talking to the English couple and I decided to go with them to Trieste – but, I repeat Inspector, what has all this to do with your trying to find my passport?'

'Well you see, Mr Kelly, we don't like not knowing who our – er – guests – are, and since you have absolutely nothing which identifies you as George Kelly we have to satisfy ourselves that you are who you say you are – which I am sure is so – and one way would be to check with the last hotel you stayed in. What was that by the way?'

'I haven't stayed in a hotel for some time. I flew to Vienna from London last week and was met by the Jannings and taken to their home.'

'You don't have a return ticket?'

'No – I won't be going back to Vienna.'

'You didn't keep the used ticket, I suppose?'

'No – I threw it away.'

'And you don't have any credit cards – '

'I don't believe in them.'

' – or traveller's cheques?'

'They cost too much and are a nuisance to change – I prefer cash.'

'Did you declare the foreign currency when you entered Yugoslavia?'

'No, I'm afraid I didn't – should I have done?'

'You should – there are signs in English saying so, but never mind, we can regularize that. Did you not think of renting a car on your travels?'

'No – if you don't have a credit card the deposit is too high.'

'But don't you carry your driving licence when you are abroad – just in case you are offered a car by one of your friends?'

'Didn't think of it, I'm afraid.'

At that point the young policeman returned carrying a tray with a pot of coffee and a bottle of slivovitz and three cups and saucers. The Inspector poured the soot-black liquid into the cups, put in three spoons of sugar and, after glancing at me for approval, added a slug of slivovitz. I noted he gave the young policeman only coffee.

I had been very glad of the break in the polite but persistent questioning and mentally checked back on my answers to make sure I hadn't contradicted myself. So far I thought I was all right, but it was obvious that my complete lack of anything to indicate that I was George Kelly had aroused his policeman's nasty suspicious mind. I could have kicked myself for not having said that I had also lost my wallet which, although I had removed all traces of Colonel Rokesby-Gore from it, did have the dollars and the lire and Andric Leskova's card, the 'importer' I'd met on the bus whose name the thorough Inspector had also written down.

We sipped our fortified coffee and then the Inspector read through the dozen or so more pages of my answers to his questions and closed the file.

'Well Mr Kelly I must admit that I find it strange that you do not have even one piece of paper with your name on it – no letters, no diary – nothing. But when you go to the British Consul tomorrow he will no doubt be able to make the necessary enquiries direct to London and you'll be issued with a temporary identity document to enable you to return to England. You'll be sure to bring it in to us, won't you?'

'Yes, of course.'

'Good – well I think that's all.' He scanned his notes. 'You don't happen to know where your English friend was going to next, do you – Richard Grenville?'

'Didn't ask him.'

'Well, never mind – perhaps to Flores in the Azores, eh?'

'Don't follow you, I'm afraid.'

He wagged his finger at me. 'You don't know your Tennyson, I see. I was a liaison officer during the war between the British and the partisans and one of my English friends gave me his Palgrave before he left – it has given me much pleasure.'

I smiled, trying to appear completely baffled.

The Golden Treasury?'

I shook my head.

'Also before your time, I expect.'

He rose and so did I, thankful that the attack – for I knew that's what it had been – had stopped, if only for the time being. We shook hands.

'You won't change hotels without letting us know, will you?'

'Of course not – and if you do find my passport before the bus goes to Rijeka tomorrow you'll let me know, won't you?'

'Certainly – but don't be too hopeful.'

In the police car being driven back to the Metropole I wondered what it was that had made him cross-examine me so thoroughly. I decided I'd better get my travel document from the Consul, show it to the police to get them off my back, find an easy mark and do a quick con to fatten my purse, and get the hell out of Yugoslavia on the double.

As I got out of the police car at the entrance to the hotel a white Rolls Royce open touring car, a model I knew wasn't made any more, drew up and I saw that the driver was Alex, the French boy I'd scraped an acquaintance with at the pool. His sister Michèle and Anna, one of the Yugoslav girls, got out of the back at the same time as a woman in her forties, or perhaps a carefully preserved fifty, got out of the front.

'Hi!' The boy waved at me and I waved back and the girls then noticed me.

'Ah, Monsieur Kellee.' The French girl came over to me. 'Come and meet my mother – Maman, this is Mr Kellee – the film writer we met at the pool.'

Her mother smiled politely and I bowed. 'I am only a rewriter – a much lower category.'

She looked at me through gold-rimmed, tinted glasses.

'That is the famous English modesty, I am sure.' We started to walk inside in a group while Alex parked the car. I could smell money – lots of it. She wore an expensively simple short linen dress that clung to her hips and buttocks and she carried a baby-alligatorskin bag. The price of either would have kept me for a week. She wore a platinum and diamond wedding ring and another ring with a solitaire diamond that could not have been smaller than two and a half carats. Even without the evidence of the Rolls I could see that I had stumbled on to real, solid wealth.

She was deeply tanned and thin to the point of scrawniness with wrinkles in her neck that no amount of make-up could conceal. Her hair was blonde – too blonde – and cut in short careless waves, too careless to be true. As we entered the lobby the manager indicated that he would like to talk to me and I watched her walk away, moving her bottom just a trifle more than was necessary and holding her shoulders back so that her small but firm breasts stood out. As she entered the lift she turned and looked in my direction, apparantly not seeing me but I knew that she did.

'You know Madame de Crespigny, Mr Kelly?' the manager asked.

'Hardly at all,' I said truthfully. 'We have friends in common, though.' For all I knew that could be true too: I've met a lot of people in my time.

'A charming lady – *vraie Parisienne*,' he added.

'Yes – what did you want to say – have you found my passport?'

'Alas, no – I trust your interview with the police was satisfactory?'

'Yes, of course. I shall go to Rijeka tomorrow to report it to my Consul.'

'You would like a car?'

'No, I prefer the bus – I always think one gets such a good idea of the country and its people on a bus.'

'It's rather a long trip.'

'I'm sure I'll enjoy it.'

'Would you like to take a picnic lunch perhaps?'

'What a good idea.'

'I'll see to it, then.' He bowed and left me wondering if he, too, were a little suspicious of George Kelly.

My suit was hanging on the inside of the door, having recovered its look of quiet distinction, and my white shirt had dried, so I would be able to go down to the dining-room dressed for dinner as a proper Englishman should be – even in a holiday hotel.

While I was dressing I turned over various possible cons for Madame de Crespigny, who, I had decided, would be my next mark. It might be supposed that the very rich are not concerned about making more money and particularly not by doubtfully legal means. On the contrary they are always interested in acquiring more and seldom have too many scruples about how it is to be done – so long as they run no risks, as they are extremely cautious, having so much to lose.

I suppose that is as shaky as most generalizations but it is true that I have found very, very few really rich women who didn't jump at the idea of turning a quick profit by an evasion of duty or taxes or an illicit

125

sale. I would sound out Madame de Crespigny discreetly the next time we met.

It was not yet seven o'clock when I went downstairs to find the youngsters I'd promised to meet for a pre-dinner drink. I could hear music coming from somewhere, the kind of noise adolescents delight in these days, and I followed my ears to an underground room from which, as I got near, I could hear not only the imitation mid-west American singing of a German or Dutch, or possibly Yugoslav, young man, but the unmistakable noise of fruit-machines' whirling dials earning money for their owners.

The first thing I saw when I pushed open the saloon-type swinging door was Alex feeding coins into two one-armed bandits at once and Anna the local girl studying the choice of records displayed above an enormous coin-in-the-slot record player. Michèle was seated at a table on which there were one Pepsicola and two Coca Cola bottles. She looked up and beckoned me to join them.

'I'll just get a drink,' I said, and went quickly to the bar and ordered a draught beer which I would make last so that I wouldn't get stuck for a round of drinks, as I was sure that even the soft ones would be expensive in this obvious tourist trap.

The rattle of one of the machines paying out for a change brought applause from Anna and Michèle, both of whom ran and helped themselves to the pile despite Alex's protest. He came back to the table and dumped what was left of his win on the table.

'Was it the jackpot?' I asked.

'No – fifty coins – or it *was* fifty before these piranhas got at it.'

'Are you winning now? If so, stop.'

'No – I am a little ahead tonight but I have lost every night until now – and I will lose all this soon.'

'If you know that why do you do it?'

'Ennui – boredom.'

'But how can you be bored here – with the beach, the boats – the beautiful countryside?'

'I am tired of the beach and the pool and when you have been to Piran once you have exhausted it. I am very bored here – I would prefer to be with my father – he is in Spain for the bullfights but my mother will not let me go with him.'

'Because he is with his mistress – that's why!' said Michèle vehemently.

'Tais-toi! Papa has not got a mistress . . .'

'Shhh!' warned Michèle, who was facing the door. I turned my head and saw that her mother had just entered. I rose, taking in the deep blue sheath of silk with a Chinese slit which seemed, but surely could not, to run up to her waist. Alex too had risen, but it was I who pulled out a chair for her and asked her what she would drink. This would be a business investment.

'Un Pernod, Monsieur, if you please.'

I signed for it at the bar and tried not to wince at the price – at this rate I wouldn't last long. I didn't think it necessary to order more cokes for the brats.

The investment paid off when, having drunk her Pernod and chatted to me about Hollywood, which she had visited, she graciously invited me to join them for dinner. After a few polite objections I accepted, but we had to wait while she downed a second Pernod which, thank God, Alex signed for. In the dining-room she was met with deference and the waiter quickly laid a fifth place at one of the round tables. Fortunately for my finances there was some wine left over from lunch, both red and white, and it was French, not Yugoslav, I noticed. During the indifferent meal fresh bottles appeared without, as far as I could see, anyone having ordered them. Madame's glass was emptied several times.

I was seated on Madame de Crespigny's right and the first time her knee touched my thigh I thought it might just be that we were a little cramped around the table but didn't move my leg away, although she soon did. A few minutes later as she turned to ask me a question her leg was laid against mine in a way I could not misunderstand.

'And you, Monsieur Kelly, what do you do besides rewrite film scripts?'

'I speculate,' I said, returning the pressure. 'I take advantage of favourable opportunities to better my lot.'

'Favourable opportunities? What is that?'

'Any chance to make a profit that I come across – you'd be surprised how often it occurs.'

'Tell me more – it sounds ver' interestin'.'

'Well – if you're sure you wouldn't be bored?' I glanced at the youngsters who obviously were.

'But no, of course not, no. I adore the business.' She caught the eye of the waiter who never seemed far away from her – I guessed that she had tipped him well on arrival – and he was at her side immediately.

'Café?' she asked the table. I accepted but Alex and the girls refused, having polished off a huge cassata each. 'Two coffees and please bring my own cognac.' I started to protest but she said that she always brought her own wine and cognac with her as it came from a vineyard 'in the family'. She then allowed her children and their guest to leave, which they did with obvious relief. She poured two large portions.

'Now, Monsieur,' she said, moving her leg away from its contact with mine. 'Tell me of these opportunities which have "bettered your lot".'

I've almost got a set piece for occasions like that: it starts with suggesting that I am a knowledgeable connoisseur in a number of fields without being too specific so that I can shy away if it becomes apparent that the mark herself is knowledgeable in one of them; I then point out that such knowledge of, say, china, silver, netsukes, prints, stamps, coins or first editions often enables me in out-of-the-way places to buy something valuable – sometimes extremely valuable – at a comparatively low price. I then give a few examples, watching my mark closely to see how she reacts to admissions of, first, sharp practice, as, for instance, misrepresenting the object I'm trying to buy, and then, progressively, to downright breaking the law, as my tale of buying objects from a museum in Mexico from the director himself, which is something that, to my astonishment, I once saw a Brazilian woman do right in front of my eyes. When, and if, my prospective mark expresses believable moral indignation I concur and backtrack to the point where she doesn't, and this gives me the lead for the particular bit of clever, unscrupulous dealing she will be invited to join and, eventually, to her cost, to finance completely. I'm good at telling these tales, for I've not only had a lot of practice but I have a knack for entertaining in this way – I was much in demand in my last prison and used to collect a cigarette from each of my audience.

But I was conscious that I wasn't doing as well as usual. I thought at first that it was because she was so rich herself that a profit of a thousand or even a few thousand dollars or pounds didn't awaken her greed as it almost always did. But when she leaned across me to knock the ash off her cigarette and banged her tit into my shoulder I realized that she was randy and more than a little drunk.

'Pardon,' she said, giving me an insolent look.

'What for?' I looked at her mouth and opened mine, at the same time gripping her leg between my knees.

She pulled her leg free, stubbed out her cigarette and drew a deep breath.

'Shall we go?'

'Yes – would you like to walk in the garden?'

She nodded. As we rose she staggered slightly, and when I gripped her upper arm to steady her she tucked it into her side, pressing my knuckles against her breast, which did not after all seem as small as I had thought.

The garden's paths were lit brightly; at the bottom, one led to a bridge which crossed over the main road giving access to the beach. It was lit only dimly while the beach itself had no lights but was saved from complete darkness by the ones on the road. We fell against each other as we walked and each time this happened she grabbed at me with her long thin fingers, which she seemed to want to dig into my body.

As soon as we reached the beach and the shadow of a building in which the deck chairs and tables were kept she stopped, turned to me and, as I kissed her as passionately as I could manage, dropped her hand down and grabbed my penis through my trouser leg, squeezing it with such enthusiasm that, even though I didn't have an erection, it was quite painful.

Stifling a cry, I shoved my knee between her legs which, thank God, forced her to let go. I then made what I hoped were convincing noises of sexual desire and, slipping my hand inside her slit skirt, I grabbed her buttocks.

'Not 'ere, not 'ere, Georges,' she said, pulling her mouth away from mine and slipping her hand down inside my trousers where my poor penis was trying to rise to the occasion.

'Where, chérie, where?' I asked in what I hoped were tones of desperate desire. 'Your room?'

'No – impossible. Michèle's room connects with mine. I must come to you – but later, much later. It's too dangerous now.' She broke clear expertly and smoothed her dress. 'Et alors, we go back and dance, eh?' she said in her normal voice.

'Dance?'

'Yes – there is a dance in the hotel tonight. You wish to dance with me, don't you, Georges?'

'Yes, of course.'

'Don't be triste – I will make you very happy later.' She laid a finger on my lips. 'It will be better for waiting – you will see. Come.'

129

She took my hand and led me back across the bridge. This, I thought, is all very well but I can't see a profit in it for me.

I could hear the music as we approached the hotel; real 'thirties dance music, a foxtrot no less. I dance well – one has to in my profession – and I hoped that she did too as I didn't feel up to carrying her around the floor.

As we reached the garden entrance to the ballroom, which was actually part of the dining-room, she stopped.

'But you don't even know my name!' she said in mock horror. 'We are so wicked!'

'What is it?'

'Claudette – but only call me that when we are alone – Michèle is very aware of such things and so are the hotel staff – we do not want the scandal, do we?'

'Of course not.'

'Good. Now we will dance for, oh – 'alf an hour – and then I will go and find my children and spend some time with them. I make them go to bed by eleven – they always come and say good night to me – and then I will wait until I am sure they are asleep and come to you about twelve. What is your room number?'

'I'm in 318. I'll leave my door unlocked.'

'Good – now let us dance.'

She did dance well and I enjoyed it. The orchestra ran through its old-fashioned repertoire of foxtrot, two-step, waltz, rumba and tango, and we did them all. During the rumba I was bumped so hard I nearly lost my balance. I turned and saw that I had been hit by the large bottom of an extraordinary looking woman. She was no more than five feet tall and if she had not, obviously, been held in by a strong girdle and metal-cupped brassière which threatened to push her breasts up to her chin, she would have been as round as a beach ball. She wore a baby-doll dress of bright pink, a red rose in her hair, and was glistening with sweat.

'Forgive me, sir,' she gasped, giving me a wide smile of white teeth interspersed with gold, 'but I love the rumba!'

Her partner was a tall young man, hardly more than a boy, at least twenty years younger. He was dressed in black and stood waiting patiently without the least trace of embarrassment or annoyance with his fantastic-looking partner.

'The fault was mine,' I said, bowing.

'Oh no, I . . .'

But at that point Claudette de Crespigny recovered her breath, exchanged brief greetings, and then pulled me back into the rumba which seemed to have speeded up.

'She is Colombian,' she told me as we walked back to the table. 'We met her last year. She *says* the boy is her stepson and that he must sleep in the same room because her husband does not like to leave her without the protection. Ha!'

'Perhaps it's true – after all if they are lovers they would pretend to be married.'

She shrugged her shoulders. 'Maybe – it could not happen in France, though.'

'I don't think it would in England either, but perhaps it is different in South America.'

'Perhaps – and, of course, she is very rich – she owns millions of hectares of coffee land.'

'Millions?'

'Well, anyway many thousands. She plays baccarat in the casino here as though the banknotes are toy money.'

'Does she win?'

'Sometimes – she took enough off me last week but *on dit* that last year she lost fifty thousand dollars here. That was after having lost heavily in London too.'

'What's her name?'

'Alsinas – Josefina de Campos Alsinas – or the other way round. Why – does she interest you?'

'Good heavens, no! I just wondered who it was who nearly broke me in two.'

She dug her claws into my thigh. 'I will break you in two later tonight,' she said in an imitation of a man's voice. Then in a completely different tone she said, 'Well, I must go now – good night,' and was walking away while I was still rising from the chair.

When I was sure she had left the room I looked over at the fat lady and was somehow not surprised to find her looking at me. I smiled and she spoke to the boy, who came over to my table.

'Good evening, sir. My stepmother asks if you would join us in a glass of champagne.'

'Good evening. I'd be delighted to.'

She was fanning herself rapidly but stopped to point to a chair between her and the boy who, as I sat down, summoned a waiter and without saying a word indicated that another glass was needed and should be filled, with the complete confidence that his wishes would be instantly carried out that only comes from having been waited on hand and foot all one's life. The glass found its way into my hand as though by magic.

'You are an old friend of Claudette de Crespigny, sir?' she said, bending towards me so that I was sure her breasts were going to pop out.

'Not as old as all that. We have friends in common, though.'

'I am Señora Alsinas and this is my stepson, Oscar.' The boy bowed his head.

'And my name is Kelly, George Kelly.'

'From Ireland – you are a Catholic too?'

'No to both. I am English, Church of England.'

'I love Englishmen – they seem very cold and very correct but really they are not.' She poked me with her fan.

'I love South American ladies who seem very warm and very correct and really are,' I said.

She laughed. 'You have known many South American ladies?'

'Not enough, alas.'

'I shall begin to think you are not English at all if you continue with such gallantries.'

There did not seem to be anything to say to that so I drank some champagne, which was sweet which is just how I like it though I always order it very dry because that's the thing to do. But if you can lose thousands gambling without bothering you could have ice-cream and caviare without apologizing.

I tried bringing out the boy with a few questions, but although he replied affably enough it was obviously not his place to talk to me, as his stepmother made very clear by interrupting him, changing the subject and seizing the initiative by questioning me.

No, I wasn't exactly on holiday, I told her, I was here to arrange a barter deal between a certain European country I couldn't mention and Yugoslavia. God knows where that bit of invention came from; it just popped out.

'But why here in Portoroz?' she asked. 'Why not in Belgrade?'

Why not indeed? 'Because,' I said, 'the Minister – I'd better just say the high government official – involved has a small holiday house near here where we can meet in private, whereas if we met in Belgrade the word would go round and speculators would be able to make a huge profit at the expense of the people.'

'How?'

'How?'

'Yes – how could speculators make a huge profit if they knew that, well, England for example was going to exchange whisky for Yugoslav Riesling?'

I looked startled. 'What made you say that?'

'I don't know. Why – don't tell me I guessed right?'

'No, but you are getting warm, as the children say.'

'Anyway you haven't answered my question – how can the speculators make money?'

As she said the word 'money' she sighed and licked her lips like an alcoholic talking about his obsession.

'I'm afraid I can't tell you that – it would be an abuse of trust.'

'And you are never tempted to do a little speculating yourself?'

'No – and anyway it would be impossible for me to do so without it becoming known.'

'Unless someone acted on your behalf.'

'Why should they?'

'For profit, innocent, honourable Englishman, for profit! For the opportunity to participate. How safe is this speculation?'

'It's guaranteed – an automatic profit.'

'I don't understand.'

Neither did I, but I am nothing if not imaginative. I was amazed at how, without any preliminary work on my part at all, this bird had voluntarily come forward begging to be plucked. It does, however, sometimes happen.

'Well I think I *can* say this much. When something which is readily available suddenly becomes in very short supply its price quickly rises – like petrol, for instance, in recent years.'

'And if you know in advance that it's going to happen . . .'

'Precisely. You see how careful I have to be.'

The orchestra had come round to the rumba again and her shoulders began to move in time with the rhythm. The boy got to his feet with a touch of weariness, but she waved him down and turned to me.

'You did it so well with Claudette de Crespigny, but the rumba is after all a South American dance – come, I will show you the South American way.'

I was surprised to find that for all her peculiarly distributed bulk she danced very well, as light on her feet as though she were a gas-filled balloon and apparently tireless. I was soon sweating as much as she was and suddenly very much aware of how tired I was. I still had a bit of fever and it had been a long, exhausting day – both mentally and physically. I was well aware that my work hadn't yet finished. It was, I saw by a surreptitious look at her small diamond-studded wrist-watch, just past ten to ten – unless the watch had only one hand – and if I were to come up to Claudette's expectations I needed some rest before midnight.

But on the other hand this mark was too good to lose: I didn't yet know how I would con her out of a few thousands, but I was confident it could be done. As I was puzzling about my next move, she made it for me.

The music stopped and as we walked back to the table she asked me if I liked gambling. I said I sometimes played baccarat for modest stakes, which I guessed to her would mean a few hundred dollars.

'I knew we were simpatico,' she said triumphantly. 'I love baccarat. Will you play tonight?'

'I don't know. I have some work to do before a meeting tomorrow, but I may go up to the casino later.'

'Good – I never go before one and the big games don't usually start before two. Perhaps I'll see you there?'

'Perhaps.'

'I think if you are a gambler that we may have something of interest to say to each other. I too am a gambler but I would very much like to bet on a "sure thing" as my racing friends at Ascot say.'

'Wouldn't we all? Anyway I'm always ready to listen.'

'Good – until later then.'

At the porter's desk I was handed a note with my key. I rather hoped it was from Claudette saying that she had changed her mind so I could get some badly needed sleep. But it was obviously not from her, being printed in block capitals like a ransom note in a TV thriller:

I HAVE COME HERE BECAUSE THE BUSINESS PROPOSITION WE DIS-CUSSED IS READY ALREADY. GOOD PROFITS WITH NO RISKS OF LOSSES. YOU MUST PHONE TO ME WHEN YOU GET THIS COLONEL NOT MATTER HOW LATE. THIS IS IMPORTANT FOR YOU.

It was signed 'Andric Leskova', Annexe Room 903. I didn't like it one little bit. Behind the innocuous words lay a clear threat: the 'Colonel', when the note was addressed to 'Mr George Kelly', and the last sentence with its disguised menace left no room for doubt. I would

134

co-operate or else.

For the moment I had no choice; I tried to phone him as soon as I got to my room but there was no reply. I left a message saying I would be in touch early in the morning. I had a shower and lay on the bed with a cigarette, looking at the ceiling. Not for the first time my life was a complicated mess; the next throw of the dice would either move me up a long ladder or slide me down a damn great snake marked 'Prison Again'.

14

I STUBBED OUT MY cigarette and wondered what the time was. In my profession timing is often critical and I hated being without a watch. I'd just have to spend some of my working capital on a cheap Israeli one the next day. The girl on the switchboard told me that it was ten thirty-eight. That gave me an hour or so's sleep before Claudette arrived to 'make me happy' and about an hour to get rid of her so I could have a catnap before going to the casino to continue with the Colombian balloon. It also gave me a little time to invent a barter deal between a Yugoslav Minister and – I supposed it had better be a British company. But what on earth could they be exchanging which would have to be so hush hush – atom bombs?

I laughed aloud, and then I thought, no, not bombs but the stuff that was needed for a nuclear power station. That would fit the bill all right. The only snag was that I couldn't remember what it was, apart from being a radioactive substance, not radium but some kind of uranium. If only there were an English library where I could look it up – give me half an hour with an encyclopaedia and I can talk knowledgeably about almost anything except mathematics. Perhaps there might be one at the British Consulate.

Somehow I'd find out about the raw material for a nuclear power station. Anyway it was pretty long odds that Sra Alsinas would know anything about it, although the young stepson might. But what on earth could Yugoslavia barter for it – something which would then be in short supply and so have risen steeply in price? I'd implied that it had something to do with alcohol but I couldn't see anyone – and certainly not a shrewd woman like her – swallowing a tale of thousands of gallons of slivovitz or Yugoslav wine being exchanged for uranium or whatever it was. No, that was too far-fetched. It would have to be a raw material of some kind – but what? Oh well, I didn't have to have all the details worked out yet; a hint about a nuclear-powered electricity plant would be enough to be going on with.

I turned out the bedside light, expecting to be awakened by a kiss like the sleeping beauty. But sleep wouldn't come. I began to shiver again and waves of nausea swept over me. It was the damned malaria; I'd got up too soon. But no I hadn't; I remembered the police car at the hotel – it was better to be ill in a Yugoslav hotel than a Trieste police cell. A mood of black gloom, which had been threatening to overwhelm me ever since I'd found myself being interrogated by Inspector Kovaks, now took hold of me. All my earlier optimism melted away, to be replaced by the deepest pessimism. I wasn't going to interest Claudette de Crespigny in any con – it was obvious that she was a near-lush bored to distraction with the chore of having to take her children on holiday and ready for a roll in the hay with almost any man. It had all been too easy and it certainly hadn't been my sex-appeal that had made her shove her knee into my leg – I just happened to be there, that's all. She was obviously used to hotel encounters and I wouldn't have been the first younger man – younger? we were probably much the same age – who'd had an eye on her money. We'd have our tumble in the sheets and I'd do my best but she was no inexperienced Dora and I'd have a hard time revealing new delights to her. And as soon as I steered the conversation towards making a fast buck – I wondered what the French for that was – her suspicions would be aroused.

Similarly the Colombian millionairess, Sra Five-by-five as I'd mentally named her. She must be used to smooth talkers trying to chip some of her millions off the pile. She'd always be on her guard. Probably her only interest in me was to annoy Claudette de Crespigny; it was obvious that the two women detested each other.

I wasn't going to get a bean out of either of them and my tiny stake would soon be used up and I'd find myself broke in Yugoslavia and if I threw myself on the mercy of the British Consul the odds were that the link with Colonel Rokesby-Gore would be made and I'd be back in an Italian nick on a diet of potatoes and cheese.

Then there was that damned suspicious police inspector who, I was sure, wouldn't just let the matter rest. He had Leskova's name in my file and I supposed the hotel notified the police of the arrival of all new guests, including Yugoslavs, so he'd spot the name the next morning and just possibly – no, probably – hell, certainly, he would question him about me. Would Leskova then mention the name he'd seen on my passport? If he did, then it would only be a matter of time before

Inspector Kovaks knew the Italian police were looking for Colonel Rokesby-Gore, for although the European police do not inter-circulate information on all wanted men, police in the border towns of friendly countries always work closely together.

I slept and awoke sweating, my headache worse. I pulled the blanket up under my chin and fell into a half-sleep which quickly became a nightmare in which I was in a bull ring dressed as a torero facing an angry bull. I was sweating with fear and my knees were shaking but when I looked for a way of escape all I could see were rows and rows of people cheering, and they all seemed to be women.

The bull gave an unbull-like cry and charged; I raised my sword and saw to my horror that it was a stage prop of painted wood and that as the bull reached me it turned into a cow with enormous udders. My wooden sword splintered on its head and I dropped my hands to protect my testicles from her great curved horn.

I awoke trembling, with sweat pouring off me. My teeth were chattering not, I realized, with fear but from another cold spell. I was reaching the peak of my recurrent malaria and ought to start a course of Paludrine, but God knows what the tablets would cost in Portoroz.

Although I knew it was foolish I dragged a chair out on to the balcony and sat there in only my dressing-gown, feeling more like a sick child in need of mothering than a ruthless, swashbuckling con man always in superb health like The Toff or The Saint, heroes of my schooldays reading. They never so much as caught a cold while I could think of more than one occasion when red eyes and a runny nose had lost me a profitable client.

I remembered the chickenpox that had put Miss Emmy off me just when I'd thought that I was dominating her. I'd made her come to my room over the garage saying that it was too risky for me to come to hers. That had really made her let her hair down. She'd had me take photographs of us with a camera fitted with a delayed action shutter and got them developed by someone she'd known in Soho. She'd kept them in a locked box, or one she thought was locked, with others equally discreet.

Then I'd caught chickenpox but she hadn't come back when I recovered. When I asked her why she'd said that a boy wasn't really a substitute for a man. It was such an abrupt turnabout I concluded that she must have found someone in London.

'I think it's time I left here,' I told her.

'I think you're right but where will you go?'

'Where the money is – London. Only I need a stake to pay my way until I can keep myself.'

'Where will you get that from, your mother?'

'No, from you.'

'From me? You've got a hope, I'm practically stony. I might manage a fiver for old times' sake.'

'You'll manage a hundred quid or the General gets the photographs you think you've got locked up.'

She stood up and stepped towards me; I backed away. 'Christ, what a bloody fool I've been. My God, if you're a bloody blackmailer now what are you going to be at thirty? A prisoner, I hope.'

'Don't worry about me. Worry about getting the money because I'm not joking.'

I didn't see her the next day. I thought perhaps she was trying to raise the cash and I could already see myself on a white cruise ship in a tropical sea. I'd have a rich widow or middle-aged divorcée hooked and I'd part her from a sizeable chunk of her money.

About tea-time my mother came to my room and told me that Miss Emmy wanted to see me in the library.

'There's nothing wrong, is there, George? You haven't been up to anything, have you?'

'Of course not,' I snapped, angry at her standing there in her clean lady's maid uniform. I wondered how many more people were really two persons – the one everyone saw and the one their sexual partner knew. I wanted to reproach my mother not because of what she and Lady Liz did together but for allowing herself to be used so cheaply. By God, I wouldn't.

In the library Miss Emmy and Lady Liz were seated in the big leather chairs and the General was standing behind his writing-table trying to look like an angry Winston Churchill. He didn't speak for at least a minute and when he did I jumped and suddenly realized that he hadn't always been an old duffer.

'You will go and bring me back all the photographs – now!'

'No,' I managed to get out.

'Do you dare to defy me? Do you know what will happen to you if I send for the police, eh?'

'You have no proof; you haven't even told me what I'm supposed to have done. What photographs?'

'You damned little barrack-room lawyer. Do you think the magistrates wouldn't believe my daughter?'

'Maybe they would but you wouldn't risk the scandal – not for fifty pounds.'

'Ah! So it's fifty now, is it? And what for, eh, what for – come on, spit it out, you ungrateful little swine.'

'It's a free gift to me on leaving your employ because you've always underpaid me.'

He got so flushed with anger I was afraid he might have a heart attack, which would put paid to my plan so I kept quiet but held my ground. If he had been going to call in the police they would have been there.

'Oh, give him the fifty pounds, dear, and kick him out. It's cheap at the price. You can make sure he doesn't take any photographs with him; we'll strip his baggage and him bare.' Lady Liz looked at me with loathing but I remembered her head buried in my mother's crotch and I gave her a smile the contempt of which I hoped would worry her. She glared and I was glad she couldn't hurt me.

'Go and get your things, boy, and bring them here. You're going to be searched before you leave this house!'

'What about the money?'

'You'll get the money at the station when you've told us where the photographs are. If you lie about it I'll have you arrested for theft.'

On the way back with my few possessions packed in an old suitcase, which the General himself had given me, I met my mother.

'What is it? Where are you going, George?'

'I'm getting out of here; they don't want me any more. The General is going to give me some money to keep me going until I get a job in London.'

'Why is it all happening so quickly? Why haven't they told me? Are you in some sort of trouble?'

'No, of course not. I'll write from London; please don't interfere, Mum.'

'All right, if that's how you want it, but wait a minute, I've got something for you.' In a few moments she came back and handed me a manila envelope. 'It's your birth certificate. You can get a short one in London which doesn't say you're illegitimate. There's a photograph of your father and me in Portsmouth I thought you might like. Chuck it away if you don't.

I took the envelope and we kissed. I didn't see her her again for over ten years.

Miss Emmy drove me to the station with the General sitting beside her. No one spoke until we got on the platform.

'Now, where are the photographs and negatives?'

'The money first, please.' The ticket collector and a porter were only yards away so I felt safe. He took a wad of notes with a paper band round them which had BARCLAYS £50 on it. I wanted to count it but didn't dare. I shoved it into my coat pocket; it seemed to weigh a ton. I saw the signal arm change and heard the train approaching.

He gripped my arm painfully just above the elbow. 'Well?'

'They're under the back seat of the car.' I wrenched my arm away and walked up the platform towards the train.

'You're a scoundrel!' he shouted. 'A damned scoundrel!'

Well he was right, of course. I had been a scoundrel and I still was. I didn't regret the life I'd led but I was ashamed of how unsuccessful I'd been. I was sure there were many men who'd done much worse things, now living in ease and comfort, who never had to look anxiously over their shoulder. They'd been lucky and I'd been unlucky, I told myself, but I didn't believe it.

I supposed it must be getting near midnight and I'd better get ready for romance. I had another shower and finished off with cool water just as there was a firm but not loud knock on my door. I wrapped the bath towel around my middle and let Claudette de Crespigny in. She'd changed into a dark dress and had added a long, flimsy white scarf which I guessed she'd used as a hood to conceal her face on her way to my room.

I knew that we should have fallen into each other's arms barely able to restrain our passion but I had a splitting headache and a grinding in my stomach which was an omen I recognized. I gathered my strength, summoned what I hoped was a loving smile and kissed her gently.

As though to make it clear that I wasn't going to get away with that she pulled me to her. 'But you are burning, chéri!' She laid her cheek on my hairless chest. 'Is it because you are so 'ot for your Claudette?'

'Oh yes, yes, come to me!' I sat down on the bed before my rubbery legs let me down. As she pulled her dress over her head I whipped away the bath towel and got under the sheet, not, as she might have thought, out of modesty, but because my poor, limp penis gave the lie to a burning passion.

Taking off her bra and panties she struck a pose for me. Her body was tanned dark brown except for the area covered by a bikini where the white skin contrasted with her black bush so different from her very blonde hair.

'I am beautiful, no?'

She was pulling in her belly, which bore marks of childbearing, and her breasts sagged a little but I'd certainly seen a lot worse.

'Irresistible!'

She slipped under the sheet and grabbed my penis which recoiled even further if that were possible. But instead of berating me for a fraud she gave a twist like a contortionist and first her feet and then the rest of her legs appeared on either side of my head until her thighs rubbed my face. For one awful moment I thought she was going to bite my penis off but then her tongue went to work expertly and her mound settled down on my face. There was a smell of eau de Cologne and an expensive scent. She had come prepared.

Taking a deep breath I plunged in and the phone began to ring. It could only be Leskova and he knew I was in. I pulled my head clear of her clutching thighs and got hold of the phone. Claudette went on with what she was doing, which was distracting to say the least.

'Is that you, Colonel?' It was his voice all right.

'George Kelly here,' I said sharply. 'Plain George Kelly – what do you want?'

'We met on the Trieste bus this morning – do you remember, Mr – Kelly?'

'I remember, but that hardly gives you the right to disturb me in the middle of the night.' I grabbed Claudette's hair and pulled her face off me – things were beginning to get beyond my control and I pride myself on my control.

'I apologize,' he said, not sounding apologetic at all. 'But it is a matter of urgency – and could mean great profit to both of us. If it were not important I should not have driven all the way from Ljubljana to see you tonight.'

Claudette began to stroke the big vein under my penis. I crossed my legs like a reluctant virgin and, covering the mouthpiece of the phone, whispered, 'Wait – don't waste it!' That she understood, contenting herself with laying her cheek low on my belly and blowing on my bewildered John Thomas.

'Do you hear me, Mr Kelly – tonight!'

'Yes, yes, I hear you – what's the time now?'

'It is twenty-past twelve – shall I come to your room?'

'No! – you can't do that. I'll meet you. In the casino – in one hour or so – say half-past one.'

'Why so late? Why not in ten or fifteen minutes?'

142

'Because there is something else I have to do first.' Claudette stifled a laugh. 'One-thirty – in the casino.'

'All right – one-thirty it is. Do you want to earn ten thousand dollars, Mr Kelly? – If you do be sure to be there. If you don't come I will think you do not want to be friendly and then I will not want to be friendly either, Colonel.'

'Oh, I'll be there!' I hung up.

The love-making could not be delayed any longer and, thanks to Claudette's variety and expertise, which made me wonder if she'd had a spell as a prostitute, and the frenzy of my fever, she was knocked out. I felt as though I'd been dragged through a wringer and certainly didn't want to get dressed and go to the damn casino, but Leskova had scared me with his not-to-be-mistaken threat.

Claudette had fallen asleep on top of my arm, which was beginning to get pins and needles. As I began pulling it away slowly so as not to wake her up – I was afraid she'd want another go on the merry-go-round and I wouldn't get away – there was a loud knocking on the door which woke her and startled me. In my feverish state I thought immediately of the police and my first instinct was to go off the balcony to the one beneath, but then I realized the police wouldn't have to knock – the hotel would just let them into the room. Besides I wouldn't get far stark naked.

I put my finger to my lips to warn Claudette and, wrapping the towel around me, went to the door just as there was another loud knock. When I opened the door Oscar de Campos Alsinas in a midnight-blue dinner jacket clicked his heels.

'My stepmother presents her compliments and reminds Mr Kelly that he has an appointment with her in the casino.'

'I was just about to dress and come along,' I said. 'What time is it?'

'Just past one o'clock. I will tell my stepmother that you will be along in five minutes.'

'Make it ten.'

'Very well, ten.' He bowed and left.

'Wasn't that Oscar Alsinas's voice?' Claudette asked. 'What did he want?'

'I arranged to meet him and his stepmother in the casino . . . '

'What! When you knew I was coming to you!'

'They invited me after you left and I thought you would be compromised if I refused. They would guess we had an assignation.'

'Thank you,' she said mockingly. 'You are quite the English

"gentleman", so concerned with a lady's honour. But don't worry – I can look after my own. Give me my cigarettes, please, and my lighter – in my bag.'

I did so – she smoked Gauloises and the lighter was the kind with a long wick such as French workmen use, not the little jewelled one I would have guessed. She lit up as I dressed and blew a great lungful of smoke towards the ceiling.

'And the other phone call – another lady, eh, Casanova?'

'You know it was a man – you could hear his voice.'

'All right – it was a man – you like both, perhaps? The English disease?'

It's funny how many women turn bitchy after love-making and it's usually the ones who've made all the going. Almost as if they are ashamed of their forwardness and want to demean the man and therefore themselves.

'No – women are more than enough for me thanks. It is a business opportunity, one in which I think there is a good chance of turning a quick profit . . . ' I waited for a response but she said nothing. Was it my imagination or had her eyes narrowed with suspicion. 'It's quite simple really – someone wants to get rid of a very large quantity of dinars – the proceeds of a big black-market deal I should guess. Anyway my contact is offering them at a third off the official rate.'

'Do you think they are genuine? Not forged?' She sat up in bed, bare-breasted. She was no fool obviously.

'No – they don't forge dinars, only hundred-dollar bills, because there are so many in circulation and people who buy them illegally can't complain. I expect the seller is offering the dinars at half price and my man wants the extra sixteen-plus per cent as commission. I'll try to cut him down to ten, that is offer to buy at forty per cent off, but I only have two thousand dollars or so in cash and traveller's cheques and I'm not sure I need that many dinars.' I got the red polo-necked sweater from the drawer and shook it out. She still said nothing but went on smoking her cigarette and watching me. 'Still, I'll probably need five hundred dollars' worth of dinars to pay hotels and so on and if I can get that amount for three hundred or even three hundred and sixty-six dollars – if he won't up the discount – I'll do it.'

I straightened my hair, put on my coat, kissed her unyielding lips lightly and turned to go. 'I'll be back in an hour or an hour and a half – will you wait for me?' I hoped to God she'd refuse but God must have had other things to do.

'Do you want me to wait?'

'Oh yes', I lied, 'very much, chérie.'

'Perhaps I will, perhaps I won't – anyway now I'll sleep a little.' She snuggled down in the bed. I thought she wasn't going to take the bait, but then she stopped me at the door.

'Georges?'

'Yes?'

'Ask you friend what rate he will give for cheques de voyageur in French francs.'

'Okay. How many?'

'Oh enough to pay the bill here. Thirty – no, forty, forty thousand francs' worth.'

'Right – he leaves tomorrow morning though.'

'Okay – if the rate is right I will sign them and give them to you at breakfast.'

Normally I wouldn't take traveller's cheques because she would report them stolen and I'd have to sell them at a discount in the right quarter, and I had no such contacts nearer than Nice, but I was pretty sure friend Leskova would take them off my hands and at quite a modest discount since he needn't know there was anything wrong with them. I'd have to stall Claudette for a day somehow – she knew that I was going to Rijeka to the British Consul early that morning and would probably agree to wait until my return in the evening for her dinars.

I would go to the Consul, swear a deposition or whatever to get the temporary document, good for perhaps a week, after which I'd either have to go to another British Consul or return to England. Actually I'd keep going by bus – the most anonymous way of travelling – back into Italy (as George Kelly) and back via Genoa to Nice, where I'd pick up my real George Kelly passport from Peter and report to the Consul there that I'd 'found' it.

It was dangerous as I'd then have the Yugoslav police looking for George Kelly; the Italian police looking for Colonel Rokesby-Gore; and an irate Leskova looking for both. There was still, of course, the ten thousand dollar proposition he was offering me, but the only things I could think of for that sort of money were murder or smuggling heroin and I was certainly very far from being a hit man, nor would I risk ten to twenty years at my age in a Yugoslav or any other prison for any amount of money. Anyway I'd soon find out what it was all about.

15

A T THE ENTRANCE to the casino I had to show my passport to get the card which would allow me to gamble, since Yugoslav nationals are not allowed to. The hard-faced man sitting at a small table refused to make an exception even when I explained that the authorities knew I'd lost my passport. Really I was glad since I didn't want to gamble. I understand enough mathematics to know when the odds are unbeatable – and I now had an excuse which wouldn't make my Colombian mark think that I couldn't afford to lose a few hundred dollars at the tables.

But as a hotel guest – I showed my key and a little card they'd given me – I could go into the casino. After a quick look through a fat, indexed-ledger to check my name against their undesirables, I was passed through.

There were not many people, less than twenty, and most of them were playing roulette at the one wheel which was operating; at the craps table a man in a black lounge suit was apparently playing but I spotted him for Security – I've developed a sixth sense about cops, house dicks and the like. All the places at the baccarat table were taken and among those waiting for a chair was Josefina Alsinas, who couldn't be missed. She was an extraordinary sight in a lime-green dress which was painful to the eyes and shaped like a circus tent and, I realized as I got closer, had a flower design in seed pearls. She wore an emerald necklace, the dark green of which fought against the horrible colour of her dress. From her head a high gold and tortoiseshell comb stood up like a crown. I couldn't resist looking down at her shoes, which were gold – probably real gold, I thought.

She waved a fan at me. 'You are a naughty man! You have kept me waiting – what were you doing – something very naughty, eh?'

Oscar was standing beside her in his beautifully cut dinner jacket, white handkerchief's three points showing and a red carnation, which

I thought was overdoing it just a trifle. He looked the picture of boredom but smiled at me politely.

'No, nothing naughty at all – I've just been going over the details of the deal I mentioned. As a matter of fact I'm meeting him here in about ten minutes.'

'The Minister?'

'No – but someone from him.' Unfortunately Comrade Leskova's appearance wasn't likely to impress anybody with his importance but, despite her ridiculous way of dressing, I had a hunch that Sra Alsinas was too sophisticated to judge people by their appearance.

'Well until he comes shall we gamble a little? My game is baccarat – and you?'

'It is the only game, but alas my passport has disappeared and they will not give me a card.'

'I will bet for you if you wish.'

'I am superstitious about gambling; someone else's money always brings me bad luck – but I'll give you moral support.'

'Only moral?' She tapped me with her fan. 'Am I so fat then?'

Ye Gods, I thought, what is this place – a refuge for ageing nymphomaniacs?

'I like women who are well covered. They are much warmer.'

'For cold nights eh? But it is warm here.' I let that one go with an understanding smile.

She got a place at the baccarat table and when the shoe reached the player on her right she cried 'banco' and while he made five successive eights or natural nines, she didn't let anyone else have a bet. As he didn't take out a single chip it meant that he had won thirty-one times his original stake. I couldn't see what value the counters were so I didn't know how much that was. Then, as it was obvious that she would go on covering the lot as long as he left it there, he prudently took his winnings and passed the bank to her.

She made a bank of a hundred thousand dinars but only about a third of it was taken up. She lost steadily but kept up a flow of light chatter; she might have been playing tiddlywinks for boiled sweets for all the concern she showed for the, to me, vast sums of money she was pouring away.

'Are you waiting for a place, Mr Kelly?' I recognized the voice.

'No – I've lost or mislaid my passport so cannot play.' He looked much more respectable than he had on the bus. Now he wore a dark blue suit, a very white shirt and a loyally red tie.

'And I cannot play because I am a Yugoslav, so . . .' He pointed to a small table with two chairs in a corner. 'A coffee and slivovitz, perhaps?'

I nodded and excused myself to Sra Alsinas, saying that perhaps her luck would then change.

'It could not get worse,' she replied cheerfully, giving Leskova an assaying look. 'You will come back?'

'Assuredly.'

After the little strong black coffees and even smaller glasses of slivovitz had come I decided to take charge of the situation.

'All right – you know that I am here under a different name than the one on my passport, but there are reasons for that and they're not the ones you think. They have to do with security, security on a very high level and something which it would not be wise to concern yourself with.'

He smiled. 'I might have believed you if it had not been for a telephone call I had tonight – from Inspector Kovaks.'

'What did he want?'

'He told me that an Englishman about whom he was making some enquiries had my visiting card . . .'

'And?'

'So I asked the name of the Englishman and he said George Kelly, so . . .' He shrugged his shoulders.

'So? So you told him that wasn't my name, I suppose!'

'My dear friend and, I hope, colleague, of course I didn't say anything so indiscreet! I merely said that we had met on the Trieste bus and that I had given you my card – without asking you your name, and that, you may remember, was true – in case I could be of any help to you should you come to Ljubljana.'

'What did he say to that?'

'He asked me if I would be good enough to come and see him in the morning at ten-thirty and make a full statement. When the police here ask you politely you go, believe me.'

'So you'll go?'

'No – because by that time you and I will be a long way from here – that is we will if you are the man I think you are.' He sat back and looked at me.

'Let's stop beating about the bush. What is this proposition of yours? I'll tell you again that if it's drugs you can save your breath.'

He lifted up his hands in horror. 'Never! I have never been so

148

foolish. No, it is not drugs, although in a way it has acted like a drug for many men.'

'What has, for God's sake?'

'Gold.'

'Gold? What gold? Do you mean to rob a gold shipment or a bank? I'm afraid that's not for me either – not because of any scruples, just that I don't have that kind of guts – and I hate firearms and can't use them. I'd miss the side of a barn at twenty feet.'

'It's nothing as foolish as that. I know you are not the violent type any more than I am. No, my friend, you work with your brains. I do too. This is much more simple. All we have to do is to carry the gold out of Yugoslavia into Austria.'

'Is that all. How much gold?'

'Fifty thousand-gram bars – fifty kilos.'

'Fifty kilos!'

'Shh – you will attract attention. Yes, fifty kilos: twenty-five in each of two specially made suitcases, but you'll only have to carry them from the car into the customs hall and back to the car.'

'*I'll* have to carry them – what will you be doing?'

'Driving the car which you, an English colonel, have hired to take you sightseeing in the beautiful Austrian Tyrol.'

I don't know whether it was the excitement or shock or just the inevitable working of the bacteria which had evidently joined the malarial bugs, but suddenly I had no more time. I shot out of my seat and almost ran to the door, trying at the same time to keep the cheeks of my arse tightly closed.

Leskova must have thought I'd panicked and was making a run for it, for he kept close to me.

'A W.C. for Christ's sake,' I gasped to him. 'Quickly – where is it?'

He snapped something to the man at the entry desk who looked doubtful and then, when Leskova said something else in an urgent voice, grinned and opened a door at the side. I hurled myself through it and into the W.C. cubicle and dropped my trousers frenziedly.

I sat there for a long time after it was strictly necessary feeling quite suicidal. I would have swapped my circumstances for a decent cell in a decent prison with, say, a couple of months to do. But I knew it would be a lot worse than that and I couldn't see that really I had any choice – I'd have to play along with Leskova. I would however find out more about this crazy scheme. Twenty-five kilos is fifty-five pounds give or take a few ounces, and the suitcase and other contents must weigh another ten pounds at least. I'm fairly strong, but carrying sixty-five or seventy pounds from each arm – and trying to conceal their heaviness – would be more than I could manage.

When I came out I was not surprised to find Leskova right outside the door.

'Are you all right?'

'I think so – for the time being, but it could happen again in twenty minutes or half an hour – and go on like that at least for the rest of the night.'

'I have something that will stop it – don't worry.'

We went back into the casino, which had a few more customers. Our little table was occupied so we walked over to one of the closed roulette wheels, out of earshot, although most gamblers are so engrossed with their play and their ridiculous systems they wouldn't take it in if you were standing next to them discussing an imminent bomb explosion. I did however notice that one of the plain-clothes security men was watching us curiously.

'This gold – the fifty kilos – is it stolen?'

'Good heavens no! It has taken its owner a long time to collect – with my help. Now he wishes to get it out and to get himself out.'

'Why?'

'You must not ask too many questions, it can be very dangerous. I will tell you this but no more; since Marshal Tito's death there has been a hidden struggle for power among his former associates. My friend now knows he is on the losing side and he wants to get out of Yugoslavia while it is still possible.

'Actually his leaving is no problem. He will fly to Vienna for the opera taking his wife just as he has done several times in the last year or so. Although as a V.I.P. he will not have to undergo customs formalities he knows very well that his and his wife's overnight bags will have been secretly examined.'

'So he has to get his gold out some other way, eh? Can't you smuggle it out over the mountains?'

'Too dangerous, there are men there who would cut their children's throats for one kilo of gold. No, the safest way is the one I suggested to him, in a tourist's baggage, a well-off respectable English tourist with a rank, a colonel. And for that tourist in Vienna there will be ten thousand dollars in good, convertible Austrian schillings waiting.'

'What if I'm caught?'

'Well it will be unpleasant for both of us – remember I am driving the car you've hired – and you will go to prison but not for as long as I will, nor in so bad a prison. We treat tourists better than our own people even in jail.'

I thought hard. It was certainly true that I couldn't remember when last a customs official had done more than make me open one bag and had then just riffled through it. Also I couldn't really see that I had any choice. If I said no, Leskova would shop me – of that I was reasonably sure – and even if by some miracle he didn't I was still in a nasty mess with a determined and suspicious police inspector investigating me. I sighed.

'When is this to take place?'

He looked at his watch. 'In twelve hours or a little less the owner of the gold will catch the plane from Ljubljana to Frankfurt, where he will change for a plane to Vienna. There he will wait for us. He is not a man to be kept waiting and in case it has crossed your mind that fifty kilos of gold can solve a lot of life's problems – you wouldn't live long enough to have any problems to solve.'

'If he's that powerful why does he need you and me?'

'Because he trusts nobody but me – for reasons I cannot tell you. I can tell you this: the work in which he has been engaged since the war is of a kind which makes it very easy for him to have you eliminated.'

'How do I know that he won't do it anyway – once he's got his gold?'

'It would be foolish. You are no threat to him as long as you don't know who he is – and you won't know. The gold is worth over half a million dollars so the ten thousand dollars to each of us is chickenfeed, and as long as he is sure you don't know who he is he'll be glad to see you get paid and on your way. Now we must go. Pack your bag – no, just leave everything; I am afraid that if you try to check out, the hotel might think it necessary to tell the police because of the irregularity with your passport. You have it hidden away? You will need it to get into Austria.'

And will the Austrians be on the lookout for Colonal Rokesby-Gore I wondered. Well, there was no help for it, I'd blackmailed enough people to know when I was the victim myself.

'Banco!' I heard Sra Alsinas shout, and I glanced over and saw by the pile of counters in front of her that evidently her luck had changed. She looked up and caught my eye.

'I'll just say goodbye to my friends and then come to you – in your room?'

'No – meet me at my car. It is a white Fiat . . .' he scribbled a number, 'parked down the driveway to the left. How quickly can you be there?'

'Give me half an hour.'

'I will be waiting there in twenty minutes – try to get there by then as it is a three-hour drive to Ljubljana, where we will change cars.' He hurried away.

I walked over to Sra Alsinas, who gave me a great pile of counters of different colours.

'Cash these in for me please – I don't know how much, but I know I am winning.'

I took them but looked around for Oscar.

'I have let him go to keep an assignation – he must have a little time for his affairs too and he is now involved with one of the boys from the beach – a pretty boy like him.'

That, I thought, explains why he is allowed to share his step-mother's room.

I brought her back her cash – just over two hundred thousand dinars – which somehow she stuffed into her silver evening bag.

'Now,' she said, patting the chair next to her. 'Tell me about your big deal – you can trust me. I know how to keep my mouth shut.'

'Groundnuts,' I said. God knows where that came from, but I knew I wasn't up to uranium or plutonium or whatever they use in nuclear reactors.

'Groundnuts?' she said. 'You mean peanuts?' She pointed to a dishful on the table. 'Why – and where from?'

'There's a great shortage of cooking oil in Yugoslavia,' I said, thinking up the story as I went along. 'A crop failure . . .' – I hoped she wouldn't ask me what crop – 'and the Government has decided to buy five million dollars' worth of groundnut oil.' It seemed a good round sum.

'From where?'

'That I can't tell you but it is an opportunity to make a great deal of money by buying up the groundnut crop before the news gets out.' I rather liked the sound of that. 'Negotiations are already under way but, of course, the Minister cannot deal himself, so I am leaving within the hour by car and will catch a plane tomorrow morning for Geneva and then be on my way to Africa.' I remembered vaguely that when I was at school there was some scandal about a scheme to grow groundnuts somewhere in Africa.

'What do you get out of it – a commission?'

152

'Yes, three and a quarter per cent.' And odd figure like that carries conviction. 'But since the Minister's little group can't buy all the groundnuts on offer and the proposition is an open-ended one I'll be allowed to deal on my own account and to cut in my friends – I act for a number of people in Geneva, Amsterdam and Tel Aviv when opportunities like this come my way.'

'What do you charge?'

'Ten per cent on the net profit on the first fifty thousand Swiss francs; five per cent after that.' It came out so pat I nearly convinced myself.

'How much do you think will be available this time?'

'The crop itself runs into two to three million dollars and even with the Minister and my friends we won't cover more than fifty to sixty per cent of that.'

'What rate of profit?' Her shrewd little eyes never left mine but I looked straight back at her, a frank, honest gaze.

'It's hard to say – but twenty-five per cent in one month is a conservative estimate.'

'Can I come in?'

'Well, I don't really see how – we work with an irreversible letter of credit which I get from my bankers in Geneva. I'll phone the people I act for in the morning and they'll transfer the amount they want to invest within an hour or two – I've got to be on my way from Geneva by tomorrow afternoon – there's really no time for you to contact your bank, I'm afraid.'

'Don't be so sure.' She sounded annoyed – there's nothing like seeming reluctance to make them gulp the hook greedily. 'Anyway I suppose you'd take cash, wouldn't you?'

'Cash?' I said as though it were quite a new word. 'Well – I *suppose* so. But surely you don't carry large amounts of cash, do you?'

'I do as a matter of fact in a secret compartment in one of my many suitcases, locked with a combination only I know. I don't believe in giving the banks money for traveller's cheques, which are a nuisance anyway. I prefer cash.'

'How much do you want to invest?'

'I think – as we have only just met and don't really know each other – yet,' she smiled coquettishly, 'that I will keep it rather small – say ten thousand dollars?'

'All right.' I tried to sound as though it were the sort of sum I usually spent in an evening.

'And I get back my money plus twenty-two and a half per cent in one month?'

'About that – perhaps a little more or a little less.'

'All right.' She rose up like some weird tropical plant. 'You are in 318, aren't you? I will bring it to you in ten minutes.'

'No – I'll come to you.'

'No – I am not sure that we would be undisturbed in my room.' She chucked me under the chin with her fan and floated away, an escaped kite.

I let myself into my room hoping to hell that Claudette had gone, but she hadn't – she was still in my bed and still naked.

'I've got to leave almost immediately, Claudette, I'm driving to Ljubljana tonight.' I dived into my suitcase, got my passport out from where I'd hidden it and stuffed it in my jacket pocket, hoping she hadn't realized what it was.

'But why, Georges, why?'

'Groundnuts,' I said desperately. I just couldn't think up another story. 'It's a long story – a big deal – Geneva and Africa . . .'

'What about the marché noir dinars . . .?'

'That'll have to wait until I come back . . .'

'You are coming back?'

'Yes – I'm leaving all my baggage here. I just have to make a quick trip to Geneva . . .'

'And Africa? You said Africa.'

'No – I'm not *going* to Africa – but the deal had to do with Africa, you see . . .'

There was a light rapping on the door – it couldn't have been ten minutes since I left Josefina. Claudette had shot out of bed and was hurriedly grabbing up her clothes.

'Who is it?'

'Josefina Alsinas – let me in.'

'Just a minute while I put something on,' I said, desperately waving at Claudette who was obviously furious.

'It's not necessary – I shall not be shocked.' She rapped again impatiently. Claudette started to go into the bathroom but instead I steered her into the W.C. by the door.

'Easier to slip out,' I whispered into her ear. She jerked herself angrily away from me. I shut the W.C. door quietly and opened the entrance door to Josefina who had changed again, this time into what looked to me like a dressing-gown which floated around her as though

154

she were wrapped in a light blue cloud through which I could see the outline of a shortie nightdress, while on her feet there seemed to be cottontail rabbits.

'But you *are* dressed,' she said, closing the door and putting the safety lock on. 'You were teasing me!'

'You didn't come through the hotel dressed like that, did you?'

'Of course not – I have the suite across the hall – didn't you know that?' She sat on the bed and let the light blue material float open to reveal two knees like pumpkins. 'Here it is – one hundred hundred-dollar bills, ten thousand dollars.' She put the fat brown envelope on the bedside table. 'You can count it later,' she said firmly, kicking off her shoes and swinging her legs up on to the bed.

'But I told you – I have to go – there's no time.'

'There is always time for love,' she said, grabbing my hand and placing it on her enormous breasts. 'You Englishmen! You are always slow to get started, but later – ! She was holding my hand like a vice. I was listening for sounds of Claudette letting herself out but I couldn't hear anything.

Of one thing I was quite certain: there was nothing known to man – or woman – that could enable me to perform again if my life depended upon it. If it weren't for the packet of lovely money sitting on the bedside table I think I might have called to Claudette and let them do battle over me. As it was, I would have to fake it.

She got out of the dressing-gown and dropped it on the floor, at the same time kicking off the cottontail slippers. She lay on top of the bed looking like the Michelin tyre man and crooked a fat finger at me but then, as I lowered myself on to the bed wondering desperately how to begin, she swung her legs off and got to her feet.

'Damn! I need the bathroom, the toilet. Where is it, over there?'

'No! No, please . . .'

'Ah, you are so impatient! But you must wait till Mama make pee-pee.' She waddled towards the W.C.

'Wait! – it needs cleaning, wait just a moment.'

She had her hand on the door when there was a thunderous knocking on the main door next to it. 'Maman, maman, vite vite, viens-toi!'

'Oh my God, what next!' I shouted through the door, 'Go away, Alex, your mother is not here.'

'I know she is with you. I saw her go into your room. Quick, she must get out before the police get here.'

My Colombian beauty had seized her dressing-gown as soon as she heard Alex's voice. Now the W.C. door opened and Claudette came out.

'The police! What do they want with you, eh?' She unlocked the door and a very worried-looking Alex pulled her out just as the indicator arrow above the lift started to move up. I slammed the door, locked it and put on the security chain.

Josefina had her dressing-gown on inside out and was struggling to change it around while keeping a tight hold on the packet of hundred-dollar bills.

'What was Madame de Crespigny doing in your toilet, you puto? Why are the police after you? Oh what a scandal!'

I grabbed her and kissed her hard while she held the money behind her back.

'I can't explain but I am British Secret Service . . .' they were already hammering at the door, ' . . . and the Reds are after me . . .'

'The Reds?'

'Yes – the Communists and they mustn't find the plans . . .'

'The plans – the groundnuts?'

'No, not the damned groundnuts – secret plans, like 007.'

'Ah!' At last she understood. 'Like 007!'

'That's right – now lock yourself in the bathroom and scream for help, pretend that I am in there with you. That will give me time to get away.' I pushed her into the bathroom. 'Lock it and start screaming.'

She did – most convincingly. I dropped from the balcony to the one below, moved across two more and found one that was open to the room. Fortunately the occupant was in the shower, singing something from *The Barber of Seville* at the top of his voice.

I walked swiftly across his room and opened the door. There was no one about but a great commotion on the floor above.

Walk, don't run, to the nearest exit, I told myself.

16

I WENT QUICKLY AND quietly down the back stairs to the ground floor; I was tempted to walk across the lobby and straight out the front but at that hour I'd be conspicuous. Also the night clerk and the watchman would undoubtedly know that the police had gone up to arrest the Englishman in 318.

A further flight of stairs led down to the bar with the slot machines from where I remembered having noticed a door into the back garden. It was dark and dead down there – obviously the bar had been shut for hours and its door was locked. At the back of the hall double doors led to a ballroom cluttered with old furniture. It had windows but they were barred.

I began to feel trapped. There was only one more door, a small one under the stairs which looked as though it led to a broom closet but, I was relieved to find, opened into a little scullery. Here there was a window without bars, secured instead by a padlocked catch. The lock was only a small one but I had nothing to force it with. Frenziedly I opened drawers, turning over soap, rags, worn brushes, chipped saucers and, at last, a butter knife with a broken handle.

It was not strong enough to snap the padlock but the end was rounded and I thought I could use it to unscrew the hasp from the window's edge. The screws were stiff but I didn't allow myself to hurry, holding the end of the knife firmly in the screw slot and slowly increasing the pressure until it moved.

As I was working on the last screw, the garden floodlighting went on and a number of men came out of the hotel and began searching. My window was partly below ground but I shrank back nevertheless. They looked for not more than two or three minutes, as the garden wasn't large and there were few places where a man could be concealed. Someone shouted; they ran back into the hotel and the lights went out. I took out the final screw, pulled the hasp away from the wood and opened the little window. Thankful I wasn't a big man, I squeezed through the narrow space and scrambled up into the garden.

I ran along the side of the bushes to the opposite corner where there was the path to the bridge to lead guests safely over the main road to the beach. I hurried along the sand, keeping out of the light from the road until I was opposite the driveway to the hotel. I stopped and looked for movement but it seemed deserted; probably they had searched there first. There were no cars about and no one in sight as I darted across the road and made my way up the driveway back towards the hotel from which I had just escaped, my heart pounding, my mouth dry, my head hot and aching and my damn bowels bubbling musically again.

Where was the white Fiat? There! and Comrade Leskova was standing by it looking towards the hotel from which he expected me to emerge.

'Pssst!' He whirled round. 'Here I am – the police are after me. Start your engine.'

'No – come and get in the boot first. Then I won't have to stop.' He opened the boot, took out a suitcase, some tools, a jerrycan and a few other odds and ends and began throwing them on to the back seat. I slipped along in the shadow of the bushes. 'Quick – get in here,' he said, pointing to the dark boot.

I climbed in and curled up in the smallest possible space, hands and arms crossed in front of my chest, knees drawn right up. It's the way I sleep when I'm alone and which yet another prison trick cyclist once told me was called the foetal position and was supposed to be significant. Leskova slammed the boot shut and my eyes and nostrils were filled with dust. The smell of petrol and oil was so strong I was sure I would vomit if I had anything left to vomit. The engine started, adding exhaust fumes to the other smells. The car moved off and after a few minutes of level driving began to swing from side to side, banging my head against protruding metal pieces. I realized that he must be going up the road which climbs out of Portoroz in a series of hairpin bends to join the main road.

I stuck the discomfort as long as possible and then I banged on the back of the rear seat and shouted as loudly as I could. Finally he stopped and opened the boot.

'What *is* the matter for God's sake? Don't you realize that we *must* drive as fast as possible? It's only a matter of time before that policeman realizes my car has gone!'

I climbed out, angrily resisting his attempts to push me back. 'I've got to shit!'

'Shit? Oh – well, hurry up.'

I squatted by the side of the road and asked him for some paper. He gave me an oil-stained bit of newspaper. I pulled my trousers up and marched round to the front seat.

'Where are those pills you said you had?'

He said something in Slovenian which I am sure wasn't a blessing and grabbed his suitcase, opened it and produced a small round tin which he thrust at me.

'Here – take four now and chew them up; four more in four hours. Quick – and then get back in the boot.'

I popped four tablets in my mouth and chewed them into a dry paste. I wanted something to wash them down but thought I'd better not push him too far.

'I won't ride in the boot,' I said firmly, getting into the front passenger seat. 'If we are stopped it's the first place they'd look and then we'd have no chance of talking our way out. If I'm sitting in the front in plain sight it doesn't look suspicious.'

'Well – perhaps you're right but I'd better put some of these things back. We've lost our head start now anyway – this car won't do much over a hundred kilometres an hour and even if they don't start after us for half an hour or so they'll easily catch us in a police car.'

He pushed the little car to the limit along the good road to Ljubljana which we reached just as the sky was getting light, having encountered a number of heavy lorries but no other cars.

Outside Ljubljana he swung off the main road and cut, right and left, through a number of back streets, coming at last to a small house with a driveway into which he turned. An abandoned truck was rotting at the end and he pulled off the driveway on to the yellowed grass of the back garden.

'Wait here.' He jumped out and disappeared into the house. Although it hadn't quite been four hours, I took four more tablets, which seemed to be working. But I was shivering again, my head was throbbing and seemed on fire. It was a cloudy, sultry morning and I felt as though I were floating a few inches above the ground. For a moment I wondered if all this weren't really a nightmare. But the discomfort and the pain of my headache were too real for a dream.

Leskova came out of the house, in which a light had appeared, accompanied by another, much larger man. They were carrying what looked like a carpet but which when they began to unfold it I saw was a tarpaulin.

Leskova pulled his suitcase out of the back of the car and told me to get out.

'We must conceal the car,' he hissed. 'Hurry, hurry!'

The tarpaulin completely covered the little Fiat and the three of us got into the front of a small truck which should have been in a museum and drove for about twenty minutes in what seemed to me to be a wide circle, before stopping at the corner of a quiet street of houses sitting in their own gardens. Leskova and I got out and the big man drove on. We walked a couple of hundred yards and then turned into a well-kept entrance and rang the bell.

The door was opened immediately and we stepped inside an oak-panelled entrance hall. The man who had let us in handed Leskova a chauffeur's cap and coat without saying a word.

Leskova indicated that I should follow and led the way to a large kitchen with a scrubbed wooden table.

'We are behind schedule, so please drink some coffee, eat some bread and confiture, and then we must go.'

'I must wash.'

'Yes, of course.' He pointed to a door which led to a tiny room with a cracked mirror, a doll-sized corner wash-basin and two antique brass taps, from one of which I got some lukewarm water. There was a bar of yellow soap and a roller towel and I managed to make myself look reasonably presentable, even to combing out my tangled hair. I returned for a big, hot and very welcome cup of coffee.

In the garage there was a black saloon car, not more than five or six years old and in chauffeur-maintained condition. Leskova, in his chauffeur's uniform, bowed, opened the back door for me and then got in the front himself, evidently deciding to start playing his part. We drove quietly off.

'Where is the gold?' I asked.

'We pick it up in Bled,' he said over his shoulder. 'It's above an hour's drive so you can get some sleep – you look as though you need it.'

The car was better sprung than the Fiat and the back seat comfortably upholstered. Although I felt ill – I knew it was much worse than a dose of the trots – the exhaustion of the last twenty-four hours (it had, I realized, only been that long since I had awakened in my Trieste hotel) overcame me and I fell into a deep sleep. I was awakened by

Leskova shaking my shoulder. I felt miserable.

'We are nearly at Bled,' he said. 'You were having a bad dream and you are very hot and your eyes are bloodshot. Have you ever had typhus?'

'No. Why? Do you think that's what's wrong with me?'

'I don't know – when did you last have an anti-typhus injection?'

'Years ago.'

'Mmmm. Well, we will be in Austria by this evening and I will take you to the nearest doctor. There is no other way with our police looking for you. Here, wipe your face and forehead – you are covered with sweat.' Leskova handed me a large, clean handkerchief, which became damp and stained. 'Keep it,' he said.

There were no clouds and the sun heated the inside of the black-roofed car until it was like a sauna; the air which came in the open windows seemed to have no cooling effect.

At the outskirts of Bled, which lies along a small, beautiful lake, Leskova pointed to a big house surrounded by a high wall. Sentries guarded the entrance.

'Tito's summer residence,' he said. 'Or rather it used to be. He would come here to escape the heat of Belgrade – much worse than this. When he came then the whole "court" followed him, all the high officials and those seeking favours. But since his death we only get the smaller fry here.'

'Like the owner of the gold?'

'Don't be curious – it is much better if you neither know nor even suspect who he is – better and safer.'

About a quarter of a mile from Tito's house Leskova turned right along a small winding road and followed it down into a valley for perhaps a mile before turning off along what seemed to be a farm track. A piece of a fertilizer bag had evidently been caught on a thorny bush and there he stopped, turning the motor off.

'We are late – but only forty minutes. We will have been seen – now we just wait. You can get out and stretch your legs – it will be your last chance until we reach the Austrian border.'

Wearily I got out of the car and staggered over to a tree, which I leaned my head against while I emptied my bladder. My urine was an orange-brown and smelled horribly – a sure sign that my body was fighting some kind of infection.

I found a place to sit against a fallen trunk and closed my eyes. If I could have summoned up even the smallest bit of faith I would have said a prayer, a prayer that my particular hell – and not only the present one but the purgatory of my life – would not go on for ever. But I knew that prayer was no answer for me.

After what seemed to be a long time, during which Leskova smoked but, thank goodness, did not talk, I heard the sound of a farm cart whose wheels needed grease, a sound I hadn't heard since I was a child. I opened my eyes.

Leskova had put out his cigarette and was standing looking back down the track. He had his right hand in his coat pocket and I wondered if he had a gun. Probably. I hoped desperately that he wouldn't have to use it; I didn't want anything to do with shooting or any violence.

From around the curve in the track, first a large grey horse and then an old wagon appeared loaded with hay. The driver was a gnarled man of fifty – or even sixty – with a leathery brown skin. He was smoking a pipe which he now put in his pocket – apparently still alight.

He and Leskova exchanged a few words and then went round to the back of the wagon and from under the hay pulled out something wrapped in burlap. When they took this off a quite new pillar-box red suitcase was revealed. Two more were produced, their protective coverings removed and stuffed back under the hay. The old man got up on the wagon again and turned it round in a space which I would have thought impossible. In a minute or so we were left alone with two medium-sized suitcases and one much larger one, all matching red.

Leskova took a folder out of the car and handed me three luggage labels from Thomas Cook.

'Fill these in with your name and address in England.'

I wrote – printed – Lt Col. R. Rokesby-Gore, DSO, The Manor House, Norley, Brockenhurst, Hants, England. Leskova tied them on.

'See if you can lift this,' he said, pointing to one of the medium-sized suitcases. I grabbed the handle and pulled; it seemed nailed to the ground.

'Try both at once,' he said. 'One balances the other. Bend your legs, not your back, and use your leg muscles to straighten up.'

I followed his instructions and somehow got both suitcases off the ground.

'Now walk to the car as though they were not heavy – concentrate! As though your life depended on it.'

I staggered towards the car thinking that my arms would dislocate at the elbows. He followed with the large suitcase.

'What's in that – more gold?'

'No – this is the bait. We will put the two with the gold on the back seat with you and you will seem eager to take them into the customs and will apparently want to leave this one in the boot. I hope that they will then want to look at this one which only contains clothes – with an English suit and English shirts on the top.'

'You've thought of everything.'

'We try to, but the clothes, I am afraid, are two or three sizes too large for you. We must just hope that the customs man is not that observant – he will, after all, have no reason to be suspicious.'

He put the large suitcase in the boot and began to put the others on the floor and back seat.

'Wait a minute,' I said. 'I want to see what's in them. I have to make sure it's not heroin.'

'That will not be possible. If we try and open the suitcases we will be in serious trouble. Don't look now, but you may have noticed that this track climbs up beyond us to a hill. We have been watched from there by a man with a rifle ever since we arrrived. He has orders if we try and open the suitcases.'

'Orders?' My mouth had gone dry.

'Gold worth so much is a great temptation and, as I told you, the owner is not a man to balk at a killing if he thinks he might lose it.'

I hesitated.

'Come – believe me, George . . .' He hadn't called me George before. 'It is *not* heroin. Why should we be so foolish as to make the suitcases so heavy? It is gold – pure gold.'

That seemed to make sense and in any case I didn't have any choice; the dice had been thrown and I was going to land on a ladder or a snake. God knows it was about time for a long ladder.

So I gave in and got in the back. He adjusted his chauffeur's cap and we drove back to the lakeside road and soon came to the little town of Bled with its castle perched high up across the water like a fairytale illustration. The streets were packed with people festooned with cameras and wearing an extraordinary mixture of clothes.

'Tourists!' Leskova spat contemptuously, but I wished I were one of them, staying in a lakeside hotel with nothing worse to worry about than the quality of the cooking. I began to think about a hotel in which Maria-Luisa and I had stayed, but I put her firmly out of my mind.

We drove through beautiful wooded country, past a river tumbling over rocks, and I dozed off, awakening when the car hit a pot-hole. We were climbing up a stony road not much wider than a cart track. Suddenly Leskova pulled off into a small clearing at the edge of woods.

'We'll take ten minutes or so to eat – I've brought food.'

I ate a tasteless, pulpy apple, a sweet orange and a pastry turnover filled with some kind of cooked meat. There was coffee from a thermos and delicious cold water from a stream.

'How do you feel, George?'

'Lousy – I think I'm dying. What I need is rest in a nice soft bed. How much further is it?

'Not far now – this road comes out about four kilometres from Tržič and just north of there is a village where there'll be a message for me to make sure we can get through the Loibl Pass into Austria.'

We reached Tržič just before two and a few minutes later came to a small village with a river running through it. Leskova disappeared into the only shop, which was also a bar, leaving me sitting in the hot back seat. He was gone for nearly fifteen minutes and when he came out he looked worried.

'They don't want us to go on to the main road to Klagenfurt but to go back to Tržič and take a back road west over the mountains to the road from Ljubljana to the Wurzen Pass into Austria – I don't like it.'

'Do you think someone has tipped off the customs here?'

'No – if that had happened the whole thing would be off. I'll do what they say, but be ready for anything.'

'What's that supposed to mean?'

Leskova just shrugged his shoulders and we drove back a couple of kilometres and then turned right, crossed a bigger road which pointed to somewhere called Kranj, and began climbing up a narrower, rutted and pot-holed road, arriving at a cluster of stone houses and a bridge over a nearly dried-up stream.

'Begunje,' Leskova said. 'Home of robbers . . . '

At that moment a man with a rifle slung across his back stepped out from behind an old truck and held up his hand.

Instantly Leskova slammed the accelerator down and the car leaped forward, revealing a power I hadn't suspected. There was a shout and, turning round, I saw the man running back down the road along which we'd come. A jeep-like car with three men in it came from somewhere and slowed down enough for him to scramble in the back.

We tore down a track that ran alongside the river, the car bouncing

164

so hard I banged my head on the roof.

'They're following us!' I shouted to Leskova.

'I know – get down!'

I lay on the back seat expecting bullets to crash into the car any minute. We were travelling at such speed that I was certain we'd break an axle, and sure enough there was a loud crack, followed by a tremendous thumping under the car, but we didn't slow down.

'A spring gone,' Leskova said. 'It's nothing – only not so comfortable.'

Comfortable! I thought as I was flung against the back of the front seat and felt my neck near to breaking. I took a quick look out of the back window and saw that they were gaining on us. I half expected to see one of them leaning over the side and firing a gun at us as I'd so often seen in the movies, but there was no sign of it. After all there were four of them and if they could catch us, as seemed inevitable, they had no need of guns.

The road dipped down and then curved sharply to cross the narrow brook over a wooden bridge. Leskova tried to brake but the rear of the car swung and hit the side of the bridge, and one wheel dropped over the side, spinning furiously as he pressed the accelerator.

It was quite hopeless. The bulge in the back axle was sitting firmly on the splintered board of the bridge.

We could hear the sound of the jeep closing the gap.

'Run!' Leskova yelled, leaping out of the car and running forward over the bridge. I jumped out but chose the wrong side and landed on my face in the brook.

'Come on, *come on!*'

I scrambled to my feet, sopping wet. The other car's brakes screeched as it came down the slope and round the curve and its driver saw our car spread across the narrow bridge.

I hadn't stopped to see what happened but as I scrambled up the bank on the other side I heard the crash. There was some screaming and I guessed that one at least of our pursuers was out of action.

'Keep up with me,' Leskova ordered and ran up the road for a hundred yards or so, then plunged off left through the trees. I followed and he zig-zagged in and out of trees until I didn't know in which direction lay the road we'd left.

Finally, as I thought my lungs were going to burst, he stopped and flung himself down. For a few moments neither of us could speak. I had a terrible stitch in my side and lay on my back with my arm across my face, feeling my wet clothes, which were the least of my worries.

'Who were they!' I asked as soon as I could talk.

'Friends,' he said grimly.

'Friends!'

'They work for the man whose gold they now have – or they did work for him. Now they will disappear – very rich and very frightened.'

'What will you do?'

'The only thing I can do is to make my way back to Begunje and see if I can hire someone to take me to Ljubljana. There I'll telephone to him tonight in Vienna and tell him what has happened and hope to God he doesn't think I had anything to do with it. I don't think he will because we belong to the same family.'

'What will he do?'

'He will have his weekend in Vienna; see the opera and come back and no one will ever know what he had planned to do. And the order will go out and those four will all die – it will take time but it will happen.'

I shivered. 'What about me?'

'You cannot pass through the border-crossing looking like you do and with no luggage – they would be bound to hold you for enquiries. But you can slip over the border by yourself if you are careful. It will be hard, though, very hard.'

I am not made for this sort of thing, I felt; I shouldn't be here in these damned woods miles from a bed or even a restaurant. Walk up and over the mountain without being seen and find my way into Austria? Who did he think I was, Daniel Boone?

But there was no choice.

'You'd better give me directions,' I said despondently.

17

'YOU LOOK BAD; I think you cannot walk for so many hours,' Leskova said. 'And if you can't go on up high there, you will die.'

'I don't have much choice, do I?'

'You can come back with me to Ljubljana; the police are not really after you.'

'What do you mean, not after me? Who was that hammering at my door, then; are you crazy?'

'That was the police but they were there because an anonymous phone call told them you were a marijuana dealer.'

'You?'

'Yes. I thought you would not go through with it so I start you running.'

'You bastard! I ought to kill you!'

He pulled down the corners of his mouth and gave a little contrite shrug; I wanted to hit him but I didn't have the strength. I think if there had been a piece of wood handy I'd have tried to smash his skull in. We stood looking at each other: I felt an overwhelming sadness at his contempt for me and I sat on the ground and leant back against a tree, quite hopeless.

'I don't know you then, George. I only want to use you; now it is different. I like you and we are friends.'

'You're no bloody friend of mine! I don't ever want to see you again! Now are you going to tell me how to get out of Yugoslavia or aren't you?'

'Of course. You must follow the river up the mountain for about five kilometres to where it comes out of the rocks. The way is steep; it will take you two or three hours. From where the river begins you must walk a little to the west of north and in about two more hours you will come to the Austrian State Forest. The frontier is its southern edge and is marked by a double fence. Make sure you are not in sight of any watch towers and find a place where you can wriggle under the wire. Don't touch it, for it may be electrified. There are no mines; Yugoslavia does not have an Iron Curtain. When you come out of the forest turn due west; you will come to a narrow country road. This goes to Feistritz, there a bigger road goes to Stau and Klagenfurt where you can get food and a bed and see a doctor. Can you follow those directions?'

I didn't think I could for a moment but there wasn't any point in saying so.

'I suppose so – which way is north?'

He laughed. 'Up there – here, look.' He held out his wrist-watch. 'It is nearly three; you point this hour hand towards the sun, so. South is along a line halfway from the hour hand and an imaginary line from the centre of the watch to the number twelve.'

'And to go north I turn a half circle, eh?'

'Yes, but line up something on the horizon which is due south so you'll know when you're facing north. Then pick another mark and when you reach it, get your bearings again. Do you understand?'

'Yes – except that I haven't got a watch.'

He handed his to me. 'You have now.'

I felt tears come to my eyes. How damn stupid! I wouldn't be in this bloody mess if it weren't for this man and now I was near weeping because he'd given me his wrist-watch. It must be because I was ill.

'Thanks, I'd better get going. Goodbye.'

'Goodbye, George. I'm sorry things go bad on us and you don't get your ten thousand dollars.'

'It wasn't your fault.' It was, but what the hell.

He turned me round by the shoulders and pointed. 'That middle tree of the three on the skyline is your first mark. Keep your eye on it; if it goes out of sight when you drop down choose another mark. Don't hurry – you have to wait for dark anyway and that's after nine at this time of year. Now – go.' He gave me a little shove and I started a journey which I can even now only remember vaguely.

I walked north – the song 'Freedom Road' sprang into my mind from somewhere – branches whipped across my face, thorns clutched at my clothes and tore the threads, I fell down, lay for a little while, got up, got my bearings and stumbled on. My fever came and went, changing places with shivering spells. I ate four more tablets although my diarrhoea had stopped. I had a terrible thirst and drank water whenever I came across it. I became light-headed and sang songs I hadn't thought about for years until I realized that I mustn't sing, mustn't attract attention. As the sun sank I climbed up and up; suddenly the peak of a mountain cut the sun from view and I was immediately chilled. At the top a cold wind nearly cut me in two. I plunged down and it got steeper and steeper until at last I could only progress sitting down and choosing carefully the next few feet, fearful of falling, of breaking an ankle or a leg and lying helpless.

But I didn't fall and somehow I must have crossed the frontier – on the down slope of the mountain and on the high hills I came across many fences but none that looked like an international border. I saw a tower with a light in it and couldn't decide whether it was an observation post for the frontier or for fire-watching.

I stumbled on, fighting exhaustion, shouting once again, oblivious of danger; cursing the Fates, moaning my bad luck, then laughing aloud at my own ineptness. If anyone could have seen me he would have thought me quite mad and perhaps I was. I heard myself chanting 'You pick 'em up, Lawd, and I'll put 'em down.' Some old joke but was it a runaway slave or just a chicken thief? And for a long time I repeated a line from a half-remembered poem – 'And miles to go before I sleep. And miles to go before I sleep' – over and over again, keeping time to its rhythm.

My thigh and calf muscles seemed to be on fire; I longed to stop and stretch out on the ground but I was afraid that I wouldn't be able to get up again. I stopped talking aloud; I had no more breath for it. I gripped my lower lip between my teeth to cause an alternative pain and at last I came out from the dark trees into a field of ripening corn. As I plunged into it a dog began barking excitedly and a voice shouted at it in German. It wasn't proof positive that I was in Austria but it encouraged me.

From the corner of the field a path took me to a narrow dirt road. The sky was crammed with stars and I found the Plough and the North Star, lower in the sky than in Hampshire, and was glad to see that if I went right the road ran north-west. I was on course by some fluke.

After about a mile, probably less, I reached a hardtop road and an old wooden sign pointing to the right, Feistritz i Rosental. I couldn't remember Leskova's directions but I stumbled on through the sleeping village and came to what was obviously a major highway. Now where?

169

I heard a heavy-duty petrol engine in the distance and the sound changing as the driver double-declutched to change down. Then, to my left, I saw the reflection of its headlights. My first impulse was to hide, but as I was in Austria I didn't have to worry – no one was looking for me. I stood in the road and waved my hand as the bright lights picked me out. I left plenty of room for the big truck and trailer to pass me if the driver didn't want to stop. But I heard the hiss as he hit the air brakes and the great dark shape squealed to a halt. As the front of the engine passed me I saw that it carried Yugoslav licence plates.

'Oh God!' I said aloud but there was no way a truck driver could be looking for me. I hobbled as fast as my swollen feet would take me to the cab. The driver held the door open and shouted something at me which I couldn't understand.

'Do you speak English?' I gasped.

'A leetle – no vairy good. What you want?'

'Where are you going?'

'Wien.'

'Vienna! Can you give me a lift – can I come with you?'

'Okay – come, come.'

Somehow I climbed into the cab; he shut the door, shoved the gear lever forward, the air hissed out of the brakes and we moved off. It was lovely and warm inside the cab. I put my wrist under the dashboard light and saw that it was just before four o'clock. I had been walking for nearly thirteen hours.

'Where are we – wo ist . . . ?'

'Okay,' he said, 'Okay – we twenty kilometres nach Klagenfurt – two hours – maybe little more – to Graz. In Graz we stop for eat, okay?'

From then on I don't know what was real and what was part of my fevered imaginings or the troubled dreams I had when I dozed off. I think we really did stop somewhere and drink milky coffee and eat bread and cheese and I have a clear picture – like a remembered photograph – of standing with a number of other men in front of a row of wash-basins and shaving with somebody's straight razor, and nicking my chin, although I don't remember seeing a scab on my face later.

Because I was in a state of semi-delirium I didn't stop and see a doctor but kept moving, imagining, I suppose, that I was still being pursued. I don't think, at first at least, that I had any idea of where I was going, only that I knew I mustn't go to Italy because the police were waiting for me there and Maria-Luisa would be waiting with them to urge them on: 'Arrest him!' she'd shriek. 'Arrest the bastard!'

Later I remember riding in many buses – starting in Vienna at the main bus station, where my friendly truck driver dropped me off, and I bought a ticket to Salzburg. Later again someone changed some dollars for me – that was in Innsbruck I think – and there was a row because he cheated me and someone else saw it and made him give me more Austrian schillings.

Then as my bus went through the Arlberg Pass I remember singing loudly and all the passengers trying to shush me up. I thought it was a game until the driver stopped the bus and came back and slapped my face – not hard but hard enough to stop me. Then he laid a rough, calloused hand on my forehead and said something in a shocked voice. And I think it was at the bus station in Feldkirch that a woman bathed my head with eau de Cologne, but perhaps I just dreamed that.

Somewhere along my route there was a huge map on the wall of one of the bus depots and I worked out how to get to Martigny right over in the south-west of Switzerland. From there I could pass into France and rest safely. As soon as I'd got over my weakness and fever I'd go on to Nice and hole up with Pietro Piedmonti until I was well enough to start the damn game again.

I slept in buses or at bus stations; I washed in the clinically clean rest-rooms and lived on coffee and pastries and hard-boiled eggs and fruit. My route wasn't direct but I showed the list of towns at each stop and there was always someone kind enough to advise me about the next leg. I can't now remember crossing from Austria into Switzerland but I know I was puzzled by the number of times we had to go through a mountain pass and I remember once asking my neighbour if the large body of water on our right was Lake Geneva. He laughed and told me it was the Walensee and indicated with outstretched arms how much bigger Lake Geneva was.

Then somehow, quite unexpectedly, I found myself at the French frontier where I was asked a lot of questions because I had no baggage. I said I had been on a walking holiday and that my rucksack had fallen off a mountain side. The immigration officer smiled and called me 'Mon Colonel' in a tone which plainly implied that he thought I was mad. There was a bus for Chamonix waiting so I got in and at its destination walked into the first hotel. The desk clerk was suspicious but my good old Colonel Rokesby-Gore passport plus a show of money allayed his suspicions and I got a room. I had a hot bath, which didn't help – in fact I felt worse. I crawled into the bed and apparently woke up the whole hotel by shouting my horrors in the early hours of the morning.

A doctor was called who gave me a shot which put me to sleep for a very long time. I thought that I dreamt that someone dressed me and carried me downstairs and put me on the back seat of a car, and then that I was a passenger in a small aircraft doing aerobatics until I was thrown violently to one side and woke up to find myself staring at trees and blue sky from a car window.

I turned my eyes and saw the back of the driver's head and his hunched shoulders working as he whipped the car round a series of hairpin bends. I knew who it was.

'Hey!' I shouted, and as he turned for a quick look I saw that it was indeed Pietro Piedmonti.

'Feeling better, George?'

As I sat up my head swam.

'Yes – but where the hell did you come from?'

'You had my name and address in your passport so Dr Clancier phoned me.'

'Who is Dr Clancier?'

'The doctor the hotel called to see you, but don't worry about that. You've been very ill but you're going to be all right now. He says you must have plenty of sleep, so lie down again – we'll be in Nice in less than two hours.'

'Thanks, Pietro.' I fell back and dozed off again until we reached Nice and climbed up into the old town where he and his family lived. But he went past his street and into a richer district, stopping outside a glossy new block of flats whose porter came out and opened the door for me.

I was too weak to stand and Pietro and the porter had to help me to the lift. It stopped at the tenth floor and they half carried me to the door of one of the flats. Pietro rang the bell.

Maria-Luisa opened the door.

18

THE SHOCK WAS like a vicious blow to the stomach and I slumped; Pietro caught me by my arms and just for a second I thought she was going to drive her fist into my face. I couldn't help flinching.

'Bring him into the small bedroom, Pietro.'

I tried my best to walk unaided but my legs wouldn't hold up; Maria-Luisa took one arm and Pietro the other. The covers had been pulled back and I was let down gently on to the bed. Pietro started to take off my shoes but she stopped him.

'I'll take over now, Pietro; thanks for everything, you've been really great and now we're all square. You kept your part of the deal and I'll keep mine.'

'That's okay. You know I like George, and I didn't only help you because, well, because I had to. You understand?'

She nodded and shook his hand. He held my shoulder and pushed me slowly back on the pillow. 'Ciao, bambino, and you listen to this lady.'

I tried to put my gratitude to him into words but he brushed them aside, saying that he knew I would have done as much for him. I wondered if I would.

Maria-Luisa hadn't said a word to me directly and my mind was in a whirl. There were so many questions I wanted to ask; what was the deal she had mentioned, what was she doing in this obviously furnished flat, and why was I here – above all that question.

She'd taken off my shoes and socks and was now about to take off my trousers.

'Maria . . . '

'Save your breath,' she said brusquely but not unkindly. 'You look awful; you've had dysentery and God knows what else. It's complete rest and nothing but liquids until the doctor says different. That's how it's going to be so don't argue.'

She pulled my trousers off, got my coat off over my head and my shirt the same way. Sitting in my dirty underwear I felt like a naughtly child being sent to bed without any dinner.

She got a pair of new pyjamas from a drawer and tore off the plastic wrapping.

'Can you get into these by yourself?'

'Yes.'

'Well get into bed and I'll bring you a glass of milk.'

I dropped my underwear on the floor, put on the slightly starched pyjamas and slipped between crisp white sheets. I laid my hot head against the cool pillow.

Maria came back and put the glass of milk on the bedside table. 'There's a bedpan under the bed. Call me by pressing this bell if you need help with it.'

'Maria . . . ' I started again. She cut me short.

'Not now, George. We'll talk later when you've got your strength back.' She pulled the curtains to, cutting the bright sunlight to an orange glow. I fell asleep almost at once.

The next forty-eight hours or so are still rather hazy but I know she held me on the bedpan with my head on her shoulder and I know she gave me a thorough bed wash before her doctor came and examined me as though I were a cadaver in a laboratory. He either had no English or decided that I wasn't capable of answering questions, for he addressed all his remarks in Italian to Maria-Luisa as though she were the mother of a sick child.

When he'd gone I asked her if I'd had malaria. She said it was a bad case of dysentery, possibly amoebic. The doctor thought he could knock out what was left with some miracle drug.

'He says you can have a little solid food now – a boiled egg to begin with. Here – sit up.' She put her hands under my arms and I breathed in her familiar smell. She lifted me easily.

'You're nothing but skin and bones – you must have lost twenty pounds.'

I polished off the boiled egg with some bread and butter and tea and felt much better.

'Are you going to tell me what this is all about, Maria?'

'You're not ready yet – perhaps tomorrow. Now go back to sleep.'

She must have been right because I fell into a deep sleep almost immediately, but this time without any of the feverish dreams I'd been having, and I awoke just as the sky was beginning to lighten, feeling refreshed and almost myself again. I picked up my bedpan and went in search of the bathroom.

I opened the door to the next room and found the light switch. There was a similar door to mine directly opposite, across a room rather over-crowded with that iron and glass furniture so admired by some French. That, I guessed, was her bedroom. There were two other doors, one which led to the bathroom, where I emptied my bedpan and washed it out, and the other to the kitchen, where I found about a third of a long French loaf and, in the fridge, milk, butter, salami, olives, cheese, pâté and prosciutto. My hunger hit me but I knew that my stomach could not stand the onslaught of the kind of enormous sandwich I wanted to make and settled for bread, butter and honey and a glass of cold milk.

'Obviously you're feeling better.' Maria-Luisa stood in the doorway in a dressing-gown buttoned up to the neck. I felt like a schoolboy caught raiding the pantry and started to stammer something about feeling hungry, but she stopped me.

'I'm going to make some coffee – do you want some?'

'Please.'

She made herself some toast and poured two glasses of orange juice. The smell of percolating coffee was delicious.

The sun rose while we were having breakfast and, not talking, we watched the clouds turn from black to pink to white. I felt awkward, not knowing where to begin but not wanting the unclear situation to continue. I opened my mouth to start the questioning but she spoke first.

'How do you feel, George? Are you quite recovered?'

'Much better, thanks – practically my old self.'

'I hope not,' she said and we both laughed. That, I thought, was encouraging. 'It's time we had a long talk, but get dressed first – your clothes have been laundered and your suit dry-cleaned – you'll find it in the cupboard.'

Obediently I did as I was told and when I came out of my room a bit later there was a copy of the *International Herald Tribune* on the table, which I always enjoy. Minutes later she came in looking very fresh and, I thought, rather business-like in a white linen jacket and skirt.

She opened a packet of cigarettes, lit one, sat down and tossed them to me; I lit up and waited.

'Now I want the truth, George. I know about Dora Bukovski and

175

that ridiculous stamp but who else have you conned since you ran away in Venice?'

'How on earth did you find out about Dora?'

'When she complained to the police in Venice your name was fed into the computer and our little jail came out as the last contact. The Venice police phoned my friend the captain and he told them he'd let you go only two days before.'

'I see.' It seemed logical enough. 'But how did you know?'

'After I'd cooled down, which took a day, I decided a spell in prison wasn't going to do you any good. You were getting away much too easily. I went down to withdraw charges and was furious with that corrupt bastard for letting you go. I gave him hell and made him promise to let me know if he heard any more about you. So on Thursday he came and told me the Venice police were after you. Next day I drove to the airport and flew there. I found out from the police where Dora was staying, and there the other American couple, the Harrises, told me that she and Gino and Catherina had followed you to Trieste but lost you when you slipped into Yugoslavia.'

'How the hell did Peter get in the act?'

'No, that's enough from me – you tell me who else you've conned first.'

'Well . . . ' My imagination began to work.

'Now wait a minute, George! Before you launch into one of your fantasies, you should know that Pietro has told me a great deal. Now I want the truth from you, the whole-and-nothing-but kind. It's got to be like that between us from now on.'

From now on! What could she mean? I didn't dare let myself guess but I knew that I was very tired of running, sick to death of my game of Snakes and Ladders. I was ready for almost any other alternative; I decided to tell her everything that had happened since I'd left her; the kindness of the lavatory attendant in the Milan station, the conning of poor Dora, and the farce in Portoroz. Maria-Luisa had been listening with a stern face but when I got to my Parisienne and my Colombian discovering each other she laughed aloud and I was relieved: perhaps I wouldn't be caned, after all.

'For a hard-boiled criminal you're a bit of an idiot, you know. So the only woman you actually got any money out of since we parted was Dora Bukovski, eh?'

'Yes – that's the way it turned out.'

'Well I've paid her off . . . '

176

'What!'

'She wasn't going to give up the chase until you were behind bars or she had her money and her pride repaired.'

'But why did you, for God's sake?'

'Before we come to that there's something we've got to get straight between us.' This, I was sure, was the crunch. I nodded.

'On the surface, you're a pretty poor specimen of a man.'

If she was waiting for me to agree she could go on waiting. I was grateful for what she'd done but not ready to grovel.

'You're weak and ineffectual – you're not even a good con man.'

Well I nearly conned you, I thought.

'You're rootless and friendless – except for Pietro Piedmonti.'

'Some friend! Spilling his guts to you.'

'He is your friend: when you know the whole story, you'll know that.'

'Go on with taking me apart,' I said, 'if you get a bang out of it.'

'All right. You're so damned screwed up you're almost beyond repair.'

'Almost?'

'Yes. Now despite all that you're a nice guy underneath; you're charming, witty and intelligent and, as you well know, you've got sex appeal as well as good looks.'

'Thanks,' I said feeling a lot less angry, 'so what?'

'Well, for starters, you're in love with me, aren't you?'

'Of course,' I said promptly because it was the right answer but no sooner was the meaningless phrase out of my mouth than the astonishing realization came that it was true. 'Yes,' I said, 'damn it – yes!'

'That's good, because, God help me, I'm in love with you.' She smiled at me affectionately and for the first time in my life I had no words for a woman.

'So,' she went on in an almost matter-of-fact voice, 'it seems that we're stuck with each other for the rest of our lives.'

The rest of our lives, the rest of our lives! Surprisingly I wasn't dismayed.

'God – if it only could be, but that's a pipe dream, Maria. How am I to earn a living except as a con man? It's the only thing I'm fit for now.'

'I don't think that's so. Now I'm not trying to be mysterious but this is your first day up and you've had a shock, suddenly finding out that we love each other and that you're vulnerable. So let's postpone my plans for us.'

It was true. My defences were down; I wasn't ready to flee. If the door opened and the law walked in I'd go quietly. Perhaps, I thought, it was just the effects of the days of fever and dysentery; when I was really recovered the old George Kelly would boot the new one out.

'All right. I'll wait until tomorrow to hear this plan. I'll consider it but though you'll think it out of character, I'm not going to be kept by you – I'm a con man not a gigolo.'

She laughed. 'Actually that's not out of character at all; it would be a certain way to lose you and probably a good deal of my money.' She held up a hand to stop my protest. 'Oh, I know it's the farthest thing from your mind at this minute but, no George, never fear; I'm not going to keep you and you've done your last con. Now how do you feel?'

'Fine,' I lied. 'I'm my old self again.'

'I hope you never will be that old self. Anyway, take things easy for the rest of the day and if you feel up to it this evening we'll go back to that Spanish restaurant where we had our first meal together and you can tell me the story of your life – only the true one this time, Mr Kelly.'

The evening was a success; the gazpacho and paella tasted wonderful after what I'd been living on for days, and Maria-Luisa was enthralled with my life, especially the early years. I did try to leave out certain things but, as I've learned since, she is a born cross-examiner and she got everything out of me, even my having seen my mother and Lady Liz together and being taken to bed by my Aunt Colly and subsequently being beaten up by my uncle. From time to time she nodded her head knowingly, and once or twice I was surprised to see her eyes glistening with tears. She put her hand over mine and squeezed it, but said nothing.

The later adventures made her laugh, and I saw the funny side of some of them too. For the first time I thought that perhaps my bad luck hadn't just been bad luck. Of course I couldn't tell her everything that had happened to me over more than twenty years, but I covered a lot of it. I'd never told anyone the whole truth before, not even cellmates, who always lie to each other, exaggerating their successes and minimizing their failures, and I realized that I'd never even told myself the truth, because I'd always partly believed that in some way I was Colonel Ronald Rokesby-Gore, or that if I wasn't I ought to be.

By the time I'd got to our meeting in Peter's Bar it was after eleven and I'd talked myself out.

'Now it's your turn,' I said. 'Did you tell me nothing but truth about your life?'

'No, I didn't. I left out some bits I'm not very proud of and I promise I'll tell you everything some day, but not now.'

'All right but at least tell me how on earth you got hold of Pietro Piedmonti.'

'Oh that was easy. I realized on thinking it over how someone as experienced as I am could have fallen for that retired English colonel boloney; I remembered that it was Peter, the 'world-famous barman', who'd sold me on you and that you must be working together. So I got his home number from the hotel and told him I'd caught you red-handed. He was scared and I gave him a simple choice: either tell me all he knew about you and help me to find you, or I'd go to the police with the whole story.'

'Blackmail.'

'The blackest. But all's fair you know. He got his wife to say he'd been taken ill and found this apartment for me.'

'And told you the lot?'

'Yes – but not before he'd asked me why I wanted to find you. I told him the truth – that I wanted you, no matter what you'd been, because I knew I could make you give it all up – oh, not because I'd reform you but because you're not only a very bad con man, you don't really want to do it. Once Pietro realized that I wasn't after your blood he told me everything – your time in prison together, the victims you'd fleeced with his help – the lot.'

'And you still thought you could make me give it up – you still wanted me, after all that?'

'It just confirmed the conclusion I'd come to about you, George. I can't understand why I didn't guess it during the time we spent together. God knows I've read enough to recognize those fantasies you were always spinning for me. I knew at the time that most of them were lies but I was so happy with you I guess I just switched off my brain and common sense. And when Pietro told me about your victims – always middle-aged women, divorcées or widows, it all fell into place.'

'Oh it did, did it?' I was irritated, reminded of the smug assurance of the prison psychiatrists I'd always fooled. She put her hand on my arm.

'Don't be angry, George. Remember we love each other – hang on to that and you'll know I don't want to hurt you.'

'What is this great psychological analysis you've made then?'

'I don't want to go into all that, George, but just think for a moment – if all you wanted was to cheat some gullible woman why didn't you just pick a very rich and stupid one and live off her in comfort for the rest of your life?'

'That's not what I wanted.'

'I know it's not. So what was it you did want? Not money, George, that was incidental: that was why you always got rid of it so fast, so that you'd have to find another middle-aged woman to punish . . . '

I laughed. 'Why would I want to do that?'

'I don't know, George, you'll have to work that out for yourself. Perhaps as we tell each other all about ourselves we'll both understand why we are the people we are or, at least, partly understand. But it's really not all that important because that's all in the past and we're going to start together on page one.'

'It sounds wonderful, but how?'

'It mostly depends on you and I don't think this is the time to ask you to make decisions which will mean your life taking a whole new direction. You're very tired. I've kept you up too long. Let's go.'

Going up in the lift all I wanted was to sit on the floor. I wasn't quite sure where I was to sleep but she helped me into my room and into bed.

I pulled her down to me and we kissed gently. Then she ruffled my hair and pressed my head down on the pillow.

'Good night, George – we'll talk more tomorrow.'

Lying in the dark I wondered what extraordinary plans this extraordinary woman had for us. But I was content just to let myself go with the tide without, as so often in the past, lying awake with my head buzzing with schemes. I slept dreamlessly for the first time in many years just as I had as a child after an exhausting day.

I wasn't even startled when some time before dawn I felt a hand pushing me to one side of the bed. Somehow I knew that it was her and not danger. She got in beside me and our bodies fitted together like pieces of a jigsaw puzzle, her breasts pressing into my shoulder blades, her lips just touching the back of my neck, the front of her thighs lying firmly against the back of mine.

'Just lie still and let me hold you,' she said. 'I woke up frightened that you might be gone, but it's all right now; go back to sleep.'

I slipped back into the same dreamless, relaxed world and was awakened by sunlight on my face. When I called her she brought me a glass of orange juice.

'Get up and shower – breakfast in ten minutes.' I wondered if I had dreamt that she'd come into my bed but I knew that I hadn't.

'Right!' I said firmly after breakfast. 'Let's have it – your plan for us – I'm to learn a trade, is that it? Because that's all I can think of.'

'You underrate yourself, George. You haven't counted those assets I mentioned to which we can add that you have a bit of rough French, Italian and Spanish which could easily be improved.'

'What does all that qualify me for besides a Male Escort?'

'The hotel business, of course.' She looked at me triumphantly.

'The hotel business? But I have no experience – who'd have me?'

'Since we're now telling each other the whole truth, George, I have a confession to make – I have rather more than the twenty-five thousand dollars I told you about – I guess it was the old native caution on my part.'

'So you're rich – how does that change things?'

'No I'm not rich but I do have enough money to buy a very small hotel or a bigger boarding-house. Not here on the Riviera, but in England.'

'Why England?'

'Because after we are married we'll both be British and we should live in our own country.'

'Married?'

'Of course – you are going to ask me to marry you, aren't you, George?'

'Of course I am.'

'Well, hadn't you better do it?'

'Will you marry me, Maria-Luisa?'

'Yes I will, George Kelly, and what's more I'll make an honest man out of you.'

'Have you forgotton your thousand bucks a month alimony? Didn't you tell me that you'll lose it on remarriage?'

'Do you want to live, or even partly live, on Artie's money, George? If we just shack up together I'll be conning him and if you're going straight I guess I had better too. No, I'll let Artie off the hook and all the responsibility of making it will be ours – yours and mine. Okay?'

'Okay,' I said, 'Okay!'

19

So THAT'S HOW I come to be writing this book in our bed-and-breakfast house in Penzance – our 'last resort' as Maria calls it – in the slack time before our second summer season gets under way. It took us a long time to find something we could afford; Maria's money had not been enough to buy a small hotel; it might have been once but inflation had killed that dream. So we put up half the price of this Victorian pile, once a suburban vicarage, and borrowed the rest from our London bank at a terrifying rate of interest.

I say 'we' because one of the first things Maria did after we were married by the British Consul in Nice was to put all her assets into a joint account which will honour cheques drawn by either of us. I protested but she said I was going to have to quit cold turkey. I'm a bit surprised that I've never been tempted to draw out a pound; it might be because it would be too easy but I think there's more to it than that.

More than once I was tempted to chuck the whole thing up; it was such damned hard work! The house was 'in need of some repair and redecoration', as the charming young house agent had airily said. The first months were the hardest grafting I'd ever done; Maria taught me to strip, make good and paint walls, to take up and replace rotting floor-coverings and even to do some rewiring, which I wasn't at all keen about as I've always been afraid of electricity. I found out that she's a stern taskmaster; I had to strip the new paint off and start all over again in the second room I redecorated because I hadn't prepared the surface the right way. God knows how she could tell; it looked fine to me.

Although it's possible to take nearly a thousand pounds a week, that's only during the summer and the odd week or two in other holidays. So, until we've paid off the loan, things will continue to be very tight for us. We got everything done in time for last summer but we'd had to run up an overdraft of about five hundred pounds on top of our loan account.

We put out the BED AND BREAKFAST sign and held our breath but caught our first guest within an hour and by seven that evening were half full. We practically killed those first guests with kindness; we're more casual now knowing that we give good value.

That summer was one of the driest, hottest and longest for years. We put the NO in front of the VACANCY on our sign by tea-time most days up to the first week in September. Then as business dropped off sharply we let the two local girls go – they start again next week – and made beds and cleaned and took up the early morning tea and cooked and served breakfast ourselves. We were able to pay the September quarter's interest and repayment and still have quite a respectable credit balance in our current account.

By September we'd been exhausted and irritable with each other but as soon as we were rested it all came right again and we went back to making love, something we'd just about given up in the hectic summer months. The occasional commercial, saving money on his expenses, and some weekenders kept us just ticking over and we decided to give ourselves a treat at Christmas.

We took the train to Nice having asked Peter to get us a cheap hotel near where he and his family lived. Maria-Luisa and Marta got on as though they were old friends. We persuaded Marta to dress up and accompany us to Peter's Bar, where she'd never been. Peter 'forgot' to charge us for the drinks.

Of course we went to 'our' Spanish restaurant and ordered the same dishes; we knew we were being corny and we didn't care. We promised to spend every Christmas there if we can afford it but other people in the tourist business have warned us that a cold, wet summer might sink us so we'll wait and see.

January and February this year were great; the weather wasn't too bad and we enjoyed having the house to ourselves for most of the time. We did a bit of repairs and redecoration; I'm getting to be quite good at it and Maria says she'll teach me to hang wallpaper next.

It was during that time that I got the idea of writing this book. Maria approved and so every morning after breakfast I sit at a small table in our bedroom and write for about two hours until she brings me coffee and we talk about the book, which she says she'll read right through when I've finished it.

'What are you going to call it?'

'I thought – *Damned Scoundrel*, that's what old General Rokesby-Gore called me when he kicked me out.'

She laughed. 'Well he wasn't far wrong, was he?'

I don't think there's anything of importance in either of our lives that we haven't told each other: I know there isn't in mine. She'd had a much rougher time than she'd admitted when she told me her story in our trip through Provence two years ago – it seems longer than that somehow. She'd done some things of which she was ashamed but she says, and I want to believe it, that I've been good for her too. Watching me has made her watch herself is how she put it.

I'm not going to write about those confessions though; I've learnt that you don't have to put absolutely everything into a book no matter how honest you are determined to be, and anyway it's my story I'm telling and I don't have the right to expose Maria. I've tried to tell the truth about myself but not the whole truth, for I've left a lot out; so many cons in so many places, many things which happened when I was growing up which, I can now see, made me what I was for over twenty-five years. The important people I pretended to be while all the time unimportant George Kelly was imprisoned inside shouting to be let out. I couldn't hear him but somehow Maria did.

I'd be a hypocrite though if I didn't admit that sometimes I miss the excitement of a daring con, of the pursuit and the catching of the prey. But I no longer want to hurt women and I know that some of them were hurt more deeply than I allowed myself to admit.

We don't have many friends, none in fact, just people we chat with at the local or the supermarket; we're still 'new people' to most of them. I overheard the publican's wife refer to Maria as 'that Yankee woman' and wondered what they call me. Before lunch on Sundays in the off season we usually go to the Saloon Bar of the Royal Hotel and sometimes get into conversation with the guests, worldly people, with whom I can talk.

We seldom make close contact with our own paying guests but occasionally the relationship gets a little closer. One of our favourites last summer was a Mrs Lamb, a jolly middle-aged widow who worked in a shop, in Leeds I think. She was boisterous, full of energy and a great organizer of games and outings, a real asset in a B. & B. place like ours. She came back unexpectedly a couple of days ago for a week's stay. She'd had an enormous win on the pools and had fled the outstretched palms of family, friends and professional beggars. As she'd told us last year that she'd felt a right traitor at deserting

Blackpool for posh Penzance I asked her why she hadn't gone there.

'I like you, love, and Maria; she's a lovely woman and I decided it would be nice to see you both again. Besides, you being a man of experience in money matters, I thought you'd give me some advice about all that brass.'

I said I'd think about it. As she was the only guest and had taken our best front double we asked her to have the evening meal with us as well. We spread ourselves a bit with a joint of beef and Guinness, her tipple. Maria produced a box of After Eights with the coffee and Mrs Lamb brought up the subject of the money, nearly a quarter of a million pounds she had sitting in the building society.

'I want to do better than a building society but, mind you, it's got to be safe, I won't gamble.'

I told her that I'd draw up a balanced portfolio but I thought she ought to put about half in an off-shore dollar fund that paid interest without deducting tax.

'I don't want trouble wi' tax man and I don't want dollars; I want good English pounds not foreign money.'

I tried to explain that she could have pounds and wouldn't be breaking the law; she'd pay her income tax but she'd have the use of it for a year instead of the government. I told her I'd put it all down in writing and she said she'd be ever so grateful. I felt quite pleased at the prospect of giving genuine disinterested advice.

This morning Maria insisted that I get on with something I'd been putting off for over a week: we are restoring a tiny room at the very top of the house which had been used for storage for many years. It's probably too small to let but Maria wants her daughter Nicoletta to come for a visit and I'd like to have my mother come some time from Ireland where she's living on her pension and her savings.

The window frame has rotted and is coming away from the brickwork and Maria has borrowed the longest bloody ladder I've ever seen. I've got to climb right up and fill in the holes so we can put a new window in. She marched me out right after breakfast and somehow together we got the ladder up; it seemed to reach to the sky.

'Come on, George; just put one foot in front of the other and don't look down. Up you go.'

When I got to the middle it started to sway and I embraced it lovingly. I wanted to climb down but Maria was holding the bottom and I knew she wouldn't let me escape. Besides I didn't want her to find out how deathly afraid I was.

'Go on, George, you're over the worst bit.'

I climbed, very slowly, to the top and hooked my leg around the last rung. I looked down; Maria seemed very small.

'Don't let go!'

'Don't worry, George, I won't – ever.'

As I started to hack away at the crumbling brick I was surprised to see Mrs Lamb come out of the house with her suitcase. A taxi had drawn up. She stopped and waved to me.

'Goodbye, Mr Kelly.'

I couldn't wave back because I was entwined in the ladder but I shouted a goodbye and told her to come back and see us some day.

When I was finally on firm ground again I asked Maria why she'd left.

'I told her I thought she was silly staying in a little B. & B. place with all her money and that she'd have a much better time splashing out at the Royal.'

'We can do with the money, you know.'

'She insisted on paying for the whole week, said she wouldn't go otherwise as she'd booked for a week.'

'That's all right, then. Perhaps I'll stroll over there this evening and have a drink with her.'

Maria kissed me; I don't know why.

'What a good idea! I'll go with you.'